To Vertus,

Fallen SNOW

Dee Blackmon

Best Wishes !

Hope Harbor Publishing Company

Fallen Snow
by Dee Blackmon

Published by:
Hope Harbor Publishing Company
P.O. Box 4942
Annapolis, MD 21403-4942
orders@hope-harbor.com
www.hope-harbor.com
www.deeblackmon.com

First Edition 2003

Publisher's Cataloging-in-Publication
(Provided by Quality Books, Inc.)

Blackmon, Dee.
    Fallen Snow / Dee Blackmon. — 1st ed.
    p. cm.
    LCCN 2003106444
    ISBN 0-9741625-5-8

    1. Criminals—Fiction. 2. Man-woman relationships—
Fiction. 3. Detroit (Mich.)—Social conditions—
Fiction. 4. Detroit (Mich.)—Fiction. I. Title

PS3602.L3253F35 2003   813'.6
                              QBI33-1394

Printed in the United States of America

Acknowledgements

First and foremost I would like to thank God
for continuing to bless me in all my endeavors.

To my creative team, I am so very grateful
that you came into my life:

Sherri Oliver, my brilliant and talented editor. Thank you
for accepting nothing less than my personal best,
and thank you for all your prayers.
Girl, you know I need them!

Greg Crymes, my cover designer.
Thank you so much for your creativity and your help.

Olivia Garrett, my graphic designer. The book looks great
and don't worry, I'm still looking for some
rhinestone New Balance gym shoes.

Contact them for their expertise:
Olivia: Olivia@Big-OGraphics.com
Sherri: Savvy Editorial
Greg: 301-735-7575

To Troy Rawlings, A.K.A. Brother Troy, of Ghost Host
Entertainment, thanks for beng a great host, a good friend,
and a wonderful person. Big things are about to happen so
stay close!

To Gerald Ringgold of Ringgold Imaging Solutions, thanks for
taking time out and
making me look good on the photo. You and T are a really
great couple. When's the BBQ?

To Amy, we were probably sisters in a past life. You know we've been through a lot together, but I couldn't have made it without you. Thank you for being my best friend!

To Dr. Thomas Bonfiglio, the Italian Stallion, for keeping my smile pretty.

To Michelle, my awesome dental hygienist, who has the most infectious laugh.

To Grace, of Grace and Elegance Beauty Salon, for always fitting me in and giving me comic relief.

To my mother, grandparents, and father, thank you for shaping me into the woman I am today. The growing pains were difficult, but I think I turned out okay. And sorry Mom for the long labor, the extra ten pounds, and the stretch marks from having me.

And last but not least, thanks to all of the family and friends that have supported me along the way.

And to those that didn't...

Dedication

This book is dedicated
to my son,
the most important person in my life.

EJ, you are the best part of me.
For years I'd lived my life in black
and white, but now I see color.
You are a wonderful son.
Thank you for allowing me the
pleasure of seeing a world full
of rainbows through your eyes.
Mom-Mom loves you!

Fallen SNOW

Dee Blackmon

Prologue

One year ago...

Belinda Jackson parked her shiny black Jaguar XK8 in front of AJ's Car Wash in her reserved spot. All eyes were on her as she pranced through the parking lot wearing a full-length black mink coat and three-inch black high-heel shoes that clicked with every step. She waved at the many familiar faces that greeted her as she passed.

Belinda's rich cinnamon colored skin was flawless and perfectly made up with a gleaming smile in place, showcasing a perfect row of pearly-white teeth. Every hair on her head was in place despite the cold November wind. And as she walked she left a heavy trail of Gucci 3 perfume, her signature fragrance.

"You want me to clean her up for you Mrs. Jackson," an employee everyone called Redbone asked shyly. The 2002 Jag was fresh off the lot and without a speck of dirt on it, but any excuse to talk to Mrs. Jackson was worth it to Redbone.

"Yes, please. By the way, is my husband here?"

"T-Money, I mean Mr. Jackson is downstairs inspecting a shipment. I'll let him know you're here."

"Don't bother," Belinda said matter-of-factly. "I'll wait for him in his office."

Belinda started through the lobby filled with waiting customers and the smell of freshly made coffee and a few dozen glazed donuts. She was on her way down the hall toward her husband's office, and she knew Redbone was hot on her heels, but Belinda acted as if nothing was out of the ordinary. Only when he grabbed her arm did she turn around with a look of surprise.

No man had dared to grab her that way in years. Not since her father when she was just a girl. Belinda's father treated her mother like a punching bag because he loved liquor more than his family. Once Belinda and her sister were old enough to move out on their own, they left.

Belinda had promised herself over the years that no man would ever hit her again, nor would she be poor. She used her body to get what she needed. And even though years had passed, seemingly nothing had changed.

"I'm sorry Mrs. Jackson, but you can't wait in Tony's office unless he's in there. You'll have to wait in the lobby."

Belinda held her rage in check. Tony had apparently said something to his employees and now she couldn't even get into his office. Just because Tony owned the car wash didn't mean he owned her as well. But of course Tony made sure everyone knew that *she was* his property.

Belinda flashed her pearly-white teeth again. She placed her hand on Redbone's chest, then ran a perfectly manicured finger up to his lips. Darting out her tongue seductively, she teased Redbone's bottom lip with her nail.

"All I need to do is freshen up Redbone," Belinda purred like a sex kitten. "It won't take me long at all.

You wouldn't make me use that scummy hole in the wall out in the lobby my husband calls a bathroom, would you?"

Redbone was so unsure of himself. He didn't see the harm in letting Tony's wife use the restroom in the office. Belinda *was* his wife after all. Redbone would pull the Jag around and then immediately go and tell Tony that Belinda was in his office. That would take all of five minutes.

"I guess it's okay if you're only using the bathroom."

"Hon, I would have been finished by now," she purred. "Now you clean up my Jag and I'll be sure to thank you properly next time I see you."

Belinda opened her black mink coat to reveal only a diamond choker, a black lace G-string and thigh-high sheer black nylons. Tony used to love it when she surprised him at his office nearly nude. That was a long time ago, however. Now she needed the G-string as a buffer between her and his anger.

There wasn't an ounce of fat to be seen, because Belinda spent at least two hours in the gym every morning. Forty-five minutes on the treadmill, fifteen minutes on the rowing machine, and then an hour with a personal trainer comprised her daily routine, Saturdays and Sundays included.

Even at the age of forty-one, Belinda was lean and toned everywhere. Her breasts were firm and perky, not droopy like so many other women her age. Belinda looked damn good and she used her looks to her advantage. Frequently.

Belinda trailed her fingernail back down Redbone's chest and to his groin. She ran the tip of her nail along the swollen ridge of Redbone's zipper.

Belinda didn't wait for him to change his mind. She hurried down the hallway to Tony's office. Checking to make sure the coast was clear, she went into Tony's office and closed the door behind her. She flung off her mink coat and sat down at the computer. Typing in several different passwords, Belinda finally found one that worked. She searched through Tony's files until she found exactly what she wanted.

Taking a mini disc out of her make-up compact, she shoved it into the computer and downloaded as much information as quickly as she could.

Anthony Jackson's entire world existed in the inner sanctum of the car wash. Beneath machines that operated solely to wash motor vehicles was a hidden three thousand square foot level he affectionately referred to as The Sanctuary.

In The Sanctuary Tony only dealt with the purest forms of crack, cocaine and heroin he could find.

Tony trusted no one and the layout of The Sanctuary proved it.

Three thousand square feet of black ceramic tile covered the floor of The Sanctuary. Tony wanted to make sure none of his employees dropped a speck of his merchandise. A constant inspection of the floors kept everyone in check.

In the center of the huge rectangular shaped room was a toilet and sink enclosed in glass. The user could see outside, and most importantly, Tony could see inside. He hadn't made his money by being stupid and trusting just *anyone* to work with his goods.

Tony reclined in his black leather office chair behind a massive oak desk and inspected the merchandise he'd just received then slid a briefcase filled with three million dollars across the table. The runner accepted the briefcase and then mopped his brow with a handkerchief. He was glad the transaction was done. He'd heard stories of men not making it out of The Sanctuary alive.

Tony nodded his head to Nymph, his right hand man, which was the signal to escort the runner out of The Sanctuary. Nymph was average height with shifty hazel eyes that saw everything. His high yellow complexion and super model good looks attracted tons of women, but he worked hard and he did his job well. Nymph was loyal to Tony, and was one of the few people he trusted.

Tony then gave the merchandise to Queenie, a three hundred pound homosexual, and K-Dog, a tall wiry homophobe, both a part of his crew. Tony gave them orders to distribute the merchandise to his employees to be packaged and sold. Queenie and K-Dog were known as a lethal pair. They had a good cop, bad cop routine that they had perfected, and managed to pull off every time. That was the main reason why Tony made them work together so often.

Tony strolled through his empire and checked on all of his employees. Four long tables were set up in a square that surrounded the bathroom, and topless women dressed in only their panties stuffed baggies with crack. Each stuffing station, in addition to the main recessed lighting, was spotlighted by bright fluorescent lamps that hung from the ceiling. The women's thin, nimble fingers were used to sling rocks all day if that's what Tony told them to do. But sometimes he told his women to service *him* during the day. A man never knew when he needed a blow job.

On wide black counters, and generally every flat surface, men and women packaged all different kinds of narcotics, from club drugs such as Roofies and Sextasy, to his main money maker, Heroin.

Computer stations were set up throughout The Sanctuary so Tony could monitor every inch of his empire, which stretched across the entire Detroit Metropolitan area. Watching the 'smurfs' was most important. Not the little blue men from the cartoon, but two hundred men and women that made multiple daily cash deposits at financial institutions all over the city. It was known that a good 'smurf' could deposit at least eighty thousand dollars a day without detection by the IRS, but Tony didn't have good 'smurfs'. He had excellent ones. That was vital for an operation of such magnitude.

There was one other thing that was vital.

Explosives.

Tony had blocks of C-4 hidden within the walls of The Sanctuary – enough C-4 to level the entire carwash within moments if detonated. Only he and Nymph had remotes for detonation. Tony didn't trust anyone else, and no one else trusted him, with good reason of course. Tony would detonate the charges regardless of who was inside the carwash. 'Casualties of war' they called it, quite a fitting statement.

"Excuse me, T-Money," Redbone said as he exited from a special elevator that could only be accessed from the employee lounge on the upper level. To the untrained eye, the elevator door looked like a bookcase.

"What is it Redbone?"

"Your wife is waiting in your office. She said she needed to freshen up and use the restroom," he explained.

"What did you just say," Tony asked calmly.

"Belinda is in your office," Redbone repeated.

Tony took a moment to take a deep breath. The one thing he would not tolerate from an employee was insubordination. He had made it crystal clear that no one was allowed in his office. And he expected that all of his orders were to be followed precisely. When an employee fucked up, Tony fucked *them* up.

"I hope you enjoyed screwing me Redbone," Tony told the young man as he waved over K-Dog and Queenie. Nymph also arrived shortly thereafter from seeing the runner out of The Sanctuary. Between his lips, Nymph held a B-40, a cigar laced with marijuana and dipped in malt liquor.

"I don't understand T-Money. She's just using the bathroom."

"I specifically gave orders that no one was to set foot in my office unless I was in there. Did I not give those orders Redbone?"

"Yes, you did but," he protested.

"Well, since you enjoyed screwing me I'm going to let Queenie enjoy screwing you."

"*What*," Redbone sputtered in a panic.

"He your type Queenie," Tony asked.

"Yeah, I've had my eye on him for awhile Boss. This is gonna be fun," Queenie exclaimed rubbing his hands along his groin.

"Well Redbone, take it like a man," Tony joked then laughed.

Redbone tried to make a run for the stairs, but K-Dog and Nymph stopped his exit and dragged him to an empty table where they promptly bent him over.

Queenie took over from there, his three hundred pound bulk overpowering the smaller Redbone. Queenie grabbed the waist of Redbone's pants and boxers and pulled down hard, baring Redbone's ass. Queenie freed himself then shoved into Redbone forcefully, moaning as he slid in to the hilt. Redbone screamed and tried in vain to fight free of Queenie's massive frame. Tears streamed from his eyes.

"Oh this shit is disgusting," K-Dog commented laughing.

"Yeah, Redbone's not gonna sit for a week," Nymph chimed in flicking ash from his cigar.

All of the employees tried not to watch Redbone being violated, but the scene was like a bad traffic accident. No one could resist the temptation to look, even though the scene was sure to be ugly.

And Redbone and Queenie were making an *extremely* ugly scene.

"What I say goes," Tony yelled at his employees. "This is The Sanctuary. Down here I'm God and don't you ever forget it!"

Tony left The Sanctuary with Redbone's screams floating somewhere behind him, and the sounds of his employees scrambling to get back to work.

When he opened his office door, Belinda was in the bathroom mirror fixing her make-up, wearing the full length mink he'd given her for her birthday. Tony scanned his desk and found nothing amiss. Well, almost nothing. His computer keyboard wasn't perfectly aligned with the edge of the desk blotter. He always left his desk a certain way so he'd know if someone had been in there. It could have been nothing, or Belinda could be up to something.

"Hey baby, I missed you this morning so I thought I'd bring you a surprise," Belinda said as she let the mink fall to the floor.

Tony clasped a hand around Belinda's upper arm and yanked her toward him.

"Don't ever fuck with me Belinda or I'll kill you."

Chapter 1

Camilla Lynn Abernathy watched as her aunt's casket was lowered into the ground. The cold November wind whipped through her wool overcoat as if she were wearing a spring jacket. The chill went right to her soul.

Cami's raven colored hair hung just below her shoulders and swirled in the wind, her curls flying wildly. She smoothed a lock away from her sandy colored tear dampened cheek and tucked it behind her ear. Waterproof mascara kept her luminous brown eyes from staining her cheeks black, which was good because her tears flowed freely. She had seen and experienced so much in her twenty-six years already, and now this.

Cami's five-foot-seven inch shapely frame shivered slightly. She still couldn't believe her aunt was really dead. How she wished she was dreaming, trapped in some cruel nightmare.

Cami closed her eyes as Reverend Whitaker said a prayer. However, she quickly opened them when the grotesque bloated images of her aunt went through her mind. Cami remembered her aunt's lifeless icy body at the morgue, and the misshapen mask of her aunt's face in the casket at the wake.

She remembered people patting her aunt's dead hand, and telling her how peaceful Belinda looked. "She looks just like she's sleeping," they'd said. What a stupid comment, Cami thought.   People were dumb and insensitive. How in hell did her aunt look peaceful when she was anything but.   And the morbid form in the casket didn't look to be sleeping. The form had looked just plain dead to Cami.

It seemed like it was just yesterday when Belinda had rescued Cami from her alcoholic mother. She had been only ten then, but Cami had been forever grateful. She hadn't known what life really was until she lived with Belinda. Belinda taught Cami what it was like to be loved, and how to give love in return.

Cami remembered when Belinda had taken her shopping for the first time. They had gone to Fairlane Mall and spent Tony's money on an entire fall wardrobe for Cami. She had never seen so much money spent in one day, but Belinda had told her that 'the best deserved the best'. In Cami's mind *Belinda* was the best.

The sound of pebbles hitting the casket snapped Cami out of her trance. It was her turn to throw clumps of the cold earth onto her aunt's casket. The final goodbye, the last chapter of a life so great that it hurt so very much to stand at Belinda Jackson's graveside.

Cami took a deep breath and fought hard to maintain her stoic façade. She wouldn't give her Uncle Tony the benefit of seeing her break down. She heaved the fistful of dirt that left her black leather glove gritty, into the six foot hole and onto the casket.

Cami's aunt was the only woman that had ever been a real mother to her. Now Belinda was gone, her life cut short by a fatal drug overdose. A powerful narcotic known as heroin had entered her veins and extinguished her very essence. It was enough heroin to kill a 350 pound man.

The only problem was that Camilla's Aunt Belinda never used drugs a day in her life. She had never even smoked a joint before, and had given Cami the beating of her life when she had been caught with marijuana at the age of fourteen.

"She looks so peaceful."

The statement reverberated through Cami's mind. Her Aunt Belinda was anything but peaceful.

Camilla knew deep down inside her Aunt Belinda had been murdered.

Chapter 2

The funeral processional meandered its way through the Motor City. The normal daily grind halted in favor of the weekend. The Detroit streets were as solemn as Cami felt inside.

When the processional finally ended at her childhood home on Wildemere Street, she didn't want to get out of the limousine. People who called themselves family and friends were clamoring to see inside the house of the infamous Anthony Jackson, a.k.a. the "Snow King" of the Motor City. Cami's Uncle Tony saw more powder than Santa Claus on any given day at the North Pole.

Cami never understood why her aunt had stayed with him. She supposed Belinda was addicted to the cars, the money, the clothes, and the diamonds, better known as the bling-bling. But never, ever was she addicted to the drugs. Cami knew that Belinda loved Tony, but she also knew Belinda loved the money more.

Cami jerked as the limousine door opened. Tony stood before her playing the role of grieving widower to the hilt. Oh how she despised him. Sure he had paid for her college education and had given her food and shelter, but she hated the way he had treated her aunt.

Cami could remember countless times that Tony had flaunted other women in front of Belinda. He had even brought one to the house once when Cami was fourteen and expected Belinda to accept it. Belinda usually didn't seem to care until he'd brought that girl to the house. Belinda had told the young woman that there could be only one queen in the castle, but Tony didn't think it mattered. He laughed in his wife's face as he took the girl into his office and had sex with her with his wife just on the other side of the door. Belinda's feelings were hurt that night, but she loved Tony's money. Nothing would ever make Belinda leave the money. Nothing, except *death.*

Besides that, Tony treated Belinda as if she was his property. When Cami turned nineteen she had moved out on her own, despite having a three year old daughter named Tisha. And Cami had still managed to survive. Nothing could have made her live with Tony another day. She was tired of watching the emotional abuse that he inflicted on her aunt.

"Camilla, are you and Tisha planning to join us," her Uncle Tony asked standing at the back door of the limousine.

Cami's heart was pounding furiously. She wanted to yell at him to kiss her black ass. She wanted to tell him that she knew he had murdered the only mother she knew, but Cami had to bide her time and bite her tongue. She needed to find absolute proof of his crime, or else she'd be lying next to her aunt six feet in the ground. Cami was positive Tony wouldn't hesitate to kill her too.

"Come on Tisha. Let's go inside the house."

"How come we can't go home? Mom, I don't want to be around all these people crying all the time."

Tony grabbed Tisha's arm forcefully and hauled her out of the limousine. He caught the child by such surprise that she let out a startled gasp. Her uncle had never touched her in anger. He'd never even touched her at all. She had barely ever seen him in her ten years on earth. Her mother had only done things with Aunt Belinda except for maybe some holidays.

"Have some respect for the dead girl," Tony barked at her.

"She does have respect," Cami spoke up. "She doesn't like the sadness. No kid would. She'll be fine. Now let her go," Cami directed and pulled Tisha's arm away from Tony. There was no way in hell she'd allow him to hurt her baby.

"Come on sweetie," Tisha heard her mother say as they walked into the front door of the house.

There were a few other kids her age at the funeral, but each of them knew that playing together was out of the question. They all stayed by their parents and were even afraid to say hello.

Reverend Whitaker followed the family into the Jackson home. He patted Cami's arm as he passed her in the foyer. He'd known Cami since she was just a girl. He still remembered the day that Belinda had brought her ten year old niece to church and introduced her to the congregation. Cami had grown into an intelligent woman despite her chosen line of work. He wasn't one to pass judgment though. He couldn't and wouldn't be a man of God if he did. However, the Jackson home gave him pause. He had heard all the rumors, and boy did Reverend Whitaker hear stories. The corrupt things the Jacksons had done sometimes surfaced at the church. However, the Reverend thought Belinda was such a sweet woman and he would have never believed her to be a drug addict.

It seemed as if lately he was losing his flock one by one. If the young people weren't going to jail they were dying in drive-bys. Gangs in Detroit were on the rise, and drugs were prevalent among kids that were as young as Tisha. Drugs they probably got from one Anthony Jackson.

Just the other day Reverend Whitaker saw one of his most devoted Deacons kissing another woman at a

Southfield restaurant during the middle of the day. The man had a family, yet he was out with another woman and cheating on his wife.

Then there was Deacon Earl. Reverend Whitaker didn't know why he even allowed Earl to stay on the church board. Earl had been cheating on his wife for years and thought that no one knew about it.

Yep, Reverend Whitaker was losing his flock one by one.

Cami locked herself in her aunt's bathroom. She was sick and tired of watching people eat off of her aunt's fine china and hearing them make comments like, "Sometimes God's children do stray, but Belinda's in a better place now."

Everything was making Cami nauseous and bile was starting to rise in her throat. Besides that, she was sweating profusely, and her stomach was cramping so badly she thought she might faint. When she felt the first trickle of blood on her leg in the kitchen as she was trying to choke down a glass of water she immediately began to panic. On the way up the stairs to the bathroom was when the trickle felt like a gush. Cami knew her underwear was saturated with blood. She also knew that she was losing her baby.

Cami opened the bathroom's linen closet and took out a maroon colored face towel. She folded it in thirds then lined her underwear with it. If only she'd had a maxi pad in her purse – there were none in the medicine cabinet. That was a given, since Belinda had had to have an hysterectomy at the age of thirty-six.

Cami rinsed her face with cool water then dried it. She had to be all right until she could make it home. She'd collect Tisha and they would leave. She only lived a couple of miles away. Cami would force herself to make it. She had no choice.

Chapter 3

As Cami came downstairs, she saw Deacon Earl Turner mingling with the crowd and lending his strength and support where needed. There were several members of First Baptist in the house, but there were just as many that she didn't recognize.

Earl scanned the crowd and found his wife, Helen, helping clear the dishes from the table along with Deacon Tim's wife, Roberta. He searched the lingering crowd once more but without success. Deacon Earl wanted to extend his regards to Belinda's niece, Cami, but she was nowhere to be found. He'd seen her in the kitchen earlier, but then she'd disappeared.

Earl saw Tisha sitting on the living room sofa with a coloring book and started forward to question the child about her mother's whereabouts.

"Tisha, sweetheart, how are you holding up," he asked the girl. She was so beautiful and smart too. Tisha had her mother's eyes and complexion. The child's smooth sandy brown skin and long, thick ebony hair was the spitting image of Cami. There wasn't too much of Tisha's father in her features, and Earl thought that was a good thing.

"I'm fine, Deacon Turner," Tisha replied. "I'm just waiting for my mother so we can leave."

"Where is your mother, by the way?"

"She went to the bathroom." Tisha continued to color.

Just at that moment, Cami came up beside Earl as he was talking to Tisha. The last thing she wanted at the moment was to deal with him.

Earl noticed Cami's pallor and was instantly alarmed. He'd seen that look before when she hadn't felt well for one reason or another. A slight sheen of sweat glistened on her skin and her lips were red and bruised from having been chewed by her own teeth. The grimace on her face was subtle, but there nonetheless. Everyone probably thought it a mask of mourning, but Deacon Earl knew better. Cami was in pain.

"Come on baby, let's go home," Cami told her daughter and began putting the Crayola crayons back in their box.

"Mom, we don't have our car. How are we going to get there?"

"Damn! Tisha you're right. I forgot we rode in the limousine," Cami remembered belatedly.

"I'll drop you off. It won't be a problem," Deacon Earl offered. It was the least he could do.

"No!"

"But we need a ride home Mom. It's too cold to walk. How come Deacon Turner can't take us home?"

Cami closed her daughter's coloring book and gathered it together with the crayons. She didn't have time for this right now. She barely kept herself from passing out. She didn't want or need a confrontation.

"Can you go and get our coats Tisha? I promise you that we won't have to walk."

Tisha ran off into the den that was serving as the temporary coat room. She was glad they were leaving.

Deacon Earl turned toward Cami after watching Tisha run off. He noticed that she didn't seem as tall last week when he saw her at church. The saying that children grew like weeds was absolutely true.

Earl turned to Cami once Tisha was out of sight. He looked around then and noticed they were relatively alone. The people were mostly in the kitchen and dining room.

"Let me take you home Cami. I want to, and you know it won't take long. I'd be back before Helen finished cleaning up."

"Fuck you Earl," Cami hissed. "I don't want a damn thing from you." She looked at Earl's youthfully handsome chestnut face that sported deep dimples and his athletically lean build. At five feet eight inches tall, Earl carried himself well. He still lifted weights on a regular basis, Cami noticed. His chest was firm and his arms were muscular. He could easily pass for a twenty-five year old man even though he was forty-one. He was so devilishly charming, always lending a helping hand. But he was what he was: a smooth talking devil. Cami learned the hard way that the biggest devils were found in the sanctuary.

"I deserved that. Can't we just bury the hatchet? Things don't have to be this way."

"And what way should they be Earl? Enlighten me please. Should you be allowed to come to my house while Tisha's at school to get your dick sucked because Helen is having a bought of depression? Do you think you can fuck me whenever you want?"

"Sister Belinda will be greatly missed, but rest assured she's in a better place now," Earl spoke up loudly as Deacon Timothy suddenly appeared.

"You listen to Deacon Earl Sister Camilla," Deacon Timothy said and patted her hand, then lifted his suit coat jacket off the couch. "It will be hard for a while, but things will get better after a while. Deacon Earl or I are always there for you. I'll see you soon."

Deacon Timothy left the living room, leaving Earl and Cami alone once again. Earl was silent for a moment or two as he released a pent up breath. They'd almost been caught. He couldn't afford for that to happen.

When Earl turned back to Cami he saw her visibly flinch and bite her lip. Her fists were clenched tightly and tremors wracked her body.

"What's the matter Cami? Something's obviously wrong. I can tell. You know I worry about you dammit. You still don't return my calls. Are you feeling alright?"

"Why don't you ask your daughter how she's feeling? Oh, I'm sorry I forgot. You haven't done that in ten years."

"Cut the bullshit," Earl snapped. "And do both of us a favor and leave Tisha out of this. Tisha is on her way out here right now. I suggest you put your coat on and take your ass out to my car. I'll be there in a minute."

Cami was in so much pain that she didn't make one of her usual sarcastic retorts. That worried Earl even more. Something was definitely wrong. He left Camilla and Tisha as they were putting on their coats. He went to tell his wife of his newly acquired errand.

Earl spotted Helen in the dining room clearing the last Pyrex and Corningware serving dishes. Mounds of mashed potatoes and candied yams were heaped in the bowls. Tony would be eating the potatoes and other food for a month.

"I'll only need a few minutes Earl. Roberta and I want to get everything cleaned up for Anthony. It will be one less thing for him to worry about."

"Well, take your time sweetheart. I'm going to give Sister Camilla and her daughter, Tisha, a ride home. She's so overcome with grief that she's virtually shaking."

"You're what," Helen asked rhetorically. She knew all about Cami. Her husband didn't think she did, but

Helen knew all right. She knew about the long lunch hours her husband used to take. Of course, he'd been coming home for lunch lately. Well, the last year or two actually. There was only that one Tuesday two months ago that he couldn't make it home for lunch. But Earl had come straight home from work that day - early, with a dozen red roses and a box of coconut-filled chocolates, her favorite.

Helen knew Earl didn't trust her to stay home alone for long periods of time. And she could understand why.

She remembered that fateful day two years ago. Earl had come home to a bloodbath. She had slit her wrists after trying to conceive a baby for fifteen years with no success. Helen cursed her body. The blockage in both her fallopian tubes remained despite two painful surgeries ten years ago.

Earl had found her that Friday morning unconscious on the bathroom floor. She'd ended up there after going on a rampage through the house and destroying the home they'd lived in for nearly twenty years with her blood.

Helen had smeared the words "I Hate God" with her blood on her living room wall above the sofa, and she had broken precious heirlooms that her mother had given her. Broken glass and splattered blood followed her as she wandered through the house. Drops of blood colored the carpeting and stained everything, even her cream-colored bedroom comforter.

Helen was just happy that Earl had forgiven her. Their marriage had been better since then. Earl told her everyday how much he loved her, and he had actually been talking about adoption. When he had first brought up the topic Helen was devastated. But, as each day passed, she warmed to the idea. She wanted Earl to have a child and be the father he'd always dreamed of being. Helen knew she had to do that for him even if that child wasn't biologically theirs.

"I'll be right back sweetheart. It will take me twenty minutes or less. I think Sister Camilla lives on one of the 'lawn' streets, either Greenlawn or Roselawn. You and I both know that's only blocks from here. By the time I get back you'll be ready to leave."

"Well, okay Earl. So long as you come straight back in twenty minutes."

A silent communication passed between them, and at that moment Earl knew that Helen knew about Camilla. He didn't know how, but she did. He wondered what else Helen knew about. He'd have to be very careful around her. Earl had to make sure Helen knew he loved her. And he did.

Earl kissed Helen lightly on the lips then headed for the front door. Camilla and Tisha were already seated in his gray Cadillac.

"Mom, are you okay? Are you sad about Aunt Belinda?"

"I am sad Tisha, but I don't feel well. When we get home I'm going to rest for a little while. I want you to watch one of your videos okay?"

"Okay I will. I hope you feel better."

"Thank you baby."

Earl opened the car door just as the mother-daughter exchange was ending. He noticed that Cami actually looked worse. He started the car and they made the short drive in silence.

Earl arrived at the Roselawn address all too soon for him. He would have liked more time, and he wanted to talk to her. Cami hadn't let him anywhere near her in years, literally. Except for that Tuesday afternoon a couple of months ago. They'd had so much fun together. Earl had left her house feeling relaxed and refreshed.

Cami had always made him feel good ever since he met her at the tender age of fifteen. She'd been so beautiful that first day that he knew he had to have her, despite her being jailbait.

Cami and Helen were like night and day. While Cami had a personality that lit up a room like sunshine, Helen was mundane and boring. She made Earl tired and sleepy. He'd look at Helen or listen to her mouth and nod off immediately.

Helen was short and petite, a little over five feet tall, while Cami was tall and had legs for days. She could have been a look-a-like for Beyoncé, a member of the popular singing group *Destiny's Child*. Cami was sexy as hell.

Earl pulled into the driveway and parked behind Cami's black Mazda Miata. For whatever reason she hadn't parked the car in the garage.

"Thank you Deacon Turner," Tisha said as she climbed from the backseat. She was mentally rummaging through her movie collection to pick a DVD to watch.

"Yeah, thanks Deacon Earl," Cami tried to mock her daughter's manners, but the statement still came out sharp and biting.

"I'll walk you inside," Earl replied and got out of the car before Cami could object.

He watched Tisha as she waited by the passenger's side door for her mother to get out. Earl opened the door and held it wide for Cami.

"You don't have to," Cami started but didn't finish the statement because a sharp stomach cramp took her breath away. She squeezed the door frame willing the pain to subside just enough to make it into her house.

"Mom are you okay," Tisha asked, a bit scared. She'd never seen her mother look that sick before.

"Cami, what's wrong with you?"

Although Cami loathed and despised Earl, she was grateful for any help she could get at the moment. She just needed to make it to the house, up the stairs, and into the bathroom. The life within her was dying and Cami could feel it being ripped from her womb. It hurt like hell.

"Earl, I need you to get me to the bathroom."

It took a few seconds for Earl to realize Cami had asked him to do something for her, because she never asked him for anything. That thought alone shocked the shit out of him and scared him to death. Either Hell had frozen over, or Cami was seriously ill.

As soon as Tisha unlocked the front door with the key she kept around her neck on a chain, Earl scooped Cami into his arms and wasted no time in getting her to the bathroom.

Cami gripped the cold porcelain sink in the bathroom. She was vaguely aware of Earl standing against the closed bathroom door. She distinctly heard the strains of the opening bars of music from Disney's Beauty and the Beast. That was a good thing, because Cami didn't want Tisha to know what was going on.

"Cami, tell me what's wrong. I'm not leaving until you do."

A pain so great wracked Cami's body that she toppled to her knees. Just as she managed to grab hold of the sink again, she felt the last shreds of life tearing from her womb. Blood ran down her legs and as she slid off her underwear Cami felt a rolling sensation in her loins. She lifted herself up, as a baseball-sized sack plopped down from between her legs onto the tiled floor.

"What the fuck is that," Earl asked and took a step forward. He thought for sure Cami was dying. Her insides seemed to be falling out before his very eyes.

"Oh God no, please no," Cami wailed in between gulps of air. She hadn't been thrilled when she'd missed her cycle, but it wasn't just Earl's baby. It was her baby too, and she loved it from the moment the plus sign popped up on the pee stick.

"That was my baby," she cried more to herself than to Earl. Death was choking, first with Belinda, and now the tiny life inside of her.

"You're pregnant," Earl asked dumbfounded.

"Was pregnant Earl. Past tense. Was. Not anymore."

Cami's ordeal was over, her body having expelled her child. She suddenly felt a lot better. The pain was lessening minute by minute. She still hurt physically, but not as badly. Emotionally however, she wondered if she would ever recover. The day would forever be etched in her mind as a day of mourning.

"Why didn't you tell me? When? That Tuesday," Earl said and answered his own question.

"That Tuesday," Cami cried. She just wanted Earl to go home. She needed space to think about what needed to be done. She didn't want to go to the emergency room, but her regular doctor's office wasn't open on the weekends. Cami was so confused and so tired. She wished she knew what to do, besides feel helpless and weepy. A doctor wouldn't bring her baby back to life. No one could.

"I think you'd better leave. You don't want to keep Helen waiting."

Cami had to get Earl out of the house. She wanted to call a friend of hers that used to be an OB/GYN. He would tell her what to do. Cami felt better now that she had a plan. Her friend, Theo, would tell her how to take care of herself. For once Cami didn't have to have all the answers.

"Cami, I –"

"Leave Earl. Now!"

Cami cleaned up as best she could once she heard Tisha lock the front door. Earl was gone and she could finally concentrate on pulling herself together.

Cami knew she had to be calm when she called Theo, or she wouldn't be able to explain what had happened to her baby.

Pulling on an old tattered jogging suit, Cami sat on the side of her bed and dialed his phone number. On the third ring, a deep male voice answered. Cami could hear strains of a college football game in the background.

"Hi Theo, it's Cami."

"Cami, what's up," Theo asked immediately on guard. He'd known that Cami had gone to her aunt's funeral that morning and wouldn't have called him if it weren't important."

"Theo, I was two months pregnant, but I just lost the baby. I don't know what to do."

Theo kicked into his professional mode. Even though he didn't practice anymore, old habits died hard.

"Pregnant?" he asked confused. "When were you planning on telling me?"

"I was going to tell you before I started showing, I guess," she replied guiltily.

"Well, are you bleeding heavily?"

"No, just a little actually."

"And I take it that when you said you 'lost the baby' you passed the entire gestational sack?"

"Yes. It sort of fell out on the bathroom floor," Cami said embarrassed. It was stupid to feel embarrassed about death, but she did for some reason. Cami knew she truly had lost her mind.

"I'm really sorry Cami. If you're not bleeding heavily, then I'd say it would be okay if you waited until Monday. If I were your doctor I'd tell you to take a painkiller, then follow up with me first thing Monday morning. However, if you do experience heavy bleeding or you're really uncomfortable, go to the emergency room okay?"

"Thank you Theo," Cami said huskily trying to mask the tears in her voice.

"Don't hesitate to call me if you need anything or you have a question," Theo told her.

"I won't. Bye Theo."

Cami threw back the covers and slid beneath them. Tisha would be fine while Cami rested for a while. She just needed a little bit of time to get herself together.

Cami closed her eyes and took deep calming breaths. Soon sleep claimed her, and for a few minutes spared her the agony of it all.

Chapter 4

As Earl made love to Helen that night he couldn't get Cami's image out of his head. Cami's body wracked with pain, her toppling to her knees in the bathroom, tears streaking her gorgeous face. Cami losing his baby – their baby.

Earl felt the beginnings of Helen's climax and did something he had never done in his life – he faked an orgasm, his mind and his heart just wasn't in it. He saw only Cami's face when he looked at anything, including Helen.

Earl wished like hell that he was married to Cami. She had been more of a woman at the age of fifteen than Helen would ever be. The things that Cami could do in bed should have been outlawed centuries ago. But Cami wouldn't have him. She wanted absolutely nothing to do with him. He still didn't know why she had allowed him back in her bed two months ago. He hadn't regretted one minute of that Tuesday afternoon, but he knew she had. Cami had refused to talk to him since then. Only a week ago when Belinda died had she uttered two words to him.

Earl wanted so badly to comfort Cami in her time of need. He knew how close she and Belinda had been. But when he had offered to come over, she had told him to go "jump in a lake." He'd tried calling twice more, but only got her voicemail. She was so fucking frustrating. Shit. Cami knew how much he loved her. Why didn't she love him?

"I'm going to take a shower honey," Earl told Helen as he heaved himself off of her and walked out of their bedroom.

Helen curled up into the fetal position as she lay on the bed thinking about Earl's behavior. She felt the moist opening at her center then drew her hand away quickly. It was as she had feared. Earl hadn't climaxed at all. He had pretended. Earl had never done that before. With the same hand, Helen wiped away the tear that had fallen.

Helen didn't need the added stress of Earl's infidelity right now. She thought he loved her. He'd been such a wonderful husband since her accident. She hadn't even noticed anything was amiss except the forty-five minutes it took to take Cami home. Helen knew where she lived. It should have taken Earl a round trip time of ten minutes – fifteen if he had done the speed limit.

Helen wiped another tear from her eye. What did Cami have that she didn't? Earl wasn't that much younger than Belinda. He could have been Cami's father. But he wanted Cami anyway. Maybe it was youth that attracted him to Cami. Lots of men went through mid-life crises and wanted younger women. Helen feared one thing more than Cami's youthfulness. She feared Cami's ability to have children. Maybe Earl was attracted to her because she could bear children. Her womb wasn't dry as the Sahara Desert like Helen's.

Helen didn't wipe the tears that fell this time. It was useless, just as she was useless. Thinking of Earl and Cami together made Helen sick. Earl having sex with Cami was enough to make Helen regret that she was still alive.

Earl kept his eyes on the staircase and listened for movement upstairs. Helen thought he was in the shower so he had a few minutes to kill before he actually had to get into the running water. He wanted to spare his wife the details of his extra curricular activities.

Earl picked up the telephone and dialed Cami's number. It was close to midnight, but he wouldn't be able to sleep without knowing if she was all right. What if she needed to go to the hospital? Earl didn't think he could live with himself if anything ever happened to his Camilla. He didn't care anymore that she didn't want to be with him. As long as he could see her at church or at her job, that was enough for him. And maybe, just maybe, Cami would ask for his help again like she had today.

"Hello," Cami answered sleepily. She didn't bother looking at the caller identification feature on the black cordless phone. That would have meant opening her eyes. She had finally gotten herself to sleep after having a private pity party. Her eyes felt so gummy from the incessant crying she had done. She missed her Aunt Belinda so much. Not to mention, her stomach still cramped a little, and her baby was dead.

"How are you feeling," Earl asked, whispering into the telephone. He peeked at the staircase again then continued talking. "Do you need to go to the hospital or something?"

"I'm fine Earl."

"What about Tisha? Is she okay?"

"Tisha's fine too. Why don't you go talk to your wife Earl. Goodbye."

"Camilla wait. Please."

Earl heard the dial tone in his ear.

Fuck!

Why was it always so difficult with her, Earl asked himself. He only wanted to check on her. She made him feel like the Devil.

Earl punched the side of the refrigerator. Things were going to have to change – with him, with Helen, and especially with Cami.

"Who were you talking to Earl?"

Earl whirled around quickly, a chill settling over his naked body. He was getting careless and he hated himself for it. He was too old for this shit.

Chapter 5

Coltrane jogged down Curtis Street then turned down Roselawn. He had been at this for three weeks now, and he was pretty certain that he had his timing perfected.

Coltrane knew that every Sunday morning Camilla Lynn Abernathy came outside at exactly 9 a.m. to get her newspaper. She'd have a white chipped coffee mug in her hand with an oblong handle that boasted of 'the world's greatest mom', and she usually wore an old Wayne State University jogging suit.

Just like clockwork Coltrane saw Camilla open her front door. He stopped at her driveway as she bent down to pick up her newspaper.

"Morning," Coltrane greeted her.

Cami tucked the newspaper under her arm and nodded her head in greeting.

"It seems that we're neighbors. I just moved in next door a couple of weeks ago. I'm Coltrane Kennedy."

Cami stared blankly at the man standing before her. His warm mahogany colored skin glistened with a sheen of sweat. He had a perfectly groomed goatee that outlined full, luscious lips.

The brotha was fine.

A thin scar marred the center of his left eyebrow and the diamond stud in his left ear winked at her through the gray haze of the cold November morning.

The sweat suit he wore covered a strong, powerful physique. Of that Cami was certain.

"That's an awfully big name to carry on such small shoulders."

"Ouch," was all Coltrane could say, standing in the driveway with his hands on his hips.

Cami closed the door and leaned against it. Why did she have to be such a bitch? That brotha seemed perfectly nice and friendly and fine as hell. He *was* her neighbor. There was no reason for her to have acted like that. All men weren't the scum of the earth. There were a few good black men left that weren't in prison or gay. It seemed at the age of twenty-six she would have met at least one in her lifetime. No such luck. She had let a man like Earl into her life.

Cami didn't know what had happened to her two months ago. She hadn't been with Earl in years. Then one Tuesday afternoon she went and blew it. She didn't even like him anymore. He was Tisha's father. That was it. Period. But she had been so lonely lately. Being held by a man for a few hours felt wonderful.

Cami's loneliness was still no excuse for her rude bitchy behavior. When she saw Coltrane Kennedy again she would apologize and actually introduce herself.

Coltrane pulled his sweat shirt over his head as he turned on his laptop computer. His cell phone rang just as he draped a towel around his neck.

"Yeah," Coltrane barked into the shiny silver Nokia.

"So, how's it going?"

"Depends," Coltrane answered.

"Well have you met Camilla or not?"

"Yeah, I met her a few minutes ago."

"And what did she say?"

Coltrane laughed into the phone. "She said I had small shoulders."

"What," the caller asked not understanding the comment.

"Nothing. What have you found out? Anything," Coltrane asked impatiently.

"I'll have something in a few hours. I was just wondering if you'd made any progress with your new neighbor," the caller probed.

"Call me when you have something. Later."

Coltrane tossed down the cellular phone then poured himself a cup of coffee. His thoughts turned to his neighbor, Camilla. She had seemed like a nice person from afar. Coltrane had seen her playing with her daughter in the backyard having snowball fights. Camilla had laughed and sang along with the ten year old. Maybe she was having a bad day, he thought. Or maybe Camilla Lynn Abernathy was a bitch.

The cellular phone rang again.

"Yeah," Coltrane answered for the second time in as many minutes.

"We gotta problem," the caller said frantically.

"What now and who fucked up?"

"Belinda Jackson is dead."

"Say what!"

"Drug overdose. Sully talked to a neighbor yesterday when he saw all the limousines pull up in front of the Jackson home. He hadn't even been at the rental house five minutes before all the ruckus started. After he found out about the overdose, he just went back to the hotel and called me. There was no sense in staying at the rental when the person we were supposed to keep tabs on is dead."

"Shit," Coltrane uttered under his breath. Belinda Jackson was their one sure shot at getting inside. He was supposed to be on an extended vacation visiting his mother. Camilla was only supposed to be maintenance for him. Now she was their only chance.

"Those were my sentiments too. You know what you have to do right? Camilla is the only one we have. You don't have any choice Coltrane. Take it from me and just get the job done as quickly as possible. If you sit around and think about it, your conscience will eat at you."

"Yeah, I know," Coltrane sighed into the phone. "She seems like such a nice woman though, from afar at least. And what about the kid? What'll happen to her?"

"Listen, keep your emotions out of it and do the goddamn job Coltrane."

"Give me a few days okay? This is going to be difficult."

He didn't have any choice. Belinda was dead, and Coltrane had a job to do.

Chapter 6

Reverend Whitaker stood at the pulpit and looked out at the sea of faces that made up the congregation of the First Baptist Church. There was a time when he had the rapt attention of every member of the congregation.

As the Reverend looked around the church he heard conversations and bickering. He heard hand-held video games, portable radios, and televisions broadcasting the Detroit Lions' pre game events. He heard the distinct snapping of gum and when he gazed to his right, he saw his assistant pastor nodding off to sleep.

When Reverend Whitaker went to seminary school as a naïve, young man, he wholeheartedly thought he could make a difference. He thought he was invincible and that he was going to change the world one soul at a time. How stupid he had been. He couldn't even get the members of his church to pay attention to his sermon.

Anything was more important than the Word of God.

Reverend Whitaker had yet to tell the congregation the news he had learned in the wee hours of the morning. One of their church members, a twenty-two year old named Terrance, was jumped out of his gang last night. He had promised his girlfriend and son that he'd get out of the gang, and now he lay fighting for his life at Sinai Grace Hospital.

How was he supposed to ask his flock to pray for Terrance? He couldn't even ask them to shut up. The Bible talked about having faith the size of a mustard seed, something so small and so tiny. But at the moment, he didn't even have it. Realizing this fact was the hardest thing he had ever done.

In the middle of reading a verse from Proverbs, he walked off the pulpit and out of the sanctuary.

Cami saw Reverend Whitaker leave the sanctuary and wondered what had happened. Whispered comments were spreading through the church like wildfire, especially when the choir suddenly started singing. A lively rendition of *I'm a Soldier in the Army of the Lord* rang out and startled the assistant pastor. Pastor James jumped to his feet and out of habit clapped his hands and stomped his feet to the beat of the song.

People snickered all around Cami, but she was more worried about her patient, kindhearted pastor leaving. In all the years she'd been coming to First Baptist, she had never once seen Reverend Whitaker not finish a sermon.

As Cami looked around her, she noticed the man sitting three rows behind her. He looked so familiar that she glanced at him again. That's when she saw him wave at her. It was Coltrane Kennedy.

What is he doing here?

Cami had never seen him at First Baptist before. Granted, she wasn't at church every Sunday, but most Sundays she was and he had never been there.

Cami nodded her head in greeting for the second time that day. Coltrane looked very good in a suit and tie. The navy blue pinstripe Brooks Brothers suit was tailored to perfection and it was accented with a white shirt with French cuffs and a navy blue and gray patterned tie. He looked delicious.

"Mom, who is that man you're looking at," Tisha asked as she saw the look on her mother's face.

"He's our neighbor honey. He just moved into Mrs. Kendall's old house."

"Oh," Tisha said drawing the word out for three seconds. The man looked like an actor to her. He looked like he could be in a Wesley Snipes or Denzel Washington movie. Tisha thought he was a "hottie."

Tisha waved her arm at Coltrane to invite him up to the pew with them. They had more than enough room. The row was virtually empty.

"What are you doing," Cami whispered to her daughter. Cami had planned to speak to Coltrane after service.

She watched as he excused himself out of his row, walked down the side aisle and entered their row. He sat down right next to Cami and displayed two wrapped peppermints in his palm as an offering.

Tisha asked her mother's permission with her eyes, and at Cami's slight nod, she accepted one and Cami the other.

They sat through the abbreviated service still wondering what happened to Reverend Whitaker. Pastor James, however, handled the collection, and since he was at a loss over what to do or say, he said the Benediction. Cami had never been to a service that only lasted a little over an hour. Most black churches were still reading church announcements an hour into the service.

Cami, Coltrane and Tisha made their way to the parking lot relatively easy. Cami assumed people were avoiding her because of Belinda's death. She supposed

people didn't know what to say to her. That was just as
well, because they mainly said stupid things anyway.

Coltrane followed Cami's lead content at not
having been dismissed thus far. He was more than
surprised when Tisha had invited him to join them in
their row. He jumped at the opportunity. It hadn't
been difficult though sitting next to Camilla Abernathy.
Her perfume was heavy but not overpowering, its sexy
musky scent still imprinted on his brain. She wore a
two-piece double breasted olive green suit with a
neckline cut lower than most, but it wasn't indecent.
Coltrane could see the slight outline of a black lacy bra
if he strained his eyes. Her long legs were encased in
black sheer nylons and black high heels. Coltrane loved
that part the most. He liked the sheer nylons because
he could see a bit of sandy colored skin peeking through.
The high heel shoes were just the icing on the cake.

Coltrane knew he was on the job, but he wasn't
dead. The day he stopped noticing a beautiful woman
was the day he'd cut off his dick.

Cami stopped beside her Miata and looked up at
the man named Coltrane Kennedy. All six feet of him
was utterly still and silent. She *was* the one that had
an apology to make. He hadn't done anything wrong.

"Look, I'm sorry about this morning. I'm having a
really bad week and I shouldn't have said what I did,"
she apologized sincerely.

"No problem," was all Coltrane said. He was vastly
intrigued at the moment.

"Do you think we could start over," she asked
hopefully.

"Hi, I'm Coltrane Kennedy, your new neighbor."

"Camilla Abernathy," she replied and extended
her right hand. Coltrane's touch brought such warmth
on such a cold day. Cami felt that touch settle in the
pit of her stomach and bloom with heat.

"And this," Cami continued, "is my daughter Tisha."

"Thank you for the peppermint Mr. Kennedy."

"You're welcome," Coltrane replied and smiled at the girl.

"Mom, we should invite Mr. Kennedy to Sunday dinner today since he's new to the neighborhood."

Cami gave her daughter the 'mama's eye' which meant that she was going to get in trouble just as soon as they were alone. Her daughter had a thing for bringing home strays. Cami had patched up so many kittens that she needed to hang a shingle on her door announcing a new pet clinic in Detroit.

"Thank you, Tisha, but I couldn't impose on your mother," Coltrane answered giving Cami an easy way out.

"No imposition," Cami replied. "Dinner's at five, so please be on time."

Cami told her daughter to fasten her seatbelt as they settled themselves into the Miata. Cami didn't know why in hell she'd just agreed to feed the man. But a few words like murder, death, miscarriage, and loneliness had a way of playing with the human psyche, hers especially.

"And by the way Coltrane, you don't have small shoulders."

With that said, Cami peeled out of the church's parking lot and headed home. She thought that maybe she'd set out the good dishes and silverware, not the plastic stuff that she and Tisha always used. And maybe, just maybe Coltrane Kennedy had the ability to make her smile.

Chapter 7

Helen stood at the kitchen counter chopping celery and onions. Her eyes were glazed with anger as she thought about her husband, Earl. If only he loved her. Earl loved every other woman except her, especially Camilla.

Helen couldn't compete with a woman that had perky tits and legs as long as hell. She saw how Earl looked at Camilla at church when he thought she wasn't watching him. Earl practically drooled when Camilla passed him for one reason or another. He'd lick his lips involuntarily and his eyes would slightly bulge when he saw her. Then he would pat Helen's hand and plaster a smile on his face. He wasn't smiling at Helen he was smiling at the thought of Camilla.

How could I have been so stupid?

Helen chopped and diced the last remaining celery stick and onion. How she loved the feel of a knife in her hand. The tang always felt so comfortable, the special contoured handle made for a better grip. Helen knew the knife well. She was quite familiar with it, she realized, flipping it over and studying its markings.

She remembered this particular set of knives. They promised to cut through anything. The knives didn't do as good a job as she thought they would the last time. Or maybe it was her fault? Maybe she hadn't used enough pressure the last time. Maybe she would try again?

Helen placed the blade against the inside of her left wrist. She stood there at the kitchen counter trying to remember how much it hurt the last time she sliced open her flesh. Helen took a deep breath and counted to three.

One...Two...Three...

"Helen, honey, what the hell are you doing?"

The knife clattered to the floor. She wondered how long Earl had been standing behind her. And why did he have to touch her? Anything but that. Helen didn't want to feel the light caresses he was giving her hand. She didn't want to love him, but she did.

Despite all the shit Earl had done, she still loved him. That thought more than any other made her want to die.

Cami and Tisha stopped at the Savon Grocery store to pick up salad trimmings for dinner. Cami grabbed a head of lettuce as Tisha bagged two cucumbers and carrots.

They cruised a few aisles until Cami found a bottle of ranch salad dressing. She grabbed a bottle of Italian dressing as well just to be on the safe side. Hopefully, Coltrane liked one of the two.

"Mom, can I get a bottle of Red Faygo? Please?"

"Don't we have some at home Tisha? I thought I just bought some?"

Tisha shook her head vigorously. "Nope. Tamika and I drank it Thursday when she came over. Can I? Please?"

"Go ahead, and grab a diet Pepsi as well."

Tisha did as she was told, and soon they were on their way. But only after Tisha had managed to coax her mother into buying a bag of Doritos and a bag of

Better Made potato chips, which were only the best potato chips in the world. Better Made potato chips were one of the finest products to come out of Detroit. Tisha couldn't wait until after dinner so she could get hold of her chips.

Coltrane waited patiently for 5 pm to arrive. He didn't want to make too much out of the fact that he was actually looking forward to having dinner with Camilla Abernathy.

Coltrane looked at his watch again for the umpteenth time. He still had thirty minutes to spare. He flipped through the channels to find the Washington Redskins game, using the picture-in-picture feature on his television to split the screen between the Detroit Lions highlights and the Skins.

As the Lions scored a pre-recorded touchdown and the Skins were on the five yard line, Coltrane's cellular phone rang. He hoped like hell it was good news this time.

"Kennedy here," Coltrane answered.

"Hey man, I have some news."

"Dammit Sully, it had better not be bad news. I'm not listening to any shit that you and Yuri have to say," Coltrane said already getting upset at the prospect of hearing bad news.

"Damn Coltrane. You sound like a bitch right now. As Martin Lawrence would say, do you need some 'quality time'? When is the last time you had some?"

"Why Sully? You offering to be my bitch," Coltrane asked, laughing at his friend and coworker. He, Sully, and Yuri had been through some pretty tough shit together. It was all good-natured ribbing.

"That's okay. Last time you fucked me you didn't even call the next day," Sully answered back, getting in another jibe before they got down to business.

"But seriously man, I have good news. I found out that Belinda Jackson has a mother in a nursing home in Washington, D.C. She also owns a brownstone in the city, fully furnished and unoccupied. Now, are you thinking of the same questions I'm thinking of?"

Coltrane without a doubt had questions.

"Why does someone need a townhouse in D.C. if they only visit once in awhile? How often did Belinda go to D.C., and does Anthony Jackson know about the home and her mother? Sully, you need to find out what else Belinda Jackson did in D.C."

"Already on it, Coltrane. I'll let you know what I find. But Yuri and I are still close by, just so you know," Sully told him, as he punched the keys on his laptop computer. He was communicating with his D.C. contact and giving instructions on what needed to be done concerning the deceased Belinda Jackson.

"Yeah, I know. I gotta go. I have a dinner invitation and I can't be late."

"With who," Sully asked preparing to rip into Coltrane. He was supposed to be on assignment now that Belinda was dead. He didn't have time for any dates. He needed to keep an eye on Camilla.

"Camilla Abernathy."

With that said, Coltrane hung up the phone and dropped it into his jeans pocket.

Chapter 8

Cami looked out her front bay window in the living room before she pulled open the door. Coltrane stood on her porch wearing blue jeans, a tan and blue colored pullover sweater, and a pair of Timberlands that looked well worn and comfortable.

Cami pulled the front door wide and waved Coltrane inside. She caught a hint of his cologne, and it assaulted her senses. It smelled of the wind and the ocean and a bit of spice.

Coltrane stood in the foyer and waited for Cami to lead him inside. She seemed quite hesitant about letting him in, but she relented nonetheless.

The inside of Cami's house was neat and cozy. A plush blue sectional surrounded a big widescreen Mitsubishi television and an electronics equipment cabinet. It was a cool setup.

"Hi, Mr. Kennedy," Tisha greeted him in the living room. She had a huge smile on her face while she thought once again about Coltrane being an actor in a movie.

"Call me Coltrane, Tisha," he replied and pulled one of her pigtails. Tisha reminded him of his sister at that age. Tisha was all gangly arms and legs and looked exactly like her mother.

"Okay. I hope you are hungry 'cause we baked a lot of good food. Mom made chocolate cake and she let me frost it with chocolate icing," Tisha explained excitedly. "And she made homemade biscuits. Mom makes the best homemade biscuits. All you gotta do is put some butter and honey on 'em and they melt in your mouth. They even taste better than Aunt Belinda's biscuits. A couple weeks ago she burned the biscuits and made our house smell..." Tisha stopped abruptly and her eyes filled with tears. She had tried hard not to bring up her Aunt Belinda because she knew it made her mother so sad.

"I'm sorry," Tisha said to her mother.

Cami hugged her daughter tightly and kissed her forehead. She had wondered why Tisha hadn't said much about Belinda. Now Cami knew her daughter had been trying on purpose not to say anything. She should have realized Tisha was trying not to make her sad.

"My aunt just passed away. The funeral was yesterday," Cami said to Coltrane by way of explanation for Tisha's behavior.

"Tisha, you can talk about your Aunt Belinda any time you want. You and I both loved her and she loved us. Talking about her will make us both sad for a little while, but it's the only way we can keep her memory alive. Okay?"

"Okay," Tisha answered.

"Maybe I should come back another time," Coltrane said, feeling like an intruder. He didn't want to see a soft side of Camilla Abernathy. He didn't want to think of her as a caring mother. Coltrane wanted to stay emotionally unattached and not get personally involved with his assignment.

"No, please don't leave," Tisha begged. "I'm fine now, and I want you to taste the cake I frosted. Mom says I'm getting really good at it."

Cami turned expectant eyes on Coltrane. For some reason he knew that Cami wouldn't beg for anything. It wasn't in her nature. The decision was going to be his, and his alone to make.

"I would be happy to stay and taste a piece of your chocolate cake Tisha," Coltrane decided. If he wasn't on an assignment, Coltrane would have gotten the hell out of there. Camilla Abernathy had piles and piles of baggage and Cotlrane wasn't necessarily sure he wanted to be around when she opened some of it.

Tisha, definitely not as shy as her mother, grabbed Coltrane's hand and led him over to the blue sectional.

"Wanna play a game on my Play Station 2," Tisha asked as she pulled over both controllers.

"It's basketball with real NBA teams," Tisha bragged.

"Sure," Coltrane answered smiling. Tisha was so much more extroverted than her mother. "Are you sure we have time before dinner?"

Coltrane heard Cami's voice behind him. He could picture her in her black leggings along with the purple oversized sweater that had a tendency to slip off her left shoulder. Her hair, which had been in long cascading curls at church, was now in one long plait that stretched to just below her shoulder blades. Coltrane actually thought she wore a weave when he saw her at church, but upon closer inspection he saw that it was her own hair. There wasn't anything wrong with a woman wearing a weave, but Coltrane liked everything all natural on a woman.

"You have about twenty minutes to play," Cami told them. "That's when the biscuits will be ready."

Cami left her daughter and Coltrane in front of the television starting the game on the PlayStation 2. As she straightened the silverwear on one of the place settings at the living room table, she heard Coltrane's first question.

"Tisha does your mother ever smile," Coltrane asked. He didn't know what made him ask the question. Cami just seemed so solemn.

"She used to Coltrane, but I haven't seen her smile in a very long time. Mom gets lonely sometimes, I think. She needs a boyfriend. Maybe then she could go out with him 'cause all she does now is work."

Coltrane didn't make any comments and Cami was glad. She didn't want to start defending herself. She wanted to get through dinner so she could worry about everything else later.

Tony sat in a bedroom he had converted into an office. It wasn't big enough to hold all of his equipment such as three fax machines, two computers, and two printers, not to mention the massive oak desk. Tony barely had enough room to walk. He felt cramped in the black leather chair behind his oak desk. But it didn't matter. Nothing mattered except getting the job done. And the job was done. He had succeeded in stopping Belinda. Now she was dead and he was quite happy about it. His wife of twenty years was no more. Dead and buried six feet under where, in a few months with any luck, maggots would penetrate the cheap casket and eat her lying, corpse. Belinda was the last person he had expected to betray him, but she did.

For years Tony gave Belinda whatever she wanted. He flew her to Washington, D.C. once a month to go to some fancy spa called Paris Alexander's Day Spa and Salon. It costs him three grand a month for that shit. She'd come home looking the same as she always did, but with different fingernail and toenail polish. Tony never even complained about his three grand being wasted on some fucking ugly ass nail polish.

Then there was the ice. Belinda had more *bling-bling* than Tiffany's. She had diamonds in the freezer, a safe deposit box, her underwear drawer, and nearly every shoe she owned. It would always take forever for her to find a matching set of jewelry.

Tony smiled despite himself. Before Belinda's betrayal, he'd loved her. Every man did. Belinda Jackson was a foxy bitch and she knew it. And she was talented in bed. Belinda could suck dick so good it made grown men cry. Tony should know. He was one of them. She probably could have sucked the chrome off a doorknob if she'd tried.

Tony laughed aloud and shook his head. Yeah, Belinda was one foxy bitch.

Tony picked up his private line and made a call. He was suddenly anxious to put all his ducks in a row, and he had a whole shitload of 'em.

"What are you doing calling me on a Sunday," the voice on the other end asked. "I'm having dinner with my family and you know this is not a secure line."

"I just called to let you know that my wife passed away. I buried her yesterday. It was such a tragedy," Tony spoke sadly.

"You have my condolences. I'm terribly sorry for your loss."

The man abruptly hung up the phone. He'd deal with Anthony Jackson later. A succulent, rare filet mignon was waiting for him. He was sorry that Belinda Jackson had to die, but those were the breaks. He knew better than anyone that shit happened, and then you died.

"Coming dear," he called as he headed for the dining room table.

Chapter 9

Cami ate and listened to the light banter around her at the dining room table. Tisha, it seemed, who had never been this talkative before, asked all the questions.

Cami knew that Coltrane had never been married, had no children, and was currently single. He was originally from Detroit, but had been living in Washington, D.C. for the last seven years. Coltrane had decided to move back to Detroit to be closer to his family. Cami wondered if he were an only child, and decided to ask a question herself.

"Do you have any brothers or sisters," Cami asked as she stabbed another forkful of lettuce on her salad plate. She'd been so absorbed with Coltrane's answers that she had barely touched her dinner plate.

"So, there is a voice in there," Coltrane teased Cami. He thought that he would only get to talk with Tisha the entire evening. Coltrane took a bite of yet another biscuit laden with butter and honey. Coltrane hated to admit it, but Cami's biscuits were the best he'd ever tasted, including his mother's. In fact, this was the best dinner he'd had in months. Honey-roasted chicken, roasted herb crusted red potatoes, and green beans. Man, the biscuits were good, he thought, taking one more bite before answering Cami's questions.

"Actually," Coltrane began, feeling the light and fluffy biscuit melt in his mouth, "I have one older brother, and two younger sisters. Miles is thirty-four, Ella is twenty-eight, and the baby, Billie, she's twenty-four."

Upon hearing the names of his siblings, Cami smiled. She actually smiled and it lit up her entire face. Coltrane saw that her eyes shone with merriment and her teeth were perfectly straight and white as snow. She was beautiful. He gave himself a mental shake. He had to stay focused, and Camilla was making it damn hard.

"Your mother likes jazz does she," Cami asked rhetorically.

Coltrane laughed. "My mother eats, sleeps, and breathes jazz. She drives my father crazy."

Since Tisha found the conversation utterly boring, she decided to talk about something she liked. Sports. All sports. Everybody had to like some type of sport, even if it was figure skating or golf. Even though golf bored Tisha to death, she still watched sometimes to see Tiger Woods win another title. Tiger was awesome and good looking.

"What's your favorite sport Coltrane," Tisha asked and saw her mother playfully roll her eyes. Everybody that knew Tisha knew she was a sports fanatic.

"That's a hard question because I watch all sports. But if I had to choose one, I'd probably say football. I used to play in college. Don't ask me what my favorite team is though. I split my Sundays literally in half when the Redskins and the Lions are both playing. What's your favorite sport?"

Cami sighed and shook her head. Coltrane didn't know what he was in for. Tisha, as young as she was, had her own political agenda when it came to sports.

"Well, my absolute favorite sport is tennis. I love Venus and Serena Williams. But I don't go around shouting that from the rooftop 'cause not a lot of people watch tennis in the hood. And you'll never hear me say

I watch golf. And my favorite male tennis players are Pete Sampras and André Agassi. But I can't tell people I like them 'cause they either don't know what I'm talking about, or they do know and they know those men are white. Then they think 'what's a black kid from the ghetto doing liking two white boys that hit a fuzzy ball with a racquet?' It really pisses me off."

"Tisha," Cami chided. Her daughter's language got worse as she got older.

"Sorry Mom, but it makes me so mad," Tisha explained. She knew she wasn't supposed to say certain words, but sometimes they just came out.

"Well," Coltrane said astounded at all he'd heard. Tisha was a firecracker and he loved it.

"Did you know that Venus and Serena are from Compton? And in case you don't know, Compton is considered the hood too."

Tisha's face broke into a smile. She'd had no idea. That gave her a lot of hope. Not all black kids from the ghetto got out by rapping or playing basketball, and Tisha was good at neither.

"Cool!"

Cami stood up and began clearing away the dinner dishes. It was fast approaching 7 p.m. and they hadn't eaten any chocolate cake yet. Tisha would kill her if Coltrane didn't get any cake. Her baby had worked so hard on it. Cami was always so proud of her daughter, and it helped that Tisha was a great kid. Rarely did she give her mother any problems.

Coltrane stood up too and grabbed the two casserole dishes filled with green beans and red potatoes. It was only fair to help with the clean-up since he didn't help with the meal at all. Coltrane also enlisted Tisha's help.

"Let's help your mother clear the dishes Tisha."

"Aww man! Do I have to," Tisha whined. She hated clearing the table and washing the dishes. Normally she was able to get out of it. Tisha always made sure she had schoolwork to do or a book to read. Her mother was a sucker when it came to Tisha's education.

"Yes, you have to," Coltrane stated firmly.

Tisha jumped up from the table and put the lid over the crystal butter dish then screwed the cap back on the bottle of honey. She put each away in their respective spots in the kitchen and came back for more. She even started running dishwater in the kitchen sink.

"I wish I knew your secret," Cami told Coltrane. "Tisha never does this for me."

"It's my rugged good looks," Coltrane answered playfully and saw another smile flash across Cami's face. The smiles were coming a little easier now. That was a good sign.

Cami washed the dishes and Tisha dried and put them away. They all talked, even Cami, about odds and ends. Coltrane hated to admit that he was actually having a good time. He found Tisha's conversation and comments lighthearted and amusing. And Cami was beautiful and mysterious. God, he wanted to know what went on in that pretty little head of hers. She always seemed to be thinking about something.

"Want to hear a joke Coltrane," Tisha asked as she stacked the last dinner plate in the cabinet and took down three dessert plates.

"Sure Tisha."

"There was a white man, a black man, and a Chinese man. The white man said – "

"Tisha," Cami reprimanded. "What did I tell you about those jokes?"

"I know Mom, but this one isn't dirty."

"Tisha, let's cut the cake. I'm sure Coltrane doesn't want to hear your dirty mouth tonight."

Tisha moved beside Coltrane in front of the cake.

"I'll tell you the joke another time Coltrane, when you-know-who isn't around."

Coltrane couldn't help himself. He laughed heartily and put his arm around Tisha's shoulders. At that moment Coltrane realized he needed to stay far away from Tisha and Camilla. But he couldn't. He wouldn't. Coltrane had a job to do, and he'd better get it done or Sully and Yuri would bust his ass.

Coltrane decided to change the topic to something on neutral ground.

"So, do you have your list ready for Santa next month Tisha? Christmas will be here before you know it," Coltrane said seriously.

"Come on Coltrane. There ain't no fat white man coming down my chimney with a bag of toys, especially in Detroit. I'd like to see a fat white man try to come down somebody's chimney. He'd get a bullet in the butt!"

Cami whirled around from the kitchen sink. She wondered if Coltrane would stop her when she strangled her daughter. Tisha was definitely in rare form. Her daughter had to be infatuated with Coltrane because she was trying very hard to impress him. Cami couldn't blame her though. They both seemed to be afflicted with the same illness.

"Tisha cut the cake. After that young lady you need to take your bath and get yourself ready for school in the morning. Besides, I'm sure Coltrane has other things to do, and we've taken up a lot of his time."

"Oh, all right."

The three laughed and talked some more over chocolate cake and vanilla ice cream. Tisha once again delighted them with chatter, but this time Cami was quick to join in.

All too soon Tisha and Cami were saying goodnight to their guest.   Both had enjoyed Coltrane's company and hated for him to leave.

"Thank you for inviting me to dinner," Coltrane said as he turned the doorknob on the front door.   "I had a good time."

Tisha and Camilla locked the door behind him. All together it had been a really good evening.

And Camilla distinctly remembered smiling.

A lot.

Chapter **10**

The ringing telephone penetrated Tony's deep sleep. He'd been up late making calls and checking on an upcoming shipment.

Tony cracked one eye open and stared at the bright red numbers that winked back at him. It was 8 a.m., not exactly the crack of dawn, but still early nonetheless.

It's probably somebody from that damn church, he thought as he picked up the phone. Church people were the nosiest people he thought, smiling.

"Hello," Tony croaked, his voice raspy from sleep.

"Good morning. May I please speak with Belinda?"

Tony came fully awake. He thought he'd called all of Belinda's friends and family and told them about her death. He'd personally gone through her address book. Maybe it was a telemarketer, Tony thought.

"Who's calling," Tony asked.

"My name is Ebony and I'm calling from Paris Alexander's Day Spa and Salon in Washington, D.C. to confirm her appointment this coming Saturday, November twenty-third."

"Ebony, my wife passed away last week, so she won't be keeping that appointment," Tony informed the perky young woman from the salon.

There was a pregnant pause over the line. Tony waited for his information to sink in. Then he'd hear the usual 'I'm sorry' and another awkward silence. He had been through it so many times with every one else that he was sick of it. He thought about putting a message on his voicemail, but he didn't think he could portray the grieving widower over a computerized prompt to push one if the party wanted to leave a message.

"I'm so sorry Mr. Jackson. I had no idea," Ebony apologized. She never would have called had she known about Belinda already.

"Of course you didn't know," Tony replied. "It's all right. You have a good day Ebony."

Tony dragged himself slowly from the bed. He made his way to the bathroom and turned on the shower. Tony stretched his nude body lifting his arms over his head. He had a lot to do today, he thought as he mentally ran down the list of things that needed to be done.

Tony was up early.

The only problem with that was the time. He normally didn't meet his employees until 5 p.m. at the earliest. Usually his meetings didn't start until well into the night.

Tony thought about going back to bed, but threw that idea out of the window. Although he hadn't gotten much sleep in the past week due to the death arrangements, he decided to stay awake anyway.

Stepping into the hot shower, he let the water run over his head and body. His thoughts easily slid to Camilla. He couldn't help but wonder how much she knew. If she had any suspicions and reported them to the police he would have heard about it by now. He had at least one man in every precinct in Detroit, and they were paid well to let him know shit like that, or better yet make it disappear.

Tony wondered if Belinda told Camilla what she'd found and heard. He didn't give Belinda much of a chance to do anything when he found her in the closet of his home office. She'd had a tendency to be a little heavy handed with her Gucci 3 perfume. Tony followed that scent right to the closet after he'd dismissed his right hand man, Nymph.

Tony had just stepped out of the shower when he heard the chimes of the doorbell echoing through the house. He dried off quickly, and wrapped the dark blue bath towel that matched the dark blue bathroom tiles around his waist.

Tony padded barefoot down the stairs and into the foyer.

"What are you doing here," he asked as he pulled the front door wide.

Maxine "Ebony" Jefferson-Brown sat mortified at her desk after she replaced the telephone in its cradle. Her friend and classmate, Belinda Jackson was dead. They'd attended Cass Tech High School together back in the day. They'd gotten into trouble together and shared secrets forever it seemed.

Maxine scooted away from her desk feeling sick to her stomach. She'd laughed the day Belinda had walked into the law offices of Jefferson, Jefferson and Brown and said that she thought her husband was going to kill her. That had been one year ago.

Maxine leapt from her desk and literally ran down the hall to her husband Brice's office. She threw open the door in a panic and nearly collided with his secretary, Angela.

"I'm sorry Angela. Could you excuse us please," Maxine asked politely. It wasn't Angela's fault that Belinda was dead.

"Of course, Mrs. Jefferson. I'll fax those documents for you right away Mr. Jefferson."

"Thank you Angela," Brice replied. As soon as his office door closed he stood from behind his desk and took hold of Maxine's hand.

"What's wrong Max," Brice asked in concern.

"Belinda is dead Brice," Maxine cried.

"Belinda?"

Brice's mind completely went blank. Maxine and Belinda had been friends for years. He'd met her when Maxine had taken Brice home to Detroit for the first time to meet her folks. The women had been inseparable. Now his wife was trying to tell him that a healthy vibrant woman in her forties was dead.

"Are you sure Maxine? How did you find out? Start from the beginning," Brice instructed his wife.

Maxine sat in one of the burgundy leather wing back chairs facing Brice's desk. She ran a hand down her coffee colored legs which were encased in flesh tone nylons to ward off the eminent chill. Belinda was dead.

"I hadn't heard from Belinda in two weeks. I figured that maybe she was out of town since Thanksgiving is coming up. You know how much she likes to take shopping trips," Maxine said and wiped a tear from her eye.

"Anyway, when I didn't hear from her I got worried Brice. Our agreement was that she'd call and check in once a week on Fridays. When I called the Friday before last I didn't get an answer on her cell phone, but I didn't chance calling the house in case Anthony answered. So when I didn't hear from her again this past Friday I thought maybe she was really busy. I knew she was coming to D.C. this weekend, but I told myself nothing was wrong. Just to put my mind at ease, I called the house anyway and pretended I was a woman from the spa. That's when Anthony told me she was dead. I should have taken her more seriously Brice. I told Belinda she was just paranoid when she said she thought Anthony was going to kill her. I should have listened to her Brice," Maxine cried. "I should have listened," she wailed even louder.

Brice folded his wife into his arms as he lifted her from the leather chair. He knew what had to be done next. They had to find someone in Detroit that they could trust. He and Maxine had to get the package Belinda had entrusted them with, to the right person. Brice had no idea who that would be though. Hopefully, his wife did.

"Who do we give the package to Maxine," Brice asked, pulling his wife out of her stupor. They would have to grieve later. According to Belinda's instructions, they had to move fast. Belinda had told them that every moment was crucial.

Maxine wiped her eyes with a Kleenex she'd pulled from the box that sat atop Brice's desk. She tried to remember everything that Belinda had told her.

Maxine took a deep breath and let it out slowly. Camilla Abernathy, Belinda's niece.

Camilla was the one person Belinda told Maxine to trust. Although Maxine had never met Belinda's niece, her friend had told her that Camilla would figure out what to do.

Maxine hoped like hell that was true.

"Max? Honey what are you thinking," Brice asked. He saw the wheels turning in his wife's head and wanted her to clue him in too.

"Camilla Abernathy. That's Belinda's niece and someone she said to trust. Belinda once told me that Camilla would know what to do," Maxine explained to her husband.

"Are you sure she won't take the information to Belinda's husband, Anthony," Brice asked. "Belinda never even introduced you to Camilla after all these years."

If whatever was in Belinda's file was delivered to Anthony Jackson, he would get away with murder. According to Belinda, Anthony would kill for the information.

"I'm sure Brice," Maxine said decisively. I know Camilla and I have never met, but Belinda wanted to keep her personal life private. At least that's the reason she gave me when I asked her about it fifteen years ago. However, Belinda wouldn't have told me about Camilla if she didn't trust her."

"Okay Max. We need to get the package from your office, and we need to get it to Detroit immediately."

Maxine heard what her husband said. But as she looked out of Brice's office window onto the streets of Georgetown in Washington, D.C., she couldn't come to grips with the fact that her friend was gone.

Belinda Jackson was dead.

Helen averted her eyes as she stepped through the front door of Tony's house. He was only wearing a towel wrapped around his narrow hips and taut butt.

"I hope it's not too early," Helen started, "I have the day off and I was in the neighborhood and wondered if you needed anything."

If it had been anyone else at Tony's door he would have gone off on them for coming by his house so early. But he liked Helen. She was cute and very quiet. He had caught her glancing at him numerous times on the rare occasions he went to church. He remembered winking at her a few times, and her turning away quickly and focusing on her Bible instead.

Tony never could understand why she was married to an asshole like Earl. He knew however, why Earl was married to Helen. She had a tendency to go along with whatever anyone told her. Helen was naïve and trusting to a fault. Tony could imagine Earl telling his wife that sucking his dick would give her extra protein and Helen readily dropping to her knees.

Yeah, Helen was gullible all right. He wondered if that was the reason she tried to off herself.

"That was nice of you Helen. But no, I don't need anything," Tony informed her.

"Oh. Well, okay then," Helen said standing just inside the foyer looking around quickly. She and Belinda were never really close friends. They worked on fundraisers for the church every now and again, but that was the extent of their relationship. Helen had always wondered how the wife of a drug dealer decorated her house, and she found out the day of the funeral. Belinda's house wasn't that much different from hers, surprisingly. Helen had expected more, such as guns on the wall, because of all the rumors.

Helen's eyes kept wandering back to Tony's towel. She wondered what he looked like under that towel. It didn't matter what he looked like, Helen thought. She was a married woman and Tony had just lost his wife.

At that particular moment Helen wondered if Earl had really gone to work. She'd seen him searching through his underwear drawer for his black Calvin Klein briefs. When Earl wore those briefs he thought he was hot shit. He'd made a comment once about being a 'Black Stallion' because he was hung like a horse.

Earl had told Helen that he had to pick up a coworker who was having car trouble. Helen had met Earl's coworker, Doug, once before when he'd had car trouble. Doug's wife was in a wheelchair and didn't drive.

Helen knew from experience that just because Earl had given her an excuse didn't mean it was the truth. And Helen was sure that Earl wasn't wearing the black Calvin Klein briefs for Doug.

Tony watched the play of emotions on Helen's face. He also saw the glances she kept giving his towel. Helen's meek and mild manner almost made him feel ashamed for what he was about to do – almost, but not quite. Tony felt his dick rub against the terrycloth towel. He still had the ache of his morning hard-on and he'd just figured out a way to cure it. It would be like taking candy from a baby.

"Since you're here, have a seat on the couch for awhile," Tony told Helen and led the way into the living room.

Helen folded her ankle length wool coat and set it on the arm of the couch. As she sat down, her cream colored wool skirt slid up her thighs a few inches. So did Tony's blue towel. Helen got a quick peek at bronzed skin covering heavily muscled thighs. Tony was a much bigger man than Earl by far, she noticed.

Tony purposely let his towel fall across his thighs. When he saw Helen peeking at him he decided to go for broke. He'd either get slapped or laid. He was betting on the latter.

Tony stretched his legs even farther apart until the blue towel fell from his waist. He watched the expression on Helen's face go from blatant shock to curious desire. Tony saw Helen's mouth fall agape and thought about ramming his dick inside of it. But then he thought he'd better play it cool and take things three steps at a time instead of five.

Helen stared at Tony's penis, hard and jutting from his body. At first she was filled with shock, but then something happened. Helen thought about all the shit Earl had put her through. She thought about all those times when Earl hadn't come home on time.

Helen thought about the day she tried to kill herself. Well, she thought, it was time for a little payback.

Helen surprised herself when she hurriedly stripped out of her clothes. But all seemed right with the world when she impaled herself onto Tony's dick as he sat on the couch. Helen wished Earl could see her now, riding Tony and glorying in the feel of his big dick.

Helen had found a new 'Black Stallion.'

Chapter **11**

"Come on Tisha or you'll be late," Cami hollered upstairs. She unzipped her daughter's backpack to make sure Friday's homework assignment was in its proper folder. Cami then put Tisha's brown bag lunch in the outer pocket of the backpack.

Checking her watch one more time, Cami called upstairs again. "Come on baby. Hurry up!"

"Geez Mom, I'm coming. You know I hate Mondays," Tisha grumbled as she took her backpack from her mother. "Can't you drive me to school this morning Mom? It's so cold outside and it's snowing," she begged.

"Tisha, your school is only two blocks away. It will take longer to warm up the car than it will to walk there. Now let's go," Cami told her daughter.

Tisha got her winter coat out of the closet along with her scarf, hat, and mittens. The two blocks she had to walk to Bagley Elementary were going to feel like two miles. Tisha would probably still be frozen during homeroom. Luckily, her desk was right next to the radiator. Tisha had gotten into the habit of holding her hands over the radiator while she finished the bell-work the teacher made the students complete during the first ten minutes of class. Mrs. Nelson, her fifth grade teacher, claimed bell-work jump-started their minds for learning. Tisha just believed bell-work was to make the class shut up while Mrs. Nelson drank her huge cup of coffee.

"Mom, I'm ready," Tisha said when she saw her mother set down her own cup of coffee.

Cami, like her daughter, put on her winter coat and all the trimmings. When she pulled open the front door, she seriously thought about driving. It was cold, but nothing they weren't used to.

Tisha stood in the driveway catching snowflakes on her tongue as she waited for her mother to lock the front door. Out of the corner of her eye she saw Coltrane coming out of his side door.

"Good morning Coltrane," Tisha called out and waved enthusiastically. Seeing Coltrane's answering smile was all the encouragement Tisha needed. She ran across her front lawn and met Coltrane in his driveway.

Cami saw her daughter take off across the lawn. She vowed that she would string her up by her toes. Coltrane was the last person Cami wanted to see at 8 a.m. and with no make-up. She didn't even have any lip gloss on. Cami cursed herself even more.

"Hi Tisha," Coltrane replied. "Off to school huh?"

"Yeah. You wanna walk with us? I know it's cold, but it's only a couple of blocks."

"Tisha, Coltrane was on his way somewhere. I'm sure he doesn't have time to walk you to school," Cami told her daughter, giving Coltrane an easy way out.

"Sure I do," Coltrane disagreed. He'd purposely waited for Cami and Tisha to leave, planning his timing perfectly. He had wanted the encounter. Coltrane refused to feel guilty over the fact that he wanted to see Cami and Tisha again. He didn't want to explore the feeling in his chest when he saw Cami. This was supposed to be a job for him and he needed to remember that. Otherwise, Coltrane was up the creek without a paddle.

"Well, we gotta go or Mom will start nagging again. She has this thing about being on time," Tisha warned.

Coltrane fell into step with Tisha and Cami then relieved Tisha of her backpack.

"When I was in school," Coltrane explained, "when a boy walked to or from school with a girl, he carried her books."

Cami saw Tisha's smile and for the first time she saw her daughter actually blush. Tisha was obviously smitten with Coltrane Kennedy.

So was Cami for that matter.

"Were you on your way to work Coltrane," Tisha asked nosily. She thought it was a good question, but her mother didn't.

"Tisha," Cami reprimanded. "Mind your own business. It's rude of you to ask a question like that."

Coltrane laughed. Tisha definitely kept him on his toes. He felt like shit having to lie, but he didn't have a choice. At least he could tell a little of the truth.

"I was on my way to my mother's house," Coltrane supplied despite Cami's instructions for Tisha to mind her own business. "And as for a job, I don't go back to work until after the holidays. I'm kinda on vacation right now."

"Cool! I wish I was on vacation so I wouldn't have to go to school," Tisha commented.

"What about you Cami," Coltrane asked, "are you on your way to work?"

"Mom's off until Wednesday, because she's a –"

Cami cut her daughter off abruptly.

"We're here Tisha," Cami announced shoving her daughter forward slightly to get her moving toward the door before she could blurt out anything else.

"Thanks for walking me to school Coltrane."

"Any time Tisha," Coltrane gave Tisha her backpack.

"Mom, did you fix me a chicken sandwich for lunch?"

"Yes, I did. Have a good day baby," Cami told Tisha as she kissed her daughter's cheek.

Tisha motioned for Coltrane to bend down, and when he did she cupped her gloved hand over his ear and whispered, "Mom really likes you Coltrane."

Cami wished like hell she knew what Tisha was saying. For some reason Tisha felt the need to tell Coltrane anything and everything. They were definitely going to need to have a mother/daughter talk later.

"What makes you say that Tisha," Coltrane asked a bit surprised by the information. He thought Cami was just indifferent when it came to him, but he'd obviously been mistaken according to Tisha.

Tisha cupped her hand over Coltrane's ear again.

"You make my Mom smile, and she never smiles. She also invited you to dinner. Mom never lets anyone come inside our house, except Aunt Belinda. And most importantly, she didn't use a cuss word. Mom always uses cuss words to people she doesn't like, or that make her mad."

"Are you sure," Coltrane asked smiling at Tisha.

"I'm sure," she whispered. "But don't tell her I told you those things or you'll get me in trouble."

"I promise," Coltrane said and hooked his pinky finger with Tisha's after she'd taken off her mitten and told him he had to 'pinky swear' about not telling.

"Bye Coltrane," Tisha said happily and kissed Coltrane's cheek before she ran off.

Cami watched her daughter run into the elementary school and meet up with her friends.

She and Coltrane both turned and headed back home.

"Thank you for being so patient with Tisha," Cami told Coltrane as they walked side by side through the snow.

"Tisha is a great girl. She's a lot of fun."

"Any chance of you telling me what she whispered to you," Cami asked.

"Nope," Coltrane replied shaking his head. "I pinky swore."

"I was afraid you'd say that," Cami said smiling. She saw the house looming near, and for the first time in her life, she found herself actually dreading parting company with a man.

The fact that Cami was interested in Coltrane was shocking. She had never even been in a true relationship before. Cami had always pulled away before it got too serious. And it was also hard to find a man that accepted her kid too. Men didn't like ready-made families. But Coltrane seemed to like Tisha, and Tisha already adored him.

Hell, Cami was starting to think she was two steps away from becoming lesbian. A relationship with a woman was probably much simpler, she thought and grinned.

"What's funny," Coltrane asked.

"Nothing really," Cami replied choosing to keep her crazy thoughts to herself.

"Would you like to come in for a cup of coffee, or do you have to leave," Cami asked Coltrane as they reached her driveway.

"I'd love a cup of coffee."

"Are you sure your mother won't mind if you're late?"

"Don't worry, she doesn't know I'm coming," Coltrane replied. "Besides, I'm sure she'd much rather me have a cup of coffee with a beautiful woman than hanging around bothering her."

Cami laughed and motioned with her hand toward the front door. As she inserted the key into the lock she heard a familiar voice from her driveway.

"Good morning Camilla."

Chapter **12**

Helen lay in Tony's bed, Belinda's bed, and adjusted the sheet around her body. After their first encounter on the couch, Tony had carried her into the bedroom for more comfort. Helen thought that a strange thing to do considering the rumors she'd heard about Tony being a drug dealer. He hadn't treated her like the cold, calculating, notorious man he was rumored to be.

For some reason, being in Belinda's bed didn't bother her even though Belinda had only been gone a week. Helen could still smell traces of Belinda's signature Gucci perfume in the sheets.

Helen nearly laughed at the irony of the situation. Somewhere in her mind she knew she shouldn't be laughing, but she just didn't care about anything. Not Earl, not Belinda, not even having a baby. After the way Tony had made her feel on the couch Helen knew she wanted to live a very long life. Her entire body had experienced an awakening that she never even thought was possible.

All Helen cared about was the way Tony made her feel. Maybe it had something to do with the pill called Ecstasy that Tony had given her after their first round of sex. That pill made her want to fuck *everything*. Right now the lamp on the dresser was even looking pretty good while Tony took a phone call.

If Helen had to explain what had taken place over the past hour, she would be at a loss for words. She had never taken any drugs before in her life, besides the pills associated with the fertility treatments. Helen wouldn't even take a simple aspirin if she had a headache. She chose to use herbal remedies instead.

But when Tony held out that little pill and a glass of water, Helen threw caution to the wind. She probably would have taken anything if it would have meant that Tony was going to make love to her again.

Make love? No, what they did together was not considered making love. Tony had fucked the hell out of her, and Helen had enjoyed every minute of it. He had been rough with her, the complete opposite of Earl, and that was very appealing. Earl had always handled her very carefully, like a piece of broken glass, while Tony had stretched every muscle in her body to suit his needs. Now with the drug taking over, she was enjoying herself even more.

Helen's hand traveled down the length of her body and stopped at the juncture of her thighs. She slid first one finger then two inside of herself.

In...out...in...out.

Helen kept up the pace, the friction causing her to moan aloud. Her legs spread wider apart as she began to approach her release for the second time in as many minutes. That was how Tony found her when he walked back into the bedroom with Nymph, spread eagled and hungry for more.

Nymph looked at Tony and smiled. He was suddenly glad that he decided to stop by Tony's house before heading to the car wash.

"Let me guess, you gave her the white one," Nymph said to Tony and started laughing.

"You know it," Tony boasted. "Church girl's rhythm was off just a little the first time, so I decided to help her out. Besides, she looked like she hadn't been fucked properly in years."

"Can I get some help here, or are you boys just going to watch," Helen asked in between moans. Some small rational part of her brain recognized that she had just invited a total stranger to have sex with her, but the drug was in full control now and she just didn't care.

"So you gonna hit this with me or do you have somewhere else to go?"

Nymph already held his answer in his hand, hard, throbbing, and ready.

"*Helllooo*, are you just-"

Before Helen could even finish her sentence, Nymph gave her something to shut her up, as Tony mounted her from behind.

Tony was definitely starting his morning off with a bang.

Chapter **13**

"Looks like you have company," Coltrane said to Cami. "I could come back another time."

Cami looked from Earl to Coltrane. The difference between the two was like night and day. Every time she saw Earl's face it reminded her of how stupid she was. Cami knew she should have never gotten involved with Earl at the age of fifteen. And she'd rather forget about that Tuesday two months ago.

Cami turned to Coltrane and said, "No. I offered you a cup of coffee. I intend to keep my word."

Earl took it upon himself to climb the porch steps without being invited. He didn't think that Cami would make a scene. But then again, he didn't know what Cami would do. Earl never thought in a million years that she would have let him back into her bed after so many years, but she had. Earl thought that maybe there was hope for them after all. Maybe Cami had finally forgiven him for taking her virginity. Their first sexual encounter wasn't exactly forced, but he had pressured her into it. Cami had loved him, but he knew she hadn't been ready for such an undertaking. He had wanted her so badly though. Earl had felt as if he had to have her or he'd shrivel up and die.

"Cami, please talk to me. Tell me how you're feeling," Earl begged jamming his foot between the door and the jamb when Cami tried to close it.

"I'm fine Earl.   Now leave," Cami said exasperatedly.

"Who's your friend," Earl asked and used his momentum to shove himself through the door and it caught Cami off guard.

Coltrane caught Cami against his chest when she lost her footing. He was dying to know who Earl was. And he wondered if Earl was someone he should tell Yuri and Sully about.

"It's none of your goddamn business who he is," Cami hissed. "Now get the hell out of my house."

"You didn't tell me to get out two months ago," Earl shot right back. "You already have someone else warming your bed."

If Cami had had a knife in her hand she would have cut out Earl's tongue happily. She had never been more embarrassed. Earl apparently wanted to a play a vicious game of 'tell all' and Cami could give just as well as she got.

"You want an introduction Earl, you got it."

Cami turned toward Coltrane and said, "Earl, this is Coltrane. Coltrane, this is Earl, Tisha's father."

"Shut the hell up Cami," Earl rasped, his anger evident in his voice.

"Oh, what's wrong Earl? You don't want anyone to know you fathered a fifteen year-old child's baby? Or is it that you don't want your wife to know her husband likes girls half his age?"

"Dammit Camilla! It shouldn't be like this," Earl croaked. Seeing Cami always knocked the wind right out of him. She was always so taxing on his nerves. Cami either hated you or loved you. The problem was that Earl remembered when Cami *had* loved him. She had made him feel ten feet tall and young again. What he wouldn't give to feel that way again.

"You're right Earl, it shouldn't be this way. You should openly acknowledge your daughter. You should pay child support, and you should tell your wife about Tisha," Cami admonished.

"You know damn well you don't need my money," Earl replied.

"You're right Earl, I don't *need* your money, but Tisha deserves it. Now get out!"

Earl felt deflated and horny. If only Cami could realize how much he loved her. They could have such a good relationship despite his marriage to Helen.

"I'll call you later," Earl called over his shoulder as he loped down the steps and made his way to his car.

Cami closed the front door and leaned her forehead against it. She couldn't believe Earl showed up when he did. She hadn't even gotten to know Coltrane well, and now he knew all her business.

The part that angered Cami so much was that she genuinely liked Coltrane. Now that he knew about her relationship with Earl, he probably wanted nothing to do with her. Coltrane was probably disgusted by what she'd done and he probably couldn't wait to leave.

"Now that you know my dirty little secret I'm sure you can't wait to leave."

Coltrane had been silent through the entire exchange. Cami had handled herself well. She by no means knew what he was thinking. If she could have read Coltrane's mind, she would have known that he had to restrain himself to not punch Earl square in the nose.

"You don't know what I'm thinking Cami, so don't assume you do."

Cami unzipped her coat and took it off. She was quite warm all of a sudden and knew it was either from her embarrassment or her anger. She knew what Coltrane was thinking, and she wasn't going to listen to his lies about how what he'd heard didn't matter. Things always mattered to people. Cami had learned that lesson long ago.

"Oh I know Coltrane, believe me I do. Right now you're thinking what kind of girl gets herself knocked up by a married man twice her age."

"Dammit Cami! Why is that chip on your shoulder so large?"

"Because men like Earl put it there. That's why," Cami lamented. The fight was slowly seeping out of her leaving behind shame and hurt.

Coltrane pulled Cami close and placed his lips gently over hers. He berated himself silently for kissing her, but felt that he had to.

God I want this woman.

That thought prickled his conscience, but he ignored the little voice in his head. He refused to think about his job while he tasted something so sweet.

Cami was the first to pull away staying Coltrane with one hand on his chest.

"Don't Coltrane. Especially if you don't mean it."

"What do I have to do to make you trust me," he asked placing a hand on her right cheek.

"I don't trust anybody."

"That's a damn lonely existence. Tell me what to do here Cami."

Cami looked into Coltrane's eyes and saw the sincerity there. At least she thought it was sincerity. How she wanted to trust him. Cami would never admit it, but she needed to trust Coltrane. By him just moving there from Washington, D.C. there was a good chance he didn't know Tony Jackson.

The bottom line was that Cami needed someone to trust, and Coltrane just might be that person.

"For starters," Cami said, "you can stick around. This is my life. It's filled with a ten year old daughter, a dead aunt, and men like Earl. And it only gets worse from here."

"How about that cup of coffee," Coltrane said compassionately.

Chapter 14

Helen relaxed in her bathtub and thought about all that had happened that morning. Her body ached deliciously. She was bruised nearly everywhere and very sore, but she loved the way she felt. Helen felt very alive and she hadn't felt this good in a long time.

Tony had given her exactly what she needed. Helen had never thought of herself as sexy, but now she did. She remembered Tony and the other man, whose name she didn't even know, doing all sorts of nasty, freaky things to her and she liked every minute of it.

Helen pulled her butt cheeks apart so the warm water could penetrate her rectum. Even that was sore, but how she had loved the feel of Tony's penis there. She had winced in pain at first, but then the other guy had started doing things to her with his tongue, and the next thing Helen knew, she was having the most amazing orgasm of her life. She would never in a million years have thought that she'd take it in the ass and like it.

Helen wished she'd had a video camera, because she almost couldn't believe she had been so uninhibited. Of course the little white pill had had a lot to do with it, but Helen clearly remembered being in control of her own feelings. She thought the pill had only made her horny as hell.

Helen rinsed the soap from her body and she decided to do a bit of shopping at Northland Mall. After a day like today, she deserved a new outfit, and maybe a pair of shoes. She even thought about treating herself to lunch somewhere decadently expensive.

Helen gingerly toweled her body dry as she gazed into the full length mirror on the back of the bathroom door. The woman in the mirror looked the same, but she felt so different.

The woman in the mirror had bite marks circling her breasts that were rapidly turning bluish purple in color. Helen remembered the other man biting her while Tony had fiercely thrust into her. She also remembered screaming with pleasure as it happened. Helen had been forever changed in Belinda's house, her bed. And it was a change for the better. She had never felt more alive than she did at that moment. The fact that Helen realized she wanted to live brought tears to her eyes.

Helen didn't want to live in hopes of having a baby. She didn't even want to live for Earl. For the first time in over a decade, Helen wanted to live for herself.

Coltrane pulled into the driveway of his parents' Bloomfield Hills home. He admired the house every time he came to visit. He and his brother Miles had saved up enough money to purchase the house for their parents six years ago. And with the settlement check that his father had received from Ford after losing the ring and pinky fingers of his left hand at the plant, they'd been able to furnish the house as well as invest a sizable nest egg for their retirement. Coltrane's father had never believed that hard work and Social Security alone would be enough to take care of his family.

That lesson alone was probably the reason his older brother Miles was pulling down beaucoup bucks working as a derivatives trader on Wall Street. Stanley

Kennedy had made his boys read the *Wall Street Journal* thoroughly everyday. They'd been the only black kids in Detroit running around the ghetto telling the crack dealer on their block that he needed to diversify. They'd had a crazy childhood.

Coltrane exited his Ford Taurus and searched through his pockets for his house keys. All his siblings had keys to the house, even though Miles lived in New York City, and Coltrane had been in Washington, D.C. Ella and Billie both had their own places. Ella was married and living in Detroit, while Billie had her own place in Ann Arbor, one semester shy of finishing her Masters degree at the University of Michigan.

Coltrane entered the house and heard the low strains of Bob Barker's voice, sounding the same as it did when he was a boy. He experienced a weird sense of déja vous. He couldn't count the times he'd come into the house and heard the sounds of The Price is Right.

Coltrane found his mother in the family room with a cup of tea in her hand, yelling at the contestant on the big screen television to go higher as he tried to come within one thousand dollars of the price of a Volkswagon.

"Hi Mom," Coltrane called out competing with the boisterous audience on the game show.

"Coltrane, you made it," Diana Kennedy said to her son simultaneously turning down the volume on the television with the sleek black remote control.

Diana's warm copper complexion shone and her hazel eyes lit up as she broke into a smile. She smoothed a stray salt and pepper strand of hair back into the bun wrapped tightly at her nape.

Diana loved it when her children came to visit. She missed all four of them on a daily basis. She wished she had them all living at home with her again especially since she had retired from nursing, but they were all spread out living their own lives. That was okay with Diana as long as they came to visit on a regular basis.

"Sorry I'm so late Mom, but something came up," Coltrane explained.

Diana looked deeply into her son's eyes. She had always been able to read Coltrane the easiest out of her four children. The others made Diana work at it a bit more, but Coltrane had never been able to hide anything. To the average person Coltrane was viewed as shy though outgoing, but in front of his family he could be himself, and let down his guard.

"You want to tell me what's really on your mind," his mother asked setting down her tea cup and moving to the love seat in order to sit beside her son.

Coltrane shrugged his shoulders. His mind automatically strayed to Cami. He hadn't been gone an hour from her house and he was already wondering what she was doing. They'd parted company with him leaving for his mother's house, and her having to make a doctor's appointment, only after assuring him that it was just a check-up.

"I think I'm falling for a woman and I know I have no business falling for her," Coltrane admitted.

"Is she married," Diana asked.

"No, it's nothing like that."

Diana ran her hand along the side of Coltrane's face. It was still hard to believe that her son was all grown up. She still remembered the day she'd brought him home from the hospital. Coltrane had been her biggest baby, outweighing his brother and sisters by nearly a pound. He and Miles were the same height, but to this day, Coltrane was still slightly larger in build.

"Son, you can't help who you fall in love with. If that were the case, I would have married your Uncle Marvin. I didn't mean to fall in love with Marvin's brother, but it happened. And obviously it was meant to happen because Stan and I have had a wonderful life together with wonderful children."

"I know Mom."

Diana patted Coltrane's hand then took another sip of her tea. Her son had her intrigued. Rarely had he brought women to meet his family, or even talked about a woman. Whoever the woman was, Diana knew she had to be someone special.

"Tell me about her," Diana told her son and settled back into the pillows to listen.

Coltrane smiled. He had no idea how to describe Cami. There weren't enough hours in the day or enough words in the dictionary to describe her, but Coltrane tried.

"Camilla is beautiful and shy and courageous. She's a single mother of a ten year old daughter named Tisha. She also has walls up about ten inches thick, and for the life of me I can't figure out a way to get past them."

Coltrane sighed like a forlorn child and rested his head back on a pillow.

"I realize we just met Mom, but she doesn't trust anyone. I don't even know how to earn that trust," Coltrane told his mother dejectedly.

Diana stood up and motioned for Coltrane to follow her into the kitchen. She put a cinnamon roll on a plate and heated it in the microwave oven. Pouring a tall glass of milk, she set both on the kitchen table for her son.

"First of all son, it's going to take time for Camilla to trust you. Contrary to what you may think, just because you tell her to trust you doesn't mean she's going to do it."

"I know that Mom," Coltrane lamented feeling his frustrations mount. He always hated when his mother pointed things out that were right in front of his nose.

"I think that if you really want Camilla, I mean truly want her, you should woo her. That means flowers and gifts and romantic dates. It also means don't try to have sex with her until the timing is absolutely perfect. And Coltrane, most importantly, don't lie to her."

"It's already too late for that," he mumbled under his breath when his mother turned toward the refrigerator.

"What did you say dear?"

"Nothing. Hey Mom, how are the kittens?"

Coltrane neatly changed the topic. He was starting to feel really guilty.

Diana's cat Trixie had had kittens six weeks ago. She promised Coltrane a kitten when her daughter Billie had informed her Coltrane's twenty year old cat, Shadow, had died.

"The kittens are weaned and litter box trained. I was going to give you first pick before I take the rest to church on Sunday. A few people were interested in adopting them."

"I'm keeping one, and you'll take one, so that leaves me with four kittens that need homes."

Coltrane thought about his cat Shadow. He'd found Shadow in an alley scared and hungry when he was just a year or two older than Tisha. That thought gave him an idea.

"Mom, would you mind if I picked out two kittens? I'm thinking of giving one to Tisha."

"That's a wonderful idea. And I'm sure you'll score points with Camilla for thinking about Tisha. I knew I didn't raise a fool."

Coltrane just shook his head and laughed. His mother was one of a kind.

"What time is Dad coming home," Coltrane asked checking his watch. He had hoped to catch his father before he had to leave, but Coltrane wanted to make it back before Cami. At the rate the snow was falling, their driveways and sidewalks would be covered with several inches of snow before he knew it. Coltrane wanted to surprise Cami and have her walk shoveled by the time she got home.

"He won't be home until two or three today. He wanted to stay for the holiday shipment that's being delivered in preparation for Black Friday."

Coltrane smiled. Since retiring from the plant his father had thrown himself vigorously into overseeing shipments of toys at a nearby Toys R' Us.

"I'm going to go and shovel the driveway for him, then he can use the snow blower later," Coltrane decided and stood from the table to get his coat. "I'll look at the kittens and pick two when I come back inside."

"All right son. I'll put on a pot of coffee for you," Diana said grateful for Coltrane's help. Her husband, Stan, thought the snow blower was for weaklings. He preferred the manual hard labor of shoveling heavily packed snow. At least Diana knew exactly where her children's stubbornness came from.

Chapter 15

Tony and Nymph sat at the dining room table with three empty bags of Dot & Etta's shrimp. They'd worked up quite an appetite that morning. Shortly after Helen had left, they'd redressed and gone out for food.

Nymph sat back in his chair and rubbed his dick. He hadn't run a train on a woman in awhile, at least six months or so. The last woman hadn't been as accommodating as Helen. Nymph had slipped GHB, a clear liquid that resembled water, but was actually a mixture of floor stripper and drain cleaner, in her rum and coke at a club. Then he and a buddy had taken her to a motel and fucked the shit out of her. Of course when she woke up the next morning screaming 'rape,' Nymph had had to take care of her. He and his buddy hadn't worn rubbers and there was no way Nymph would go to jail because of some crazy whoring bitch.

After making sure she was scrubbed clean, Nymph had taken her back to her car at the club. She was later found behind the steering wheel with a gunshot wound to the chest, an apparent mugging victim with the contents of her purse strewn about the car and ground, her cash and credit cards stolen.

It was nice to fuck a woman and not have to kill her, Nymph thought.

"What time is the shipment arriving," Nymph asked Tony as he took a gulp from his can of ice cold Budweiser.

"Seven p.m.," Tony replied. "Tyrone is also driving in from Chi-Town tonight."

"Tyrone," Nymph asked rhetorically. "The last time you used that motherfucker he brought us heroin covered in shit. He didn't even bother to rinse off the pellets first. I'm going to shoot that bitch in the ass if he tries that again."

Tony laughed, remembering Nymph's face when he had to clean the shit off the pellets.

"I had a talk with him about that," Tony said. "It should be all right this time."

"It better be Tony, or I'm bustin' a cap in his ass," Nymph warned again.

Some men were just straight up punk bitches, Nymph thought. And Tyrone was one of them.

Earl came home for lunch to an empty house. Even though Helen's car was gone he still looked through the house for her. He just couldn't believe that she wasn't there to meet him for lunch. Even on Helen's days off, she still stayed home to meet Earl for lunch.

Earl searched the house and found a note on the refrigerator door. He read the note once, twice, three times. There had to have been a mistake. The Helen he was married to wouldn't have left him a note. She would have been at home.

Earl read the note once more trying to make some sense out of it:

Earl, gone shopping.
Eat shit and die.
Helen

Earl stood baffled in the kitchen. Something had to be wrong. Helen would never write a note like that.

Chapter 16

Cami made her way home through the snow after leaving the OB/GYN office. She'd had a regular pre-natal appointment scheduled, but since she'd had a miscarriage, she went in for a follow-up exam just like her friend Theo told her to do.

Cami's doctor had examined her and then took some blood to make sure her level of the pregnancy hormone HCG was lowering properly. Everything else her doctor had done had been routine.

The thought of shoveling snow depressed her as she turned down her street. Every year she promised herself that she would buy a snow blower. And every year she had talked herself out of it, rationalizing that the money was better spent on Tisha's college tuition. But now Cami had wished like hell that she'd just bought the damn snow blower seeing the mass of snow all around her neighbor's houses.

Cami slowed her Miata preparing to turn into her snow-covered driveway. But to her surprise, it was nice and clear. She quickly looked around and saw Coltrane salting her front porch. Both of their houses were shoveled and salted. Cami couldn't believe it. No man had ever done anything like that for her, let alone a man she just met.

He probably wanted money, Cami thought as she opened her car door.

Coltrane had known the exact moment Cami had spotted him. He'd seen the play of emotions on her face raw and unguarded. Coltrane saw delight and surprise give way to mistrust. Before she'd gotten out of the car however, Cami had her normal shuttered mask carefully in place.

"So, how was your doctor's appointment," Coltrane asked settling the bag of rock salt against the porch steps. He thought Cami looked adorable in her multi-colored knit hat with the ear flaps adorned with pom-poms on each end.

"It was fine," Cami answered. "So, what do I owe you for this," she asked reaching into her purse for her wallet.

Coltrane stayed Cami's hand by covering it with his own.

"Don't insult me Cami. I don't want your money."

"Well what do you want," she asked sarcastically.

"Dammit woman!" Coltrane barked. "Hasn't anyone ever done something nice for you?"

"No they haven't," Cami admitted. "No one besides my aunt or Tisha."

That knocked the wind right out of him. He didn't know what he'd expected her to say, but it wasn't that.

"I'm sorry," Cami apologized. "Thank you for shoveling."

"You're welcome."

Coltrane looked deeply into Cami's eyes and saw the sincerity there. That was a lot better than the mistrust he saw in her eyes earlier.

"Would you like something warm to drink? Coffee maybe?"

"Coffee would be great," Coltrane replied.

"There's one more thing," Cami said hesitantly with a half smile. "I usually shovel Mrs. Monroe's walkway too. She watches Tisha a lot for me, so I try to help her out because she's older," she explained.

"No problem. Just have that coffee ready."

Cami went up her shoveled porch steps and into the house. She quickly looked out the window and saw Coltrane already shoveling Mrs. Monroe's walkway. She still couldn't believe what he'd done.

Noticing that he was making quick work of his task, Cami rushed into the kitchen and readied the coffee maker before she even took off her coat.

Once the strong brew began its descent into the coffee pot, Cami ran back to the window tossing her coat over a chair as she went. Coltrane had finished shoveling and had nearly finished salting the walkway.

Cami pulled open the front door as Coltrane walked toward the house. His heavily muscled body moved effortlessly, which was surprising since he was a rather large man.

"Coffee's almost ready," she told Coltrane as he took the porch steps two at a time.

"Thanks," he replied as he took off his gloves and chafed his hands. "It's cold enough out there to freeze the balls off a brass monkey!"

Cami poured Coltrane a cup of coffee. She remembered from earlier that he liked his coffee 'black like his women' as he put it, whereas Cami heavily sugared and excessively creamed hers.

She handed Coltrane his coffee mug after he'd taken off his sheepskin coat. She eyed the coat speculatively. Cami would be willing to bet the coat was warmer than anything she owned. It looked comfortable and toasty and would probably put up a good fight against 'old man winter.'

"Nice coat," she remarked truly meaning it.

"Thanks. This coat's my best friend on a day like today," Coltrane joked.

"Have a seat," Cami told him as she sat down on the sectional in the living room. "So tell me, how's your mother?"

Coltrane sat down as instructed and smiled. At least Cami was making an attempt at conversation and not biting his head off. That was a good sign.

"She and my father are both well."

"Was she upset that you were late," Cami asked taking a sip of the scalding brew.

Coltrane curled his fingers around his own coffee mug, feeling the first tingles of circulation and warmth flow through his fingers. He wished he'd had sheepskin gloves to keep his fingers from turning to ice.

"My mother is the most laid back woman on the planet. She rarely gets upset with the family."

"Your parents live in Detroit," Cami asked as she started to relax. Letting her guard down a little wasn't too bad. They were getting to know each other and it was fairly painless, Cami thought. She wasn't used to meeting men as nice as Coltrane.

"Used to," Coltrane answered in between sips. "They're in Bloomfield now. There were three crack houses on their block and too many drive-bys."

"That's good that they were able to move. I've been thinking about moving too."

"Yeah? Where," Coltrane asked hoping Cami didn't say somewhere too far. He'd just met her and the idea of losing her so soon didn't sit well with him.

Cami shrugged her shoulders.

"I don't know. I really hadn't thought it through. All I know is that I need a change," she admitted for the first time. She felt that way even before Belinda died. Now with Tisha as her only family, there was nothing holding her back.

Coltrane was captivated by Cami. She was such a mixture of hot and cold. She kept surprising him at every turn.

"Before I forget," Coltrane began, "would you mind terribly if I gave Tisha a kitten?"

"A kitten," Cami repeated, baffled. Coltrane wanted to give her daughter a kitten.

"My mother's cat had kittens and I took two, one for me – and hopefully one for Tisha. I even bought all the necessities."

"You really want to give my baby a kitten," Cami asked. She was utterly dumbfounded. Tisha hadn't ever gotten anything from anyone besides her and Belinda.

"Yes, I really do."

Cami was so overwhelmed that she leaned forward and captured Coltrane's face in her hands. Her fingers caressed the soft, wiry hairs of his goatee, then traced the outline of his full luscious lips. They were warm from the coffee and very, very smooth. Cami so hated a man with chapped lips. She liked a man with lips just like Coltrane's.

Cami leaned forward even more, tentatively settling her lips over Coltrane's. She was timid at first, but then grew bolder as each moment passed.

The kiss was gentle and tender, yet erotic and passionate. And when Coltrane parted his lips, Cami knew it was a kiss that she would never forget. Cami felt that kiss all the way to her toes, and that worried her immensely. She tried to tamp down the growing panic that bloomed within her. Cami hadn't been prepared for such powerful feelings to course through her body.

She hadn't been prepared for Coltrane Kennedy.

Coltrane wasn't sure who pulled away first, but when the kiss ended he pulled Cami by the nape of her neck into his arms. He was doubly shocked first by the kiss, and second by her submissiveness. Coltrane didn't think Cami was the type to make the first move, but she had surprised him.

Coltrane sifted his fingers through the strands of Cami's pony tail. It was silky soft and long. He liked the texture of it and understood why he had first mistaken her real hair for a weave. It had that 'too good to be true' appearance.

Cami was the first to break the silence.

"I don't know what to say."

"You don't have to say anything," Coltrane replied and placed a kiss atop her head.

Cami casually glanced at her watch. She'd have to get ready to pick up Tisha in a few minutes. Time had literally flown by.

"What is it," Coltrane asked when he noticed Cami starting to fidget.

"I have to pick up Tisha."

"Mind if I walk with you?"

"I'd like that."

Chapter **17**

Helen unlocked the side door, carefully balancing her packages with one hand. She'd had fun at Northland Mall browsing through the stores and buying whatever she liked. She'd even bought an expensive pair of black leather boots with a matching leather handbag from Marshall Fields.

Normally Helen would never have spent money frivolously, but today wasn't a normal day.

Today Helen was alive and spent every second enjoying herself. She'd already wasted years of her life and didn't plan on wasting anymore.

She had decided that with or without Earl she was going to make a change. She had thought all day about what she was going to say to him. She'd decided that she would give him an ultimatum. He could either stay with her, or he could leave. Helen did truly love Earl, but knew she would never be happy if they continued their marriage in its present condition.

Helen made her way through the kitchen after closing and locking the side door and through the living room. She found Earl sitting in the living room's queen recliner, a magazine plopped haphazardly on his lap and a beer at his side. She hadn't expected him home. He was supposed to be at work. Helen deduced that Earl must have put his car in the garage. He was funny about dirtying the Cadillac with snow, ice and salt – all the components that made up a Detroit winter.

"What are you doing home," Helen asked setting her packages on the couch.

"I took the afternoon off because I was worried about you. You weren't home for lunch and I found a note telling me to 'eat shit and die.'"

"And yet you're still alive," Helen quipped sarcastically.

"What the hell is that supposed to mean?"

"What do you think it means," Helen fired back.

"What's wrong with you Helen," Earl asked quizzically.

"The question is what's right with me Earl."

Helen took off her coat and took her time hanging it in the front closet. She knew she had Earl on the fence and she wanted to keep it that way. If the situation weren't so serious she would have laughed. The look on Earl's face was priceless. He was confused and it showed.

Helen stood in front of the recliner and looked down her nose at Earl. She wondered if he had ever truly loved her. He couldn't have loved her since he'd cheated on her with so many women. Cami wasn't the only one. Helen knew about two other women that Earl had cheated with. One was a co-worker that Helen had met at the company's Christmas party two years ago. Helen had walked in on them having sex in the women's bathroom, of all places. She hadn't said anything about it because Earl never saw her come into the bathroom anyway.

Helen knew Earl loved her the day they got married, but she couldn't remember the exact day that things had started to go wrong. Maybe it was her desire for a baby, or maybe it was Earl deciding he needed other women to satisfy him. Or maybe Helen was just a fool in love. Whichever it was, things were about to change.

"I've come to a decision Earl," Helen started. "I can't live with you knowing that you cheat on me Earl. It makes me feel like shit, and I won't put up with it. I deserve better than that. And don't you think that yours is the only dick that works. I've had bigger and better just this morning," Helen spat.

"Son of a bitch!" Earl jumped to his feet toppling the precariously perched magazine. In his haste the beer can's contents bubbled onto the carpet as well. The vein in his neck protruded angrily and his light brown-skinned features turned a dark violent red.

"Doesn't feel so good knowing your spouse cheated does it?"

Helen remained cool, calm, and very collected.

"Who was the son-of-a-bitch!" Earl shouted.

"Actually, there were two sons of bitches, but that's beside the point. You need to go, pack yourself a bag, and leave. Right now."

"You can't be serious Helen!"

"Oh I'm very serious. Go point your dick in Camilla's direction. Maybe she gives a damn."

Earl was stunned into silence. He'd never expected this from his docile wife, especially not the part about Helen cheating. She obviously had more gumption than he'd thought. Earl knew he had to change tactics. Fast.

"Helen, you know I love you."

"Save it Earl! Now hurry up and get your shit. I have a date tonight."

Earl didn't need to know that Helen's date was with a Blockbuster movie rental of *Waiting to Exhale*. She felt a kinship to the women in the movie at a time like this. She needed all the support she could get.

Earl angrily stomped off into the bedroom. Helen heard him noisily stuffing clothes and toiletries into a suitcase, then the distinct sound of a zipped garment bag.

Within fifteen minutes Earl had packed and marched sullenly through the house and out to the garage. Since Helen had parked on the street there was no reason to go outside. She stayed put on the couch until she heard the Cadillac's muffler scrape the end of the driveway as Earl sped away. Earl was finally gone, and a huge cloud lifted from above Helen's head. She was going to be all right after all.

Chapter 18

Tony and Nymph were taking a ride to the East side of Detroit to pay a visit to Chico, one of the many runners who reported to Nymph. Chico claimed that his girl had an emergency and he had to spend Tony's money on hospital bills. Chico also claimed that he'd have Tony's money in a couple of weeks.

"Chico is full of shit," Nymph said. "I'd bet my ass that he's doing a line with that bitch of his right now."

"I know he is," Tony replied. "He's done this to me one too many times. I can't have the rest of my guys thinking they can rip me off and get away with it. I'm going to make Chico my example," Tony revealed pulling a .9mm Glock from his waistband.

"It's about time," Nymph said as he pulled up in front of Chico's house. "That motherfucker needs to be taught a lesson."

Tony knocked on the front door while Nymph waited at the back door. Within minutes Nymph had collared Chico and shoved him through the back door. He and Tony both knew Chico was a punk bitch, and punk bitches always tried to run. Nymph was there to make sure that didn't happen.

Chico's light tan complexion turned ruddy from fear and lack of oxygen. Nymph had him by the throat cutting off his air supply. He ran a hand through his curly jet black hair and took several deep breaths. His brown eyes were wide and as huge as saucers. He knew he was in for trouble.

Nymph and Chico made their way through the house and unlocked the front door for Tony. Chico had the nerve to act as if he wasn't about to run out the back door to get away from his boss.

"Where's my money *puta*?"

"Tony, I really did have an emergency," Chico started in a heavily Puerto Rican accented voice. "I can have it for you in a week. Honest."

Nymph searched the filthy dilapidated house. Mice scurried at his feet and other small rodents inhabited various corners and empty bedrooms. After opening every door and closet and finding it empty, Nymph checked the only place he hadn't looked yet.

The bathroom.

Nymph opened the creaky wooden door and looked past the dingy blue shower curtain to find a wretched looking black woman smoking a crack pipe in the bathtub. Her skin was cracked and leathery, probably from years on the street. Track marks marred her forearms and she was so skinny that her ribs protruded from under her skin. Her glazed eyes barely took in Nymph's sudden appearance.

Nymph hauled her out of the bathtub and dragged her downstairs wearing only a pair of stained white panties that smelled of urine. Her hair was dirty and matted to her head and she was as high as a kite.

Chico nearly shit his pants when he saw Tony put on a pair of black leather gloves. There was only one reason a man needed to wear gloves inside of a house. That's when Chico started pleading for his life.

"Tony, I promise you that I'll get your money. I can have it for you tomorrow in fact," Chico said.

"Have you been spending my money on this crack ho? You've been giving her my drugs haven't you puta?"

Taking Tony's cue, Nymph pulled out his pair of leather gloves and slipped them on.

"C'mon Tony, please. I don't even know her," Chico lied pointing at the prostitute.

"So now you're giving my stuff to strangers," Tony yelled.

"No Tony. She means nothing to me."

"Nothing huh? In that case..."

Tony pulled out his Glock and shot the prostitute in the head at point blank range, execution style.

"Oh God, please Tony," Chico begged and dissolved into tears. He fell to his knees and made the sign of the cross.

"Don't die like a bitch," Tony uttered disgustedly as he placed the hot muzzle in the center of Chico's forehead and pulled the trigger.

"Torch it," Tony told Nymph, "and then let's get the fuck out of here."

Nymph retrieved the liquor bottle he'd seen on the kitchen counter and sprinkled the amber liquid over the bodies. He took out his trusty Zippo and set fire to the curtains first, and then the two dead bodies. The lighter his father had given him on his thirteenth birthday, was still his favorite toy.

Nymph found Tony standing by his Benz polishing his personalized license plate that read: SNWKING.

"What's next," Nymph asked getting into the passenger side of the car.

"We check on the shipment from New York. Then we wait for Tyrone."

"Bet. Let's pick up some food on the way."

"I can't believe that bitch cried," Tony said laughing as he pulled into the street. "Next time find me a man with a goddamn spine."

"Sure thing, Tony. Sure thing."

Earl pulled into the parking lot of a Southfield Hotel. He'd elected to stay in the Detroit suburb to be closer to his job. Earl didn't know how long Helen would be in her mood, but he only planned to stay at the hotel a few days.

After having been married for so long, Earl wasn't sure he wanted a separation, let alone a divorce. He'd always had affairs with younger women including Cami, but he'd always had Helen. Part of the appeal to his affairs was fooling Helen. Now that she knew about his infidelity, it took the fun out of it.

Earl honestly didn't know what he wanted. Naturally, he wanted the best of both worlds, but Helen and Cami were making it impossible. He wanted Cami because she made him feel young, and virile. One session of lovemaking with her, and Earl felt like he could conquer the world.

Helen on the other hand, made him feel drained and empty, but he stayed with her because after nearly twenty years of marriage he was just too old to start over. Besides that, it was cheaper to keep her around.

Helen wasn't exciting at all. At least she hadn't been until now. In a way her infidelity aroused him but he was still upset about it, if that made any sense.

Earl realized that without Helen he would have to do his own laundry, and fix his own meals. But this would be a small price to pay for his freedom.

Knowing that he could go to Cami free and clear gave Earl great satisfaction. He even wondered if he could stay at her place while he and Helen got their act together. One of Cami's main objections had been his marriage. Maybe now Cami would accept him into her bed again if that weren't an issue anymore.

Earl pictured Helen in his mind and replayed their argument. He'd noticed the tight Levi's jeans that she so rarely wore. Helen also had on more make-up than normal and she was wearing new perfume. And if Earl remembered correctly she'd admitted that she slept with not one, but two men. That thought pissed him off more than he cared to think about. Earl had taken for granted that Helen would always be there. Regardless.

But here he was sitting in front of a hotel with a hastily packed suitcase.

With a long-suffering sigh, Earl went to check in.

He hoped Helen would come to her senses soon.

He knew she would take him back. She didn't have any choice. Helen couldn't and wouldn't make it without him.

Chapter **19**

Coltrane watched Cami's face as she anxiously waited for Tisha's class to come through the elementary school's front door. She watched for Tisha like a hawk with nothing distracting her.

Cami saw Mrs. Nelson lead the class to the door and dismiss them. She spotted Tisha immediately and her face lit up like a Christmas tree. Cami waved excitedly when Tisha saw her.

"You've missed her," Coltrane noticed from watching Cami's expression.

"Of course I've missed her. She's all I have."

"Not anymore," Coltrane blurted before he could think better of it. He was sure he'd kick himself tonight over his lovesick declaration, but couldn't take the statement back. If Yuri or Sully had heard him just now, they'd pull his ass off the assignment immediately.

Coltrane was having a hard time separating business and pleasure. He knew what his job was and he knew what he was supposed to do. Implementing it, however, would be difficult.

Cami let the statement pass without comment as Tisha came running over.

"Hi Mom," Tisha greeted Cami and received a kiss on the cheek. "Hi Coltrane!"

Tisha was much more excited by the fact that Coltrane had accompanied her mother to pick her up. She took that to mean that he must have believed her when she told him how much her mother liked him. Maybe, Tisha thought, her mother would finally have a boyfriend and she would be happy. Tisha missed the days when her aunt Belinda would come by and they would all go for ice cream and to the movies, or bike riding at the park. Her mother and Belinda would laugh at all her jokes no matter how corny they were. Now her mother rarely laughed at all, and they never did anything fun anymore. Tisha missed that. She missed it a lot.

Tisha even missed the happy faces that her mother used to make on top of her pancakes at breakfast. Blueberries were used for the eyes, a plump strawberry for the nose, and a piece of slightly bent bacon for the mouth made Tisha smile at least twice a week.

Now Tisha ate cold cereal most mornings and breakfast was boring. Her mother never laughed, and she didn't smile much either. She just got the job done.

Tisha even remembered her mother going on a date once or twice, but it didn't last long. She was always home early, and Tisha never got a chance to meet any of the men. Her mother always told her that the first man she met that was important to her, Tisha would meet him. So far Tisha hadn't met anyone, except for Coltrane.

"Hi Tisha," Coltrane replied.

"Thanks Coltrane for coming to pick me up from school," Tisha said with what was akin to hero worship.

"What am I Tisha, chopped liver," Cami asked her daughter smiling.

Tisha laughed. "Of course not Mom. It's just that you always pick me up. Coltrane is a nice surprise."

"I'm glad you feel that way Tisha," Coltrane told the ten year old. "I'll try to walk with you when I can. How's that?"

"Cool!" Tisha exclaimed.

Cami shot Coltrane a puzzled look. He was making a very big commitment and she didn't think it was a good idea. Cami didn't want to see Tisha's feelings hurt because Coltrane decided he wanted a new flavor of the month.

Cami immediately chided herself. Not all men were bad. It wasn't as if he promised Tisha that he'd walk with her everyday. Coltrane had made it clear that he'd do it when he could.

Coltrane held Cami's gaze and didn't back down. He knew she was thinking all types of sordid things. Only when Cami looked away did Coltrane continue his conversation with Tisha.

"I have a surprise for you when you get home," Coltrane taunted.

"A surprise? What is it?"

"You'll have to wait and see," he replied.

"Aww man! Do I have to?"

"Yes," Cami answered. "How was school today?"

Cami successfully changed the subject knowing that Tisha would chatter about the surprise the entire walk home.

"It was okay. Mrs. Nelson asked me to sing in the Christmas pageant. I'm not sure if I want to though."

"Can you sing," Coltrane asked, finding his current company utterly fascinating. He'd never met anyone like Cami or Tisha.

"Of course I can sing Coltrane. Mrs. Nelson wouldn't have asked me if I couldn't," Tisha answered in a voice that made Coltrane feel stupid.

"Why don't you want to sing sweetheart," Cami asked her daughter as they entered the house. Tisha tried to explain amid the unbuttoning and hanging up of coats.

"Mom, if I sing I'll have to wear a dress. The last time I wore a dress to school Tyrell made fun of me. He said my legs were too skinny."

Coltrane was silent while the mother/daughter exchange continued. He too had taken his coat off and then followed the duo into the kitchen. Cami busied herself with coring an apple and placing a spoon inside a Yoplait strawberry yogurt.

Cami set Tisha's snack on the dining room table then lifted her daughter's chin.

"Don't ever let anyone stop you from doing what's in your heart Tisha. You look beautiful in a dress, and I know this for a fact because you're my daughter. And we both know that I didn't have an ugly baby."

"Besides, in six or seven years Tyrell is going to wish that he was nicer to you."

"Okay Mom. I'll sing."

"Good!"

"Would you like a slice of apple Coltrane," Tisha asked as she held out the saucer filled with wedges of a juicy golden delicious apple.

"Thanks Tisha, I would," Coltrane replied only to have the plate snatched away from his hand.

"Only if you agree to give me my surprise right after," Tisha bargained expertly.

"Deal."

As promised, after Coltrane swallowed the last bite of his apple, he went next door to get the kittens. Coltrane figured he'd let Tisha take first pick between the two.

Coltrane grabbed the bags filled with cat food, a litter box and kitty litter, a pet carrier for travel, and last but not least, a collar to hold the kitten's tags. Oh yeah, he had to grab the kittens too.

When Coltrane walked into Cami's house with the bag in one hand and both kittens inside the pet carrier,

Tisha was waiting on the couch with barely contained excitement.

Coltrane sat the bag down on the floor as well as the pet carrier. When he opened the carrier's door, the kittens bounded out, playfully batting each other and mewing.

"Oh my gosh!" Tisha exclaimed and sat on the floor laughing.

"I'm giving you first pick Tisha," Coltrane informed her while he also sat on the floor.

"You mean I get to keep one," Tisha asked truly surprised.

"Of course. That's your surprise. I even bought everything you need. I forgot to buy a scratching post, but I'll pick one up tomorrow."

"No one's ever given me a present before. Well, I mean no one besides my Mom and Belinda. Thank you Coltrane. Thanks a lot."

"You are very welcome."

Cami's eyes filled with tears while watching the exchange. Her emotions had been so raw and at the forefront since Belinda's death. She'd yet to even truly grieve over losing her aunt. Her entire body felt numb.

Cami felt like a hollow shell. She was hurt that Belinda died and angry over the fact that her aunt was murdered and she couldn't do a damn thing about it. If only Belinda could have left her clues about Tony's crimes. Cami would have gone to the police immediately. Tony thought he was untouchable, but Cami wished like hell she could prove he murdered Belinda. She would love to see Tony's ass rot in a tiny jail cell for the rest of his life. Death would be too kind for the son-of-a-bitch.

Coltrane saw the tears in Cami's eyes when she looked directly at him. He could only imagine what she must have been feeling. Coltrane winked at her and he

received a watery smile for his efforts. There was
something about Cami and Tisha Abernathy that set
his heart racing. For that reason alone, he was utterly
disgusted with himself. Coltrane knew better than to
become attached, but he couldn't help it.

They both watched Tisha as she played with the
kittens. Both kittens were orange Tabbies, but while
one had four white feet, the other had a white eye patch
and a white underbelly. The kittens climbed and clawed
their way up Tisha's red sweater. She giggled and
laughed happily.

"Have you decided which one you want Tisha,"
Coltrane asked.

"I'd love to keep both of them, but one of them is
yours so that wouldn't be cool."

Tisha looked at both kittens and tried to make a
decision. It was so hard to choose because they were
both so cute. Finally, Tisha made a decision. She would
take the one with the four white feet.

"I want this one Coltrane. He has four white feet
and it looks like he's wearing boots. That's what I'll
name him. Boots," Tisha said wanting to say the name
out loud to see how it sounded. "And the other one
should be named Patch because of the white patch over
his eye."

"I think that's a good idea Tisha," Coltrane told
her and picked up the kitten. "I couldn't have thought
of a better name. I'll help you get the litter box set up."

"Okay."

Tisha jumped up with the kitten in her arms and
toppled over a stack of mail on the coffee table. She
turned to pick it up, but her mother shooed her aside.

Cami bent down to retrieve the pile of bills and
junk mail. She hadn't felt like sorting through the mail
since Belinda's death. She had been so preoccupied
with everything else going on that paying bills wasn't

uppermost in her mind. The bills were all current and not due for another couple weeks, so she didn't feel like she was shirking her responsibilities.

Cami had neatly restacked the pile of mail when she found a sealed envelope addressed to her under the coffee table. The handwriting looked familiar, but Cami hadn't remembered seeing it arrive. The letter must have gotten shuffled in with the bills. It was weird, Cami thought, because she had checked each day when the mail arrived for anything personal. She hadn't seen this particular letter and she would have noticed it because of the familiar writing and the fact that it didn't have a return address.

Cami held the letter in her hand and flipped it back and forth. She didn't know why, but her heart began to beat like a racehorse. She focused on the postmark, and that's when it hit her.

The letter was from Belinda and it was postmarked the day she died.

"Oh my God," Cami moaned over and over again.

"Mom what's wrong," Tisha asked worriedly.

"Cami, what is it," Coltrane asked at the exact same time.

"It's from Belinda," Cami managed tearing open the flap of the letter.

When Cami opened the letter and read the first line she dissolved into hysterical sobs.

Chapter 20

Maxine and Brice sat in the law office's conference room. She had finally gotten copies of Belinda's entire file made. Over the past year, Maxine hadn't realized how much stuff Belinda had sent her. There were dozens of papers with information Maxine couldn't decipher. She hoped like hell that Belinda's niece Camilla knew what to do with it. Maybe there was something in the paperwork that proved Anthony Jackson murdered his wife, Maxine hoped.

She still couldn't believe her friend was dead. Belinda was always so vibrant, playful, and sexy as hell. Maxine had envied Belinda's body from the moment they met. She still remembered the day Belinda had joined the after school dance program in high school. Belinda had filled out a leotard in ninth grade better than the thirty year old dance instructor. All the other girls in class were instantly jealous and refused to show Belinda the dance steps to their latest piece. Maxine had volunteered and a friendship bloomed immediately. After that first meeting, they were inseparable.

Sophomore year Maxine and Belinda altered their class schedules so that they had all the same classes together except for one. They'd spent the majority of class time passing notes back and forth. It was a wonder that they hadn't gotten in trouble or had failing grades.

And every Friday Belinda brought a bag to school with her clothes in it and spent the weekend with Maxine. Fridays were always special to Belinda because she enjoyed hanging around Maxine's parents. Maxine's father didn't hit her mother like Belinda's father did.

They'd talk about boys and their latest crush in Hollywood. They'd listen to music for hours while experimenting with make-up. And she would never forget the time Belinda showed her how to properly stuff a bra.

While Maxine had an athletic build, Belinda was all curves and full breasts. Maxine laughed when she thought about trips to the mall with Belinda. Belinda had always gotten the best looking guys. Maxine had given up hope until she met Brice. Brice hadn't given Belinda a second glance, and Belinda assured her that that was a good sign. She had been right.

"Hi sweetheart, sorry I'm late." Brice hurried into the conference room. "My meeting ran over. Have you called your brother yet?"

"No, but I was about to. I tried his cell earlier and left a voicemail. I'm sure he's working right now, but maybe I can catch him anyway."

Brice punched in his brother-in-law's cell phone number on the speaker phone. Peter answered on the third ring.

"Wallace here."

"Hey Peter, it's Brice."

"And Maxine," she chimed in.

Maxine and Brice listened to tons of background noise about cops being bastards and arrested persons claiming they were innocent.

"Sounds like you're right at home," Maxine joked.

"Yeah, I've been working so much that I'm going to change my address to 1300 Beaubien," Peter grumbled looking around the downtown Detroit Police

Department's Headquarters. Peter hadn't had a day off in a month. He swore up and down that he was going to spend Thanksgiving like a normal person eating loads of Turkey and watching the Lion's play football.

All the hubbub and normal activity of Headquarters made Peter's shoulder slump. Just thinking about a day off with a cold beer and the ball game on the television made his mouth foam.

To perk himself up however, he went over and poured himself a cup of coffee. His partner Julio had already beat him to the strong mud-like brew and was adding a shit-load of sugar and cream to make it bearable. Julio's coffee mug brought a smile to Peter's face. The inscription 'Our Day Begins When Yours Ends' was a favorite in the homicide division. They needed sayings like that to make them smile lest they cry. Peter had seen so much shit working in Homicide that it was a wonder he didn't wake up screaming every night of the week.

"What's up sis'? I got your voicemail earlier, but I was busy. What do you need me to do," Peter asked waiting for Julio to finish with the cream.

"Do you know of a man named Anthony Jackson?"

"You mcan *the* Anthony Jackson? As in, the drug lord, Anthony Jackson? As in the man they call the 'Snow King'?"

"Snow King," Maxine said aloud. I guess we're talking about the same man."

"What in hell do you want with him? That motherfucker's bad news Maxi. There are a dozen NARCs that would give their left hand to bust his ass, but he covers his tracks well. Too well," Peter added before knocking Julio's hand away from the last glazed donut.

"To make a long story short," Brice started, "we think he murdered his wife."

"You gotta be shittin' me!"

"We aren't," Maxine sadly informed him. "He was married to my friend Belinda."

"Belinda? You mean Belinda, as in BeeBee? She was married to Anthony Jackson?"

"Yes. Brice and I don't have proof, but we have a file of information that needs to be delivered to her niece."

"Who's her niece," Peter asked around the last bite of donut. Julio was still milling about and starting on his second donut. His partner was going to be wearing a donut around his middle if he didn't slow down.

"A woman named Camilla Abernathy. I have her address but her number is unlisted. I need you to deliver the file to her. We can't trust anyone else."

"Is the proof in the file," Peter asked reaching into his pocket for his notepad and pen.

"I'm not sure. Brice and I can't decipher the information, but maybe Camilla can."

"All right, what's her address?"

Brice read the address to Peter and patted his wife's hand.

"We'll overnight the file to you, Peter, and have it delivered in the morning. Is that okay?"

"That'll be fine Brice. I'll deliver it to her tomorrow. I'll call afterwards. Hey, I gotta go, but hug Grandpa for me. Tell him to keep you in line Maxi."

"I will. Thanks Peter, this means a lot. I loved Belinda like a sister."

"I know Maxi. You know I'll help you anyway I can. Love you."

"I love you too Peter. Bye," Maxine said and hung up.

"That was your sister," Julio asked wiping his mouth with a napkin.

"Yeah, that was Maxi."

"She all right?" Julio nosed around as much as he dared without seeming suspicious.

"Yeah man, she's fine."

"It's just that that call seemed important," Julio commented.

When Peter looked directly into Julio's eyes red flags went up immediately. Something was up and Peter didn't like the smell of it. He and Julio were partners, but their relationship hadn't turned into a friendship. Julio was new to Homicide and Peter had had the distinct pleasure of getting him as a partner. Peter didn't trust Julio with jack shit. And he wasn't about to tell him anything about Maxine.

"My family's calls are always important," Peter retorted. "I have paperwork to finished up so I'll catch you later."

"Yeah. Sure thing."

Julio stood far off to the side of the main entrance to Police Headquarters. Cops went to and fro constantly, but no one paid him any attention. A miasma of smoke curled upward from the tip of his Camel. The cigarette sported a length of ash, but Julio didn't care. He was intent on making a phone call.

Julio used the speed dial function on his cellular phone and depressed the number eight, then the talk button.

"What," Tony answered.

"It's Julio. I got some news."

"What the fuck is it then? Don't keep me in suspense."

"My partner got a call from his sister. From what I could gather, something is supposed to be delivered to Belinda's niece. I think it's something about you. His sister asked about you first then brought up Belinda."

"Who is your partner's sister," Tony asked not the least bit alarmed.

"All I know is her first name, Maxi, which is probably short for Maxine. Peter asked 'was there proof in the file' then he asked what the niece's address was."

Julio ground out his cigarette with the toe of his shoe, then immediately lit another one. He hunched his shoulders against the cold and pulled up his coat collar around his ears.

"They're talking about Camilla," Tony mumbled more to himself than Julio. "When's the goddamn file supposed to be delivered?"

"He didn't say. The call sounded urgent so probably by FedEx, maybe in a day or two?"

"So what the fuck are you going to do about it?"

"I can get a couple guys together in a day or two."

"Get the motherfucking file Julio, and if you don't you'll wish your sorry ass did."

The phone disconnected in Julio's ear. A couple guys, in a couple days – how the hell am I going to do that Julio wondered to himself. Julio ground out his second cigarette. However he was going to do it, Julio knew he'd better not fuck up or Tony would kill him for sure.

Chapter **21**

Coltrane lifted Cami from the floor and held her in his arms. The letter dropped listlessly from her hand and drifted to the floor. It landed written side down Coltrane noticed when he tried to scan the contents to find out what made Cami burst into tears. He held her closely until she got hold of herself somewhat.

Tisha stood beside her mother still clinging to the kittens. Her eyes filled with tears as any child's would when seeing their parent cry. Tisha felt helpless and afraid because her mother never cried. Cami usually showed little or no emotion at all.

"Please don't cry Mommy," Tisha begged, her lower lip quivering and on the verge of crying.

Cami lifted her head from Coltrane's shoulder at Tisha's calling her 'mommy.' Her daughter never called her 'mommy' unless she was really upset or afraid. Tisha was always so brave and independent, but every child had a breaking point.

Cami wiped her eyes and picked up the letter. Before reading the entire thing she sat down on the couch and faced Tisha.

"I'm all right Tisha. I'm sorry if I upset you, but I was surprised to find this letter from Belinda. It made me very sad," Cami explained.

"You miss Aunt Belinda real bad don't you," Tisha asked and sat down next to her mother.

Cami nodded her head yes.

"I miss her too," Tisha sighed. She stroked Boot's fur while she rubbed Patch's head.

"What does the letter say that made you so upset," Coltrane asked. He figured the direct approach would work best.

"She wrote it just before she died," Cami answered unfolding the letter to read the rest. "Give me a moment to finish reading it."

"Just try not to cry this time," Tisha requested shakily.

"I won't cry sweetheart. I promise."

Cami turned her attention back to the letter:

Dear Camilla,

This is going to sound crazy but I don't have much time. I've been secretly spying on Tony for a long time now, but this time I got caught listening to a phone call he made from the house and I know too much for him to let me live. I was hiding in the closet of all places. It was such a dumb thing to do. I don't have much time because it's already 4 p.m. and I've been in the bathroom for ten minutes already. He'll come after me soon.

Mailman coming up the block and I have to get this to you. K-Dog and Queenie are outside watching the house probably to make sure I don't try to leave. I think Tony's on the phone in his office talking to Nymph planning my murder. God I don't know what to say. Don't trust Tony. You already know that. You've always been smarter than me. I should have left him years ago but I was so stupid. Going to try to escape, but if I don't make it, put Tony behind bars forever. To do that you need to get Caroline, and find out what's really in her heart.

Proud of you baby girl. You were and always will be my daughter. I'll always love you as my own. Take care of Tisha and don't make same mistakes I did. God I love you Camilla. Don't know how else to say it.

I thought I could handle Tony, but I know now that I was in way over my head. Find a good man Camilla. There will come a time when you're going to need to trust someone. You can't conquer the world alone. I don't care if you find a man that's poor as dirt or ugly as sin, just make sure that he loves you.

I wish I could see you get married, but know I'll be there in spirit. I know you'll be beautiful. One more thing. I know Earl is Tisha's father. I've always known. I've wanted to kill the motherfucker for the past eleven years. He should never have touched you. You were just a young girl and he forced you to grow up way too fast. But I wouldn't change Tisha's birth for the world. She's always been our angel hasn't she? Teach her the right way Camilla, not the way I taught you.

Remember that I'll always love you both!

Belinda

Cami slowly exhaled a deep breath. She'd promised Tisha that she wouldn't cry and she intended to keep her word even though it would be difficult.

Cami silently reflected on the letter. Belinda's thoughts were so jumbled and her writing was sloppy. That was very unlike her. Belinda must have been scared to death and in a big hurry. Cami couldn't imagine the torment Belinda suffered knowing that she was about to die.

And the biggest question of all: Who the hell was Caroline and how was Cami going to find her?

"You okay baby," Coltrane asked squeezing Cami's hand with one of his own. What he needed to do was pump Cami for information about the letter. But for the first time in a very long time, Coltrane was focused on the person more than just the assignment. In fact, at the moment Coltrane didn't give a damn about the assignment. Coltrane wanted Cami to be happy. And he wanted to taste her sweet lips again.

"I'll be all right," Cami replied. "Thank you for asking."

"What did the letter say," he asked still holding Cami's hand.

"Yeah Mom, what did Aunt Belinda write," Tisha echoed curiously. She knew it must have been very important if it made her mother cry.

Cami looked at Coltrane before answering her daughter. With a slight shake of her head, Cami silently let Coltrane know that she would discuss it with him later. The last thing she wanted Tisha to know was that Uncle Tony killed Aunt Belinda. The news was already saturated with stories about murder around the city. Cami felt that Tisha didn't need to know about a murder that hit so close to home.

"Belinda wanted us to know how much she loved us Tisha," Cami said, telling only part of the truth.

"I think that's way creepy Mom that Aunt Belinda wrote that letter and then died. Don't you?"

Cami avoided that question like the plague. It was creepy all right. For starters, Cami didn't think that she'd get to sleep the next few nights. The thought of Belinda sitting in her house knowing she would die soon creeped her out. A lot.

"I think we should cherish the fact that Belinda loved us enough to write us a letter. You know how Belinda was always doing whacky things. I'm sure she's smiling down on us from Heaven Tisha," Cami reassured her daughter.

"Do you think she's an angel now Mom?"

"I know she is honey."

Cami hugged Tisha and kissed her on the cheek. There were days when Cami wouldn't know what to do without Tisha. She kept Cami on her P's and Q's for sure. They were a team and all each other had.

"Come on Tisha. I'll help you set up Boots' litter box," Coltrane interrupted the interlude. He didn't know what was in the letter yet, but it was evident that it was something he needed to know. Something that Yuri and Sully needed to know too.

Cami mouthed the words 'thank you' just as the phone rang. She was grateful for the small respite. Sometimes Tisha could ask a million questions in the span of five minutes. Her daughter was so curious and precocious.

"Hello," Cami answered pulling the kitchen's wall extension over to the refrigerator. She had to figure out what to do about dinner. Finding Belinda's letter totally halted her mind.

"Hi Cami, it's Jackie."

"Hey girl. What's up?"

"You sound like shit Cami. You feeling all right?"

"I'm fine," Cami replied. "It's just been a shitty weekend with the funeral and all."

Jackie sighed sympathetically over the phone. She was one of the few friends Cami had.

"I have a huge favor to ask you Cami."

Jackie didn't wait for an opening. She just forged ahead with her question.

"I know you're not working until Wednesday, but I was wondering if you could cover for me tomorrow night. Jermaine's sitter has the flu and my mother's still out of town. She won't be back until Wednesday, which is a day too late for me. I can't leave Jermaine with Michael again. Not after the last time. His sorry ass sent my baby to bed hungry. The bastard's a sorry excuse of a father."

"Sure Jackie. I'll cover for you tomorrow night."

"Thank you so much Cami. I owe you big time girl. Besides that, I twisted my ankle a little on the treadmill this morning. I could use a day to rest it," Jackie replied.

"No problem Jackie. I'll see you Wednesday."

Cami hung up the phone just as Coltrane and Tisha came bustling into the kitchen each holding a kitten. Cami tried not to flinch as Coltrane's eyes bored into hers. He was obviously searching for something, but she didn't know what.

Cami knew however, that it was the first time in her life that she had ever felt truly comfortable with a man. Coltrane had a certain magnetism and it was drawing Cami in like a moth to a flame. Coltrane made her want to smile. And Tisha was obviously gaga over him.

Cami didn't know when her life had started to twist and turn upside down. All she knew was Coltrane made her want to get her life straightened out. She, like every other girl in the world, had some type of dreams of grandeur. Cami did want a husband with the proverbial white picket fence, the kids, and a dog. Well, a cat in their case. She wanted to work a 9 a.m. to 5 p.m. job, Monday thru Friday, and put money into her company's 401(k). Cami wanted it all and she wanted it for Tisha too.

Tisha deserved to play on a tennis team at a school that actually had tennis courts with nets properly attached. Cami's daughter loved to watch soccer and lacrosse. Tisha deserved to play those sports in a school that offered them, and she deserved not to be teased about liking such sports.

Cami and Tisha wanted and needed so much that Cami was finally putting her foot down. She was going to strive to be a better mother and help her daughter achieve her dreams.

Cami also knew she needed to get Tisha away from murder and mayhem, not only in the city, but from the likes of Tony Jackson.

That thought brought Cami back to Belinda's letter. Once again she asked herself who the hell was Caroline. As far as Cami figured, she didn't even know anyone named Caroline. That wasn't even a common name – at least not around Detroit.

"Penny for them," Coltrane interjected.

"What," she asked blinking rapidly after having been dazed for several long seconds.

"Penny for your thoughts," he repeated.

"Oh, sorry. As you've seen, it gets pretty crazy around here sometimes," Cami said by way of an explanation for her behavior. She was very surprised by the fact that Coltrane was still sticking around. Enough had happened in two days to make the man head for the hills. But there he was walking her daughter to school, shoveling her snow filled driveway, and comforting her here and there. Cami felt that

Coltrane was going above and beyond and he wasn't even obligated.

"I don't mind crazy one bit," Coltrane replied.

"Mom, what's for dinner," Tisha asked still petting her new cat Boots. She was still ecstatic over the idea of having her very own pet. "I'm absolutely starving," Tisha added.

"I haven't had a minute to figure that out yet Tisha," Cami replied. "I'll whip something up though."

"What do you say about eating out tonight," Coltrane suggested. "My treat of course."

Tisha pumped her fist into the air mimicking the esteemed Tiger Woods when he made a good golf shot. This was turning out to be one heck of a day, she thought.

"I don't really feel much like going out tonight," Cami said and shrugged her shoulders. "I don't think I'd make very good company."

"Aw come on Mom," Tisha begged. "We never eat out for dinner."

Before Cami could object again, Coltrane chimed in with a compromise. He wasn't about to let her off the hook that easily. He knew she was bummed out over Belinda's letter, but he also knew Cami and Tisha had to eat.

"Why don't I pick up some take-out then? That way you don't have to go anywhere," Coltrane coaxed hoping like hell Cami would agree.

"Come on Mom," Tisha pleaded. "It'll be fun. You'll see." Tisha batted her brown doe eyes playfully, and was rewarded with a yank on one of her braids from her mother.

Cami finally gave in to all the cajoling and agreed to the compromise. They would get take-out and stay home for the evening. Cami could deal with that. The thought of a crowded restaurant set her teeth on edge.

She needed time to herself to figure out Belinda's letter. A restaurant wasn't going to let her do that. Come to think of it, Cami was sure Coltrane wouldn't allow it either. Nor did she want to think about the letter when she was with him. If anything, Cami was grateful that Coltrane helped her forget her problems and that felt really, really good.

He felt really, really good.

Cami remembered the kiss they shared earlier. His lips were so soft and his mouth was purely sinful. Coltrane kissed like a man on a mission. A mission to find the layer of ice that surrounded her heart and melt it. And if he succeeded with that, Coltrane would have more tricks up his sleeve than the *Wizard of Oz*.

"You still have to do your homework before we eat," Cami reminded her daughter.

"I know. I don't have that much, because I did most of it in school."

Coltrane sidled up next to Cami and interlocked their fingers together. Her hand was silky soft and warm, not cold and clammy. He hated cold and clammy hands on a woman. It just didn't feel right to him. But everything on Cami seemed to be warm and soft.

"So, what would you like to eat?"

Coltrane asked Cami the question, but it was Tisha who spoke up.

"A corned beef sandwich from Lou's Deli sure would be good," Tisha announced and rubbed her hungry stomach.

"Are you sure that's what you want," Coltrane asked. He didn't have a preference as to what to get. He only wanted to give Cami a night off from cooking. Coltrane might even get her to relax a little.

"I always want Lou's Deli," Tisha informed Coltrane, "but I think we should get White Castle cheeseburgers."

Cami smiled at Tisha's answer. Sometimes Cami loved her daughter so much that it hurt.

"Why White Castle and not Lou's," Coltrane asked.

"Because White Castle is Mom's favorite, and I think it will cheer her up. Even though she complains that she'll get fat, she can eat at least ten White Castle cheeseburgers," Tisha said and giggled.

"Ten huh?"

Coltrane chucked Cami under the chin and grinned. If all he had to do was stop by White Castle to make her happy he would have done it already.

"Are you telling me that your mother has a weakness for White Castle Tisha," Coltrane asked still grinning.

"Yep."

"Tisha you're giving away all my secrets," Cami playfully chastised. "Now Coltrane is going to think he can get away with anything as long as he's carrying a bag of White Castle."

"Come on," Coltrane began, "I wouldn't do anything like that."

Cami crossed her arms over her chest and gave Coltrane the 'I Don't Believe You' look.

"Very often," Coltrane added guiltily after having been subjected to the 'look.' He could spot a black woman giving him that 'look' from a mile away. Every Sunday his mother would threaten him and his siblings from the church's choir section with the 'look.'

Coltrane never understood why white women could never successfully pull off the 'look.' He thought it had something to do with attitude and the whole ancestral slavery issue. Coltrane knew that the 'look' had to be linked to picking cotton. Maybe women passed the 'look' down from generation to generation. However it originated, it was effective.

"Well, I guess I'll be on my way to White Castle to pick up some cheeseburgers," Coltrane stated and kissed Cami on the cheek.

"Don't forget the fries," Tisha added. She couldn't eat a burger without having french fries to go with it.

"I won't."

As Coltrane started to leave the kitchen, Cami grabbed his hand. When he turned around he saw a maelstrom circling in the fathomless pools of her brown eyes. Coltrane saw fire and ice, wariness and surrender. So many emotions vied for attention, but at the forefront Coltrane swore he saw love. It was gone in the blink of an eye, but it was there nonetheless. Somewhere. He knew for a fact that Cami wasn't the hard ass she portrayed. He didn't know how he knew it, but he just did. Coltrane was steadily chiseling away at the brick wall that surrounded her. And he was enjoying it, a little too much. Coltrane was in so much danger and he wasn't doing anything to take himself out of the fire. Why would he? Cami was absolutely breathtaking.

"Thank you for getting dinner," Cami told him with a genuine smile on her face.

"Geez Mom. You're smiling like he had to kill the cow to get the beef," Tisha teased. "He'll be right back. White Castle isn't that far away."

Cami immediately dropped Coltrane's hand, embarrassed by her display of affection. Tisha had never seen her with any man. Cami made it a habit to keep any man she dated away from her home and her daughter. Not that it had been a problem. Cami never really dated anyone. Nevertheless, she didn't know what had come over her regarding Coltrane.

"You're welcome," Coltrane replied. "I'll be right back."

Chapter **22**

Cami had just polished off her seventh White Castle cheeseburger when Coltrane topped off her glass of Faygo Redpop. It wasn't her fault that she had eaten so much. For one, Cami had been famished. And for two, the cheeseburgers were so small at White Castle that eating three or four would have been a snack. Coltrane had already eaten eleven and was still going strong. Even Tisha had managed five plus all of her french fries.

Cami was enjoying herself immensely and she promised that she would stave off the regret until tomorrow.

However, things don't always go as planned.

"I'm going to get so fat," Cami complained. "I'm going to have to work out first thing in the morning."

Tisha laughed. Every time her mother ate a lot she swore up and down she'd get fat.

"I told you she would complain Coltrane," Tisha boasted.

"You're not going to get fat," Coltrane told Cami. "Besides, it doesn't matter. However you look I think you're beautiful."

When Tisha saw her mother's eyes go all mushy she started cracking up. Never in her life had Tisha seen that expression on her mother's face. Tisha thought that with Coltrane around things might be okay.

Tisha laughed even harder when two french fries hit her on the nose and forehead. Her mother had launched an attack against her.

"What was that for," Tisha protested picking the french fries up off the carpet.

"You know what that was for," Cami replied pointedly.

"Now girls," Coltrane chastised jokingly.

Cami and Tisha looked at each other as a silent communication passed between them. Then before Coltrane could figure out what they were up to, Cami and Tisha each simultaneously threw French fries at him. And when the one Cami threw landed in Coltrane's pop, Tisha fell out in a fit of giggles.

"Sorry," Cami lied with a smile.

"You two won't know when it's coming, but I'll have my revenge," Coltrane promised.

He tried to sound menacing when he made the statement, but it didn't work. And when he laughed spookily, he sounded more like the Count on Sesame Street Cami thought.

"Mom, will you and Coltrane watch a movie with me," Tisha asked.

"Honey, Coltrane might have other plans this evening," Cami replied.

"Tisha, I'd be happy to watch a movie with you," Coltrane spoke up.

"Did you finish your homework?"

"I finished while Coltrane went to White Castle," she replied. "It was long division and it was mad hard Mom. I've been working on it all day."

"Well, why don't you go take your bath while I clean up, then we'll watch the movie," Cami said.

"Yes!" Tisha exclaimed, then scurried through the house and up the stairs into the bathroom. The sooner she finished the faster she could put on a movie.

"You two are so good together," Coltrane complimented. "She's a wonderful girl."

"She is," Cami agreed as she collected the debris from the table. She stuffed empty cheeseburger boxes into the garbage and set the used glasses into the sink to be washed.

As Cami washed her hands and dried them, Coltrane moved behind her and sliding his arms alongside her waist began to help dry Cami's hands with the towel. His gentle touch was warm and welcoming. Cami leaned back against Coltrane's chest and let her eyes drift closed momentarily. It felt so good to be held – too good.

"I know you don't trust me yet baby, but you will," Coltrane whispered into her ear. "Very soon."

The ringing telephone interrupted the atmosphere in the kitchen and broke the hypnotic spell Cami had fallen under. She reached absentmindedly for the wall extension only to have the line click in her ear. The caller had apparently hung up on her. It didn't matter though. There wasn't anyone Cami needed or wanted to speak with. The only people that mattered to her were in the house.

That thought made Cami stop in her tracks. Did Coltrane really matter to her, she wondered even though she knew the answer. He wouldn't have ever stepped foot in her home if he didn't matter to her.

Cami's emotions and nerves were so frazzled as of late, that she didn't know whether she was coming or going. She *would* like to be cumming however, as long as she was in Coltrane's arms, she thought.

Get a grip Cami. It's only been two days and you're ready to jump his bones.

"Mom, I need a towel," Tisha yelled from the bathtub.

"I'll be right back. Tisha always gets in the tub without checking for a towel first."

"Take your time. I need to make a call anyway. I missed my father this afternoon."

"Okay. Make yourself comfortable."

As soon as Cami went upstairs Coltrane hurried into the living room and scanned the letter Belinda had written. He wasn't necessarily shocked by it, just saddened. Belinda knew she was going to die. And Coltrane had no idea who Caroline was. He wondered if Yuri or Sully knew and took out his cell phone after replacing the letter on the coffee table exactly as it was. Coltrane listened for Cami's voice and heard her talking to Tisha. He dialed Yuri quickly and kept his eyes on the stairs.

"It's me," Coltrane virtually whispered.

"What's up," Yuri asked around a mouthful of Chinese noodles.

"See what you can find out about a woman named Caroline that's connected to Belinda."

"Will do. What else do you have?"

"Belinda wrote a letter to Cami the day she died. She said Tony was going to kill her. Apparently this Caroline woman knows something."

Coltrane listened for Cami again and heard her and Tisha talking about pajamas in Tisha's room.

"So it's Cami now," Yuri commented cautiously. "You sound awfully comfortable saying Ms. Abernathy's name."

"Do you have anything else to say," Coltrane bit out.

"Yeah. Sully found out that Belinda's mother is living in a D.C. nursing home. She has Alzheimer's. Sully seems to think that no one knows about the mother. Apparently Belinda set up a trust that pays all her mother's expenses in cash, and Belinda was the only visitor. That explains the trips to D.C. At least some of them."

"I have to go. Cami's on her way downstairs."

"Hey man, be careful," Yuri warned. "Don't get involved or you'll be making a big mistake."

When Coltrane didn't immediately answer Yuri forged on quickly.

"Coltrane, listen to me. You know what happened to Natasha. I loved her and because of my love she's dead. I don't want you to hurt the way I do every goddamn day. Do your job and keep your fucking emotions out of it."

"It's not like that," Coltrane lied.

"Yeah right, man. While you're at it just piss on my leg and tell me it's raining."

The line went dead just as Cami and Tisha entered the living room.

"Did you get in touch with your father," Cami asked turning on the television.

"Yes, I did. So, what movie are we going to watch," he asked taking a seat on the sectional and making himself comfortable.

Tisha snuggled in next to Coltrane and placed Patch on his lap while Boots curled up in hers. The kitten burrowed down deep into her pink pajamas with the matching pink robe. Tisha stroked the kitten from head to tail as Coltrane did the same.

"What do you want to watch," Cami asked waiting beside the DVD player for Tisha's selection.

"*Save the Last Dance* Mom. That's my favorite."

Cami took the DVD off the shelf and placed it into the machine. The opening credits started at once and Coltrane patted the seat beside him. When Cami sat down he pulled her closer until she was sidled up against him just as Tisha was.

Coltrane thought about what Yuri said. Cami wasn't going to die like Natasha. He would never let that happen. Yuri was just talking about himself. He was still hurt over losing Natasha. Coltrane could handle his assignment and he could handle Cami. Yuri didn't know what he was talking about.

As the movie ended with an excited Tisha cheering for the female main character, the doorbell rang. Cami stared at the front door for a few seconds before getting up to answer it. She hoped like hell that it was Mrs. Monroe and she needed a cup of sugar or something terribly unimportant. That would save Cami a trip next door to let Mrs. Monroe know that she would need to keep an eye on Tisha while she covered for Jackie tomorrow night.

"Who is it," Cami called after she couldn't see her visitor through the peephole. Whoever it was stood just to the side of the door, out of sight.

"Who is it," she repeated when there was no reply.

"Open the door Camilla. It's Earl."

"It's late. Go home," Cami said through the closed door.

"Open the damn door Camilla!" Earl yelled.

Cami darted a worried glance into the living room and saw Tisha and Coltrane playing with the kittens. She knew Coltrane had to have heard Earl yelling through the door.

"Go home!" Cami yelled through the door again and started back into the living room. Coltrane looked up at her just as she heard the front door open.

Cami was certain the door had been locked because she'd checked it after Coltrane came back from White Castle. Either Earl turned into a magician or he had a key to her house. He'd even unlocked the deadbolt so he had keys to both locks on the door.

Cami whirled around as Coltrane stood up and shoved Tisha behind him. He heard Cami tell Earl to go home twice, but he'd evidently let himself into the house. Cami looked so shocked that he didn't think she had given Earl a key at any given time. Coltrane focused on the familiar weight of his ankle holster that housed a .38 special. The thought of busting a cap in Earl's ass was tempting. Too tempting, so he focused his attention on Cami instead.

"What the fuck are you doing," Cami hissed. "And how the hell did you get keys to my house?"

"That's not important right now. What's important is that I've left Helen. I want to move in with you," Earl stated cockily. Cami had to let him stay at her house. There was no way he was going to stay in a hotel indefinitely.

"Motherfucker are you on crack? You need to get the fuck out of my house. I'm not going to tell you again."

"Dammit bitch! Why do you have to make things so hard? I have every right to be here."

"You don't have jack shit! Now get out!"

"I think I need to have a little talk with Tisha," Earl announced with a smug grin. Using Tisha was a last ditch effort.

"Be my guest," Cami said calling Earl's bluff perfectly. Earl didn't want to be a father. He never did. He wouldn't say a word to Tisha. Cami knew it and so did Earl.

Earl was enraged. The vein in his neck stood out grotesquely. Cami could never just give in. He hated that about her. Earl was finally giving her what she had wanted all those years ago. He was willing to play house with Cami and she was treating him like shit. Earl decided then and there that he wasn't going to let Cami get away with it anymore. Enough was enough.

Cami was caught totally off guard when Earl reached out and coiled his hands around her throat. When he applied pressure Cami fell back into the closet door located in the foyer. Her surprise diminished quickly however, when she heard Tisha yelling and she saw Coltrane materialize instantly behind Earl.

"Leave my mother alone!" Tisha shouted at Earl repeatedly.

Coltrane took a deep breath and reigned in his temper. He didn't want to kill Earl, merely hurt him. Badly.

Coltrane moved so fast that Cami barely saw him. One minute Earl had her by the throat, and the next thing she knew he was sprawled on the foyer tiles with a bloody nose.

"The lady asked you to leave," Coltrane stated calmly even though his insides were anything but calm. He was furious, but he didn't want to say or do much in front of Tisha. Especially Tisha because the sorry piece of shit was her father. What a waste, Coltrane thought. Earl was nothing but a deadbeat, nothing more than a sperm donor.

"I think you broke my fucking nose," Earl shouted at Coltrane, who he was seeing for the first time. He'd been so pissed at Cami that he hadn't even bothered to look past the foyer.

When Earl got his bearings, he realized it was the same man he had seen that morning. Cami couldn't possibly have something going with someone else. The bitch never dated and she never let anyone in her house either. This was a new development that Earl hadn't counted on. Cami involved with another man? Until she'd let him back in, literally, two months ago, Earl had thought Cami had turned into a lesbian. It was like the bitch had a lojack on her pussy for years. If a dick got too close, her pussy alerted the five-o and they'd secure the perimeter. Cami was strictly hands off.

Earl wiped a trickle of blood from his nose with the back of his hand.

"I can't believe you broke my fucking nose over this bitch," Earl said again still disbelieving as he saw more blood on his coat.

"I don't break 'em with the first hit," Coltrane replied. "But if you touch her again I'll be sure to finish the job."

Cami stepped over Earl's legs and opened the front door. This was the straw that broke the camel's back. She didn't think she could take much more bullshit before she completely cracked. Her life was rapidly spinning out of control right before her eyes and every time she tried to get a hold on it, her grasp slipped as usual.

Same shit. Different day.

"I hate you," Tisha yelled at Earl. She was so happy that Coltrane punched him in the face because she was too little to do it herself.

"I wish Coltrane was my father instead of you! You've never given me anything. Coltrane has at least fed me and he brought me a kitten. I'm not stupid. I hear what you say about me to my mother, and I don't care if you don't want me, because I don't need you."

"I wish you would go away and leave my mother alone. She doesn't like you and neither do I. You're an asshole and you'll never be my father. Never!"

Tisha stood her ground with her fists balled up at her sides and watched Earl stumble to the door. She was so angry that tears fell one by one on her pink robe. She hoped she never saw Deacon Earl again. And she was never going to church again either, no matter what her mother said.

"Camilla I'm sorry," Earl spoke remorsefully. He'd never meant for things to get so out of hand with her or with Helen. Tisha was right. He was an asshole and he'd just realized it.

"Just leave," Cami uttered shakily. The fact that Tisha knew Earl was her father had been a staggering blow. Cami had tried so hard to shelter Tisha from the pain, but her daughter ended up hurt anyway.

Earl hunched his shoulders against the cold, got in his car and drove away.

Cami immediately shut and locked the door, then went over to Tisha. The only problem was that Tisha didn't want to be bothered with her. When she tried to pull Tisha into her arms, Tisha turned away at once not wanting even a simple hug.

Instead Tisha latched herself onto Coltrane and cried her eyes out. Coltrane wrapped his arms around Cami's daughter and held on tight. Tears soaked his shirt as Coltrane lifted Tisha and she wrapped her thin arms about his neck.

"I'm going to bed now Mom," Tisha said in between sobs from the crook of Coltrane's neck. "And I don't want to talk about *him*. I don't ever want to see *him* again."

"Tisha, I know," Cami started but was cut off by her daughter's plea.

"Mom please, I don't want to talk right now. Coltrane can tuck me in. Goodnight."

Coltrane looked to Cami for approval and when she nodded her head he carried Tisha upstairs.

"Second door on your left," Cami called up the stairs to Coltrane.

Coltrane glanced around a lavender room with rag dolls and teddy bears piled high in one corner, a princess white chest of drawers with gold trim on one wall with the matching dresser on the other. He turned down the lavender and white twin sized comforter and deposited Tisha between the sheets.

"I gotta take my robe off first," Tisha informed him indignantly as if he had no common sense whatsoever.

"Sorry," Coltrane replied and helped her shed the robe. He lay the pink robe at the foot of the bed and pulled the covers up to Tisha's neck.

"Are you okay Tisha," Coltrane probed. He knew she had to be upset over the scene that had taken place.

"I don't know," she replied honestly. "I feel kinda angry and sad at the same time. I'm mad that he's my father, but it hurts my feelings that he doesn't want me."

Tisha sighed and a fresh sheen of tears glistened in her big beautiful brown eyes, her mother's eyes. Coltrane wiped her cheek as one enormous crocodile tear fell. Tisha made a feeble attempt at a smile.

"And he always treats my mother bad," Tisha stated with conviction. She began a new tirade as if she'd never stopped talking. "I hate him for that. People at church think he's so good all the time, but he's not. He doesn't care about anybody. I wish I were never born 'cause then Mom wouldn't have to deal with him," Tisha declared.

"Hey, I don't want to hear you say that ever again," Coltrane admonished. "I happen to like Earl."

"But Coltrane, he –," Tisha began and sat up in bed disrupting the covers before Coltrane cut her off.

"I like Earl for one reason Tisha: *He gave you life*. I will always be grateful to him for that. It's his loss because he's missing out on a beautiful, intelligent daughter with a great sense of humor. You always remember that."

"I will Coltrane. Thanks."

"Anytime sweetheart. Goodnight."

"Are you going to walk with me to school tomorrow," Tisha asked hopefully.

"I'll be there sweetheart."

As Coltrane pulled the covers back up and tucked her in he heard Tisha say, "I love you Coltrane." His heart squeezed almost painfully and he knew it was too late. Too late to get the hell out of 'Dodge'. Too late to ever forget the likes of Camilla and Tisha Abernathy. They were ingrained in his soul, and would be forever. Most of all, it was too late not to fall in love. Yuri was right after all. Coltrane was in deep shit and he knew it. The best thing to do was have Yuri or Sully take over his job. But there was no way in hell Coltrane was going to let that happen. Cami and Tisha were his and he was going to keep it that way.

"I love you too Tisha."

With that said, Coltrane turned off the lamp with the checkered lavender and white shade and made his way out of the room and back downstairs.

He found Cami in the kitchen splashing two fingers of brandy into a glass. She gulped it down greedily, gasped, then splashed another finger and drank that too.

"You heard," Coltrane deduced. He knew for a fact that Cami wasn't much of a drinker. She pretty much stayed on the strait and narrow path. She worked and she took care of Tisha.

"Not all, but most of it," she confessed.

Coltrane pulled Cami into his arms and kissed the crown of her head. God, she'd had a tough time as of late. And things were only going to get worse. Coltrane knew that for a fact. He held Cami even tighter and noticed the constant tremors that wracked her body.

"Aw shit, you're shaking."

"I'm angry," Cami replied.

"Come on, sit with me."

Cami allowed Coltrane to pull her into the living room and onto the sectional. He chose the end with the built-in chaise lounge, sat down first, then pulled Cami down to sit between his legs on the chaise. Coltrane wedged himself back into the pillows to give Cami more room.

He picked a random channel on the remote and the television sported one of those shows where neighbors took turns redecorating each others' homes on a bargain budget, often at the expense of good taste. Perfect, Coltrane thought. They needed something that wouldn't make them think about anything except the shocked look on the homeowners' faces as they saw the fiasco that was their "new" living room or kitchen.

Coltrane felt himself harden as Cami's firm, round booty nestled deeper into his crotch. He ignored his arousal, however, and started in on her shoulders. Coltrane massaged the taut muscles and little by little he felt Cami starting to relax. He worked tirelessly, squeezing and kneading through the knit of her sweater, working his way down her back, inch by gratifying inch.

"That feels so incredibly good," Cami barely whispered sinking a little further into Coltrane's chest.

Coltrane continued his ministrations until Cami's even breathing told him she was asleep. Rather than disrupt her, Coltrane pulled the blanket that Tisha had retrieved from the closet earlier over them. He glanced at the wall clock and saw that it was almost 11 p.m. He wanted to give Cami at least an hour of sleep he told himself. Coltrane would never admit that she just felt too good in his arms and he didn't want to release her. Not yet anyway, but maybe in an hour.

Coltrane and Cami slept on the sectional until his dick woke him at 3 a.m. Cami had rubbed him a little too much the right way in her sleep. She had managed to turn herself sideways with her cheek resting against his chest.

"Wake up baby," Coltrane told her and rubbed her cheek until her eyes popped open.

"What time is it," Cami mumbled.

"Just after 3 a.m. I should leave, but you need to lock the door behind me," Coltrane informed her.

"Oh, okay. I hope I didn't drool on you."

Coltrane chuckled. Cami looked dazed, sleepy, and cute.

"It's okay if you did. I'll get Patch in the morning. He seems to be enjoying his brother's company."

Coltrane hitched his head in the direction of the two kittens curled up together asleep on the floor.

"Okay," Cami replied sleepily.

"I'll see you in the morning, baby."

Coltrane kissed Cami's warm sleepy lips, shoved his arms into his coat sleeves, and left. He waited until he heard the click of the locks before he went into his house next door.

Chapter 23

Tony opened his side door and Tyrone came hurrying inside like a bat out of hell. Normally he didn't accept deliveries at his house, but he always made an exception for Tyrone, because he claimed that Queenie made him nervous at the car wash.

Tyrone had on a dark blue hoody and a pair of black jeans. An older woman was hot on his heels wearing a pair of black spiked heels, a mink jacket, and ripped blue jeans. It was odd, but Tony thought they sort of resembled each other.

"It's colder'n a motha out there," Tyrone said tossing his Sean John coat on the kitchen table. He rubbed his ashy hands together and breathed on them to warm them up. He blinked his small beady eyes rapidly as he looked around the room. He caught Nymph sneering at him and that made Tyrone smile. He probably shouldn't have been smiling at Nymph, but it was a nervous habit. Kids used to tease him about it in grade school, mostly because of his large round head, skinny tall body, and small beady eyes. With the added smile the kids told Tyrone that he looked like he belonged on the short bus.

Tony shook his head and chuckled. Tyrone talked extremely fast, sometimes so fast that you could barely understand him. Tony would even swear that most times Tyrone was making up words. The son-of-a-bitch took

Ebonics to a new level. That was another reason Nymph didn't like Tyrone. His voice was just plain annoying. But Tony didn't care. Tyrone was just dumb enough to be stupid, but smart enough not to get himself caught with Tony's powder. For that reason alone, Tyrone could say whatever the fuck he wanted.

"C'mon sit dat ass down 'ere wit me bay," Tyrone told the woman after she tossed her mink jacket on top of Tyrone's jacket.

When she sat down in the kitchen chair on Tyrone's lap and draped her arm around his neck, she noticed Nymph staring at her. She winked her right eye that was thickly rimmed with black eye liner and mascara, and smiled. She pulled her shoulders back to accentuate her breasts, which just happened to be bare and exposed by a sheer black blouse. Each nipple had a gold hoop that glittered and swayed when she flicked them with her finger.

"See somethin' you like sugar," she asked Nymph.

Nymph's gaze finally made it up to her face and he cringed. The titties were one thing, but the bitch was ugly. Her top two front teeth were missing, her face was pock marked and scarred, and her braids looked dirty and funky. For some reason she even had the same small beady eyes as Tyrone, but they couldn't have been related. Not with her sitting on Tyrone's lap.

But it was like Nymph's mama always told him: Pussy ain't got a face. He could fuck anything. Nymph would just put a bag over her head.

"Depends," Nymph replied.

"Where's my shit," Tony asked Tyrone.

Tyrone unzipped the lining of the woman's jacket and took out bags filled with pellets of heroin.

"Is it clean this time Tyrone?"

Nymph balled up his fist ready to deck Tyrone.

"It's clean awwright," Tyrone promised. He turned to Nymph. "Why you ov'dere grimmin' me like you gon' Ike me or somethin'? What da deal-y yo? Ma, go'n calm da motha down. Get'm off my case."

Nymph and Tony looked at each other and laughed.

"It's fine baby. Mama will take care of you. You know that baby."

Tyrone's mother turned in his lap and gave her son an open mouthed kiss sucking his tongue at the end.

"Motherfucker what the fuck is wrong with you? You mean to tell me you're fucking your mother," Nymph burst out disgusted. "Where the fuck you from? West Virginia? Man, black people don't do that shit."

"Hey man she sucks my dick so good 'till I can't leave 'er 'lone. Show'em bay. Show'em hows good you is."

Tyrone's mother knelt down in front of Nymph and stuck out her tongue. Her tongue rested in between her missing teeth and sported not one, but two piercings.

Nymph watched her unzip his pants and fill her mouth with him. Granted, the piercings felt good, but the missing teeth were an added bonus. Then she started to caress his balls and the blow job felt even better. It didn't matter what she looked like now. Tyrone was right, she did suck good dick. But when she pressed a finger on Nymph's prostate *hard*, he screamed like a baby and had the best orgasm of his life.

"Holy shit! Tony, you have got to let this bitch suck you off. Whatever freaky shit she does with her fingers will blow your fucking mind."

Tony counted out five thousand dollars and handed it to Tyrone.

"Now that that's out the way, I think you should send your mother my way," Tony announced settling himself comfortably in the chair.

"Awwright Tony. Just don'ts be too long 'cause I'm gon' be next."

Chapter 24

Coltrane showed up as promised at a quarter to eight to walk Tisha to school. The morning was bright, the air was crisp, and it was colder than a witch's tit. Coltrane shoved his hands deeper into his coat pockets to keep them warm. He heard Tisha's footsteps as they bounded down the stairs along with her shouted, "Just a minute Coltrane."

Tisha pulled the front door open with a smile plastered on her face, one snow boot in her hand and one on her foot.

"Good morning Coltrane."

"Morning Tisha. Running late this morning?"

"Yeah. Mom wanted to talk this morning and I didn't want to listen. She wanted to talk about *him* but I'm over it. She might be kinda mad though, so don't do anything to piss...to make her mad," Tisha amended. Sometimes the bad words slipped out all by themselves. She tried not to cuss like the other kids at school, but it didn't always work out that way.

"I'll keep that in mind," Coltrane told her and closed the door behind him.

"Keep what in mind," Cami asked as she came down the stairs and into the living room.

"That you missed me and couldn't wait to see me this morning," Coltrane replied half jokingly.

Cami gave Tisha the eye thinking that her daughter said something to Coltrane.

"I didn't say anything Mom. I swear."

"Morning baby," Coltrane greeted and pulled Cami into his arms for a quick kiss.

Cami ducked her head quickly, slightly embarrassed about the display of affection, especially in front of Tisha. She wasn't yet sure how Tisha would respond to her being in a relationship. But one good thing was that Tisha already adored Coltrane.

Cami stopped herself. Was she in a relationship? They certainly hadn't discussed anything about a relationship. Cami had no right to assume anything about Coltrane.

But that doesn't stop you from doing it does it?

"Mom, we're gonna be late," Tisha said as she pulled on her coat.

Cami put on her boots quickly and bundled herself up with coat, hat, scarf, and gloves. Pulling the front door open, she waved Coltrane and Tisha ahead of her.

"Do you have your math homework Tisha," Cami asked as they plowed through the snow.

"Yes. I even double checked my bookbag, so you can trust that it's there."

"How did you sleep last night Tisha," Coltrane asked making his attempt at conversation. He hadn't been around a ten year old since his sister, Billie, was that age. And even then Coltrane was a teenager about to graduate high school and on his way to the Navy. Needless to say, he didn't know that much about ten year olds, let alone kids period. But Tisha was special to him. She had a way about her that was shockingly mature. Coltrane suspected that wasn't typical of a girl her age, but it was welcomed all the same.

"I slept okay. What time did you leave last night?"

Cami shot Coltrane a quick look. She tried to convey that she had an impressionable daughter, even though they hadn't done anything last night except sleep.

"I left not too long after you went to bed," Coltrane answered. In his mind 3 a.m. wasn't *too* long after 9 p.m. "Why do you ask?"

"Because you should've spent the night. Mom's bed is way bigger than mine so you would've been really comfortable.

"Mom, be sure to give Boots and Patch fresh water throughout the day. I've already left food for them in the bowl.

"Coltrane, can you come over for dinner again tonight? It's fun when you're at the house."

Coltrane blinked in response. Tisha had gone off on so many tangents that he could barely keep up. And why was she thinking about his comfort in her mohter's bed. Although it didn't sound like a bad idea, he wasn't going to admit that to Tisha. Cami, as usual, was quick to come to his rescue. It was the first time that Coltrane ever truly appreciated what parents go through on a daily basis.

"Tisha, I have to work tonight. Miss Jackie asked me to cover for her."

"But Mom," Tisha whined, "Tuesdays are always 'beauty night,' but I thought we could do something different if Coltrane came over. Please don't go."

"I'm sorry Tisha," Cami apologized. "I promise I'll make it up to you though."

"Whatever," Tisha mumbled.

Cami felt guilty as hell. If Tisha could hold out a little while longer, Cami was going to get a new job, a job that didn't require her to work nights and come home smelling of cigarette smoke and cheap liquor.

"How about if Coltrane came for dinner before I left? That's if he's not busy?"

Two pair of expectant eyes turned to him for an answer. If it were any other time or place, or any other woman, he would have felt trapped. But somehow with Cami, he felt eager to comply.

"I'll be there for dinner," he affirmed.

"Yes!" Tisha exclaimed.

"Have a good day at school sweetie," Cami told Tisha as they neared the entrance of the elementary. For some reason this part never got easier to Cami. She missed Tisha more than ever the older she got, even when she was in school all day.

"See you later Tisha," Coltrane said.

Tisha kissed her mother and didn't think twice about kissing Coltrane on the cheek. She was glad Coltrane was around. Her mother was starting to smile more, just like old times.

"Bye Mom. Bye Coltrane."

Tisha huddled in with the other kids and entered the building, turning back to wave one last time.

"Coffee," Cami invited.

"Coffee," Coltrane accepted.

Coltrane had started the morning in a very good mood. His mood changed however when he noticed the same two men that he'd seen upon leaving his house a little while ago watching Cami's house. They were parked about seven houses down the block, but Coltrane noticed them nonetheless. He especially noticed when the sun glinted off the lens of a pair of binoculars. Coltrane would place a call to Yuri and Sully. He'd get them to drive by and get a tag number.

Things were starting to get very interesting.

And potentially very dangerous.

Helen applied her makeup perfectly in the

bathroom mirror. She'd traded in her usual slacks that she wore to work in favor of an olive green wool skirt that was much shorter than she would normally dare to wear.

Helen was also rested. For the first time in over a decade she wasn't awakened by the sound of Earl's snoring. She was grateful she put him out for that reason alone.

Helen dropped her Fashion Fair compact into her new leather bag that matched the black leather boots she was wearing. Out of habit she went to the refrigerator to take something out of the freezer for dinner. When the rush of cold air hit her in the face, Helen remembered something vital. She could easily pick up a salad on the way home. Old habits died hard, she thought.

Checking the wall clock in the kitchen, Helen hurried to grab her coat, or she'd be late. However, the side door opening stopped her in her tracks.

"Good morning Helen," Earl greeted her with a large bouquet of two dozen red roses. He noticed Helen's perfectly made up face and short skirt. She looked damn good for a change. She smelled good too, Earl thought and knew Helen was wearing a new fragrance.

"I'm late and I'm leaving," Helen announced by way of greeting.

"Let's not do this Helen. We can work things out. I'm sorry I've hurt you, but I promise I'll change. I'll be faithful to you just like old times."

Helen took a long, hard look at her husband and knew he was lying. The son-of-a-bitch couldn't even look her in the eye.

"Let me guess," Helen started, "Camilla wouldn't let you stay with her so you think I'd be stupid enough to take you back."

Earl's delayed reply told Helen all she needed to know.

"It's nothing like that Helen. I love you."

"Lock the door on your way out. I'm late for work," Helen said as she brushed past Earl and left him standing in the kitchen with two dozen red roses.

Helen didn't want to reconcile – not now, not ever.

The ringing telephone woke Tony out of a deep sleep. It was just like yesterday morning when the perky spa chick called for Belinda. Tony thought he'd go mad if one more person called for Belinda and he had to tell them she was dead.

In some small way it almost pricked Tony's conscience, since he did kill her and all – almost, but not quite.

Tony grabbed the phone on the sixth ring and mumbled a sleepy "Hello."

"What's this I hear about a package being delivered today? A file of proof," the caller asked. His voice was deep, quiet, and laced with anger.

Fuck! Tony sat straight up in bed dislodging the sheet that covered his naked body. He was going to kill Julio by cutting out his tongue and shoving it down his throat. The motherfucker ratted him out and he didn't even know what was in the file.

"It's nothing. I'm taking care of it," Tony answered the caller.

"If it was nothing then the file wouldn't exist you arrogant son-of-a-bitch," the caller shot back.

"Did Belinda know about me," he asked.

"No," Tony lied. Tony had checked his files after Belinda died and realized they had been tampered with. But there wasn't anything totally incriminating in his files. His computer, however, had everything. But there was no way Belinda could have figured out his password. At least he hoped not.

"If anything surfaces about me, I swear to God you'll spend the rest of your miserable life trading favors for cigarettes and getting ass fucked every night in the shower."

"Don't you threaten me you piece of shit. Don't ever forget who got you to where you are. If you ever threaten me again I will personally cut up that white trophy bitch wife of yours and serve her to you on a platter for breakfast!" Tony spat fiercely.

Tony slammed down the phone and covered his face with his hands. If he didn't handle things fast, the shit was going to hit the fan.

Fuck! He said to himself again.

Chapter 25

"Call me when you get home from work," Coltrane told Cami as he prepared to leave her house.

"It's going to be really late, probably around 2 a.m. I'm not going to wake you up."

"Call me," Coltrane demanded then kissed Cami gently on the lips. "See you in the morning Tisha."

"Bye," Tisha replied forlornly. She wanted Coltrane to stay, but he couldn't. He would have been able to though if her mother wasn't covering for Jackie.

Cami shut and locked the door once Coltrane left then cleaned up the dining room table quickly and washed the dishes. She would love a dishwasher, she thought longingly. It would save so much time. Cami vowed to herself that when she moved, she'd get a house with a dishwasher. And a garage with an automatic garage door opener, she added.

"Alright Tisha, get your walkie-talkie and turn it on."

Tisha set down her Play Station 2 controller and walked over to the entertainment center. She opened the cabinet and grabbed the walkie-talkie and a two-way pager from the bottom shelf.

"Mom, I think I'm offended because this is almost like having a baby monitor. I'm ten years old."

"Don't be offended Tisha. Anyone can use a walkie-talkie, and it allows Mrs. Monroe to check on you easily while I'm gone. Now tell Mrs. Monroe that we're up and running please."

Tisha turned on the blue walkie-talkie and depressed the black button on the side of it.

"Mom's leaving now Mrs. Monroe."

"I'm here sweetheart," Mrs. Monroe responded. "You tell your mama to have a good night."

"I will. Over and out."

Cami took her coat out of the closet and began to put it on.

"I wish Coltrane could stay with me tonight Mom. Sometimes I get bored."

"I know sweetie, but remember what I told you. It will only be a little while longer. I've already put in an application at Ford. They just have to call back."

"Tyrell's mother got laid off from Ford last week," Tisha said. "Tyrell's mother said it's 'cause the economy is down. What's that mean Mom," Tisha inquired.

Cami dropped her purse by the door and wrapped her arm around her daughter as she sat beside her.

"Well it means that Americans aren't spending money like they did before, especially after 9/11. So, companies rely on people to spend money and when people don't, the companies have to lay people off to stay in business. But once the stock market rallies back, and it will, I bet Tyrell's mother will get her job back."

"Are we going to run out of money Mom?"

"Even if I don't find another job for a while, I have enough money saved to take care of us for a long time. Now, no more worrying, that's *my* job. Lock the door behind me and I'll page you when I get to work. I love you Tisha."

"I love you too Mom."

Tisha did as she was told and locked the door after receiving a kiss on the cheek.

Cami walked into the doors of The Chocolate Factory, located in downtown Detroit. The very same doors that Belinda had taken Cami through eight years ago, the day after her eighteenth birthday. Doors that opened into what the male population in Detroit knew as a strip club.

Once Cami had given birth to Tisha, Belinda had informed her that on her eighteenth birthday she was coming to work with her at The Chocolate Factory. Belinda told her that stripping would allow her to take care of Tisha during the day while her baby was awake as well as go to college. Not to mention the money.

If she wasn't a dancer, Cami would have been on welfare waiting for W.I.C. coupons every month to buy milk and cereal for Tisha. Cami would have never been able to afford to buy a house at the age of nineteen if it weren't for the club. The nights that Belinda worked, Cami was off and the nights that Cami worked Belinda stayed with Tisha. It was perfect.

Until two months ago when Cami had realized she was pregnant. That had been enough to make her reevaluate her life. Actually, she'd been starting to reevaluate her life for the past six months. Cami had always wanted more than being a dancer. The job was beginning to suffocate her, and each time she got up on stage she died a slow agonizing death. Cami knew it was time to leave.

"Hey Cami. We got a newbie in back named Shameka. Help her out alright? And we got two Pistons and a Lion in the V.I.P. section. Work it for me."

"Sure thing Macky," Cami told the owner of the club.

When Cami stepped through the door of the dancers' area in the back of the club, she spotted

Shameka immediately. A fair-skinned woman with long, curly hair and huge breasts that the men would love, was huddled in the corner virtually kissing the celery green painted walls. She looked nervous as hell and tight as a drum. Cami went over and introduced herself before she even took off her coat.

"Shameka, I'm Cami. How ya doin'?"

"Hi," Shameka replied timidly. "Macky said you'd help me."

"Macky was right. The first thing you need to do is take a deep breath. And the biggest piece of advice I can give you is try like hell to make it to the bathroom when you throw up."

"Throw up," Shameka repeated. "But I'm not sick."

"You will be after your first dance. Don't feel bad though. It has happened to all of us."

"I'll keep that in mind," Shameka said dryly.

"Do you have kids," Cami asked while taking her coat off and putting it into her personal locker which she kept locked with a combination lock. Otherwise the girls that worked at the club would steal her shit. Everybody claimed to be a charity case.

"A two month old son," Shameka replied. "His father left me when I was six months pregnant and my dad put me out. Welfare only goes so far, if you know what I mean."

Cami scanned the lounge area of the locker room and saw a few girls standing around waiting to take the stage. Cami didn't miss the pocket mirror being passed around filled with straight white lines. The three girls inhaled the powerful narcotic through a rolled up dollar bill. And when Cami checked the mirrored wall that housed a vanity counter filled with make-up, she saw Desiree (which was pronounced 'Desire' for her stage name) sitting on a stool shooting up by sticking a heroin-filled needle between her toes so she wouldn't have track marks on her body. Desiree was an older dancer that started the same time as Belinda.

Belinda had always made her money and left the drugs alone. It was ironic that Desiree was the one that had introduced Tony to Belinda twenty years ago. Cami didn't think that Desiree had ever forgiven Belinda for being the one to marry Tony.

The difference was that Belinda stopped dancing four years ago, while Desiree was forced to dance to pay for her drug habit. Belinda was dead and Desiree was still alive, still shooting up, and still pining after Tony.

Cami watched as Desiree put the empty needle in her make-up bag along with her lighter and a bent silver spoon that was discolored from constant use.

"Look Shameka, I'm not going to try and be your mother. You're grown and can make your own decisions. But if you know what's good for you, you'll stay away from the girls that are back here with us right now. The rest are okay, but these are the ones that will get you into trouble. Leave the drugs and the liquor alone. If Macky catches you, you're out. Make your money then leave and go home to your son — simple as that. And like Chris Rock says: 'No Sex in the Champagne Room!'"

Shameka shook her head each time Cami told her something new. And come to think of it, she was starting to feel a little queasy.

"Thanks for your help," Shameka said and smoothed her hand down her pink satin negligee.

"You're welcome."

Desiree took off her robe and went to wait by the curtain. She was up next and the current song being played was almost over.

A few minutes later Ebony and Ivory came off the stage. They were a black and white duo that did a shower act. Men liked nothing better than to see two naked, wet girls grinding the soap off each other.

"Those men ain't giving up shit tonight," Ebony ranted as Desiree passed her and took the stage.

"Man, them players are all bustas," Ivory chimed in. She was a white girl that was newly converted to the ways of the 'Dark Side.' She claimed that once she went black she never went back.

"That one Pistons' guy just signed a ten million dollar contract," Ebony told the girls. "It was all over the news yesterday. He got mad paper and all he gave us was thirty goddamn dollars."

"I can't believe that shit," Brown Sugar agreed packing her pocket mirror back in her make-up case and putting it in her locker.

"Men are assholes," Angel added and checked her make-up before going on stage. She was next after Desiree.

Shameka's face lost all color when she saw Angel go on stage and Desiree sit back down on the stool to count up a handful of wadded up bills.

"What's wrong," Cami asked undressing and hanging up her clothes in her locker.

"Macky said I was after Angel."

"You'll be fine. Take a deep breath and remember what I told you. Now I have to get ready, but I'll be here when you're done."

Shameka took her place near the stage and tried like hell to breathe. She prayed Angel's song would never end, but she'd never be that lucky.

Chapter 26

Coltrane paid the twenty dollar cover charge to get into The Chocolate Factory and sat at a table all the way in the back of the club. He was so far back and off to the side that he was virtually sitting in the door. The seat was perfect. He wanted to stay out of sight, because the last thing he wanted was for Cami to see him.

Coltrane pulled his baseball cap lower over his eyes and was grateful for the crowd. He knew how to disappear in a crowd and this time wasn't any different. He ordered a beer and coughed a little from the trail of perfume the waitress left behind her. She was forgiven though, when Coltrane saw her barely there skirt rise higher above her exposed butt cheeks. He sat back, got comfortable, and settled in to watch the show. He didn't know if Cami used her real name or not, but Coltrane would recognize her anywhere. Her image was forever stamped on his brain.

Coltrane nursed his beer and waited patiently. The smell of liquor permeated the club and a hazy layer of smoke floated near the ceiling. He could barely see, but he saw enough. Black leather booths lined the outer walls, while shiny black lacquered tables filled in the rest of the area around three stages. The outer stages were circular, and smaller than the main rectangular stage that extended half the length of the club. Polished silver poles lined each stage about every six feet with a special pole in the center of the mirrored V.I.P. table at the end of the main runway. From above, the stage layout ironically resembled a huge phallus.

Three metal cages were suspended from the ceiling, each containing a writhing latex-clad dancer. The Chocolate Factory also sported two rooms for private dances, and of course the infamous 'Champagne Room'. The club's rule was 'no sex in the Champagne Room', but most of the dancers had sex anyway. Anything to make another dollar.

Coltrane watched an older stripper dance and work her ass for money, but the men weren't very generous. The woman looked hard, haggard, and nasty. The DJ said something about 'Desire' but Coltrane thought her name should have been 'Disease.' She looked like the kind of woman that would make a man's dick fall off if he fucked her. The dollar bills she picked up were more pity than payday to get her off the stage. Nevertheless, Coltrane sat back and waited.

"Hey Cami. I didn't know you were working tonight."

"Hi Redd. I'm covering for Jackie."

"You want Busta tonight," he asked taking his job seriously as The Chocolate Factory's 'spin master' as he nicknamed himself.

"Busta then Christina," Cami replied. "I'll let you know after that."

"Bet."

Cami sat down on one of the stools at the counter and read her page from Tisha, then replied.

Mom U R late

Sorry baby. Helping a new girl.

Worry when U R gone

Know baby. On stage next. GTG. ILU.

LU2

Cami put her pager in her locker and locked it up. She checked her make-up one last time blinking one eye at a time to make sure the rhinestones that lined her eyelids above her lashes were still in place. She checked herself in the full length mirror and adjusted her zipper. The leopard print jacket and skirt were sleazy and slutty and oozed sex appeal. It was perfect. Not to mention the matching bra and G-string.

Cami positioned herself center-stage, just behind the curtain and waited for her cue from Redd.

"Here at The Chocolate Factory we have milk chocolate, dark chocolate, and we even have white chocolate. But tonight gentlemen we have a very special chocolate treat for you. But first I want to know are you ready to rock the boat?"

The lights suddenly went out and the club was plunged into blackness. Thunder rolled and the wind roared through the huge sound system.

Cheers erupted around the club and the men flocked to the stage like kids in a candy store as strobe lights flashed like lightning.

"I said are you ready to rock the boat?"

Shouts rang out around the stage.

"Man, this is the shorty I was telling you about," one man said.

"She is *fine*," another agreed.

"I want you to give it up for Stormee Cee!" Redd announced.

As Cami heard the opening beats to Busta Rhymes' *Make It Hurt* she threw the curtain wide and commanded the stage.

Cami worked the zipper of her jacket down exposing more and more skin as the music surrounded her. She worked the sides of the stage first, making the center stage VIP table wait. She wanted to make them sweat a little first, and in the end the ballers always loved it.

Cami stripped off her jacket and threw it to the back of the stage. She made her way downstage blocking out the images of the men all around her. The lights from the stage bore down on her and the miasma of smoke that curled about her made her nostrils burn.

Stripping out of the scrap of material that was supposed to be a skirt, Cami made love to the pole directly in front of the V.I.P. section. And when the bra came off, the paper started flying.

Cami lost herself in the music and tried not to concentrate on the fact that men were stuffing money into her G-string as she danced in front of them.

The fact that the professional athletes had dropped several Benjamins at her feet and one in her G-string was a good thing. They turned out to be high-rollers after all.

"I hate that bitch," Ebony told Brown Sugar as they looked on while Cami danced. "She pulls in the loot every motherfucking time. Macky has got to cut her hours or the rest of us will never survive."

"I know Ebony, I'm sick of the shit too. Why should we make a couple hundred a night when she's making a couple grand," Brown Sugar chimed in.

Cami worked the pole even more, doing intricate twists and spins. The song was more than halfway done and she could get off the stage soon.

As she gyrated on the floor provocatively, her eyes locked with Earl's standing beside the V.I.P. table. He always showed up at the club when he'd done something really stupid. Cami was supposed to be stupid enough to magically forgive him then fuck him. The only thing that wound up happening was that Cami took his money. And it would be no different tonight.

Just as the song was about to end, Cami worked her way over to Earl. He had a handful of twenties with a few fifties mixed in that he'd been throwing on stage. She turned away from him and eased down slowly, making her ass bounce as she thrust it into Earl's face. He still had a large band-aid over the bridge over his nose and a huge bruise under his left eye. Earl's eyes glazed over and he licked his lips without realizing it. She looked back over her right shoulder and locked eyes with Earl. Reaching suddenly between her legs, she gave Earl the finger and snatched the wad of bills out of his hand.

Cami only needed ten thousand dollars more to finish Tisha's 529 College Savings Plan. She'd take Earl's money gladly, especially since he wasn't paying child support.

"Oh snap," one man said and laughed.

"Will you marry me," the Lion shouted at her and gave the other athletes some dap, demonstrating some handshake that they'd made up.

Finally the song was over and Cami left the stage for a brief respite before her next dance. She'd have just enough time to change into another outfit and check on Tisha.

Chapter 27

Peter cruised slowly down the block looking for Camilla Abernathy's house. He'd received the FedEx package before he left for work and was just now getting around to delivering it at 9 p.m. He hoped it wasn't too late, but Peter didn't have a choice. Despite him having a bitch of a day, Peter had promised Maxine he'd deliver it. The fact that Belinda was dead was what made him swing his car around on the Jefferies Freeway and make a trip to Camilla's house.

Peter pulled his blue Ford Explorer into the empty driveway. He'd seen lights on in the house and thought maybe Camilla's car was in the garage. He'd at least check to see if she was home.

As Peter neared the front door he heard the television set playing. At least someone is home, he thought as he tucked the package under his arm and rang the doorbell.

"It's me. Detective Wallace is at the house now with a FedEx package tucked under his arm," the voice said as Julio listened on his cell phone.

"I don't care what you have to do, but get that package from that woman," Julio informed him. "And wait until Peter leaves before you make your move. The sonofabitch is an expert shot."

"You got it. *Adios.*"

Cami's pager went off just as she sat down at the vanity counter after having changed and gotten a Vernor's ginger ale for Shameka to drink. Shameka had been on stage twice and given three lap dances, and had puked three times. If she puked once more she'd set a new first-day record at The Chocolate Factory.

Cami focused on her pager as she read Tisha's page.

Mom, man at door. Scared.
Tell Mrs. Monroe

Cami waited anxiously for another page. No one should have been at her house this late at night. She hated being away from Tisha at night. Especially since Belinda was gone. Mrs. Monroe only used to keep an eye on Tisha once or twice a week at most. Belinda would have stayed with Tisha any other night when Cami worked.

She is checking now
Don't U answer door
I won't Mom. Promise
Is he gone?
Not yet. Says his name's Peter Wallace. 5-0
Don't answer Tisha
Gone now. Slip of paper in mailbox. Come home?
Yes. Early
Wait up?
You'll be tired
Wait up. ILU
LU2 baby

Peter heard the neighbor's front door open as he stuck the slip of paper with his name and cell phone number through the mail chute. He unsnapped his shoulder holster that contained his standard-issue .40 caliber Glock, then started down the porch steps. He saw an older woman peeking through a crack in her front door and between the metal bars of her screen door.

"Who are you," she called out cautiously.

"My name's Peter. I'm looking for Ms. Abernathy," he replied wondering what business of hers it was anyway.

"She ain't home. Nobody's home so you best be leaving."

The woman purposely opened the door a little more, just enough for Peter to see the double barreled shotgun she brandished beside her. The woman was obviously protecting someone. People in Detroit wouldn't just open their doors to tell a strange man that their neighbor wasn't home. If Peter had to guess, he'd say a kid was in Camilla's house and he or she was alone.

"Ma'am, I'm with the Detroit Police Department. If you could please tell Ms. Abernathy to contact me at the number I left in her mailbox, I'd appreciate it."

"Police huh? You ain't in uniform," she observed.

"I'm a detective with the Homicide Division," he replied.

"So if I was to call the Homicide Department they would vouch for you?"

"Yes, ma'am."

Peter was tired, he was hungry, and he was cold. The last thing he wanted to do was dick around with the next door neighbor. Sometimes he wished he was the token cop in Mayberry. His day would consist of rescuing cats out of trees and there'd be no such thing as murder. And he wouldn't be freezing his ass off talking to the next door neighbor.

"That package for her," the woman asked.

"Yes, ma'am. It's important that she receive it."

"Leave it on the steps. I'll see she gets it."

"Sorry ma'am, but I can't do that. I need to give it directly to her, if you could please tell her to call me? The number's in the mailbox."

"Peter what?"

"Peter Wallace."

"Uh-huh. Will do Peter Wallace."

Peter walked further down the driveway to get into his Explorer. Knocking off the snow and salt caked on the soles of his shoes, he climbed in and drove away. Peter would gladly be a Deputy to any white man if it meant living in a town with no crime and a boy like Opie dogging his heels.

Chapter **28**

Coltrane sat mesmerized as he watched Cami dance to Christina Aguilera's song *Dirrty*. She worked the stage wearing black heels with leather ties that laced up her leg. It looked like something straight out of Dominatrix 'R Us.

Cami's body was tight and toned, not an ounce of fat anywhere. Her raven colored locks were curled wildly about her shoulders, making Coltrane wonder how her hair would look spread across his pillows. Her hips swayed provocatively and he couldn't keep his eyes off of them, and she'd already stripped out of a tiny black skirt that had hugged her ass like a second skin.

Coltrane couldn't believe that this was the same woman that ducked out of his kisses if she was in front of her daughter. The woman that he had gotten to know was actually rather shy and withdrawn. But the woman that he watched on stage commanded an entire club full of men, men that shouted marriage proposals, as they emptied their wallets onto the stage.

And one of those men happened to be Earl. Coltrane had seen him walk in a couple hours ago. The son-of-a-bitch was borderline stalker.

Coltrane focused his attention back on the stage just as Cami stepped onto the table of the three men that sat center stage in the V.I.P. section. The shirt she wore was white and thin and see-through with the letters

N-A-S-T-Y spelled across the front in rhinestones. Her dark nipples were puckered and hard, straining against the thin fabric.

Coltrane watched as Cami poured the contents of each man's bottle of beer onto her shirt, ripped it off then squeezed the brew from the shirt into each man's mouth. A nearby waitress tossed Cami a bottle of Vodka, with which she poured each man a shot directly into their mouths, holding the bottle between her legs, emulating a glass dick busting a nut. The men loved it and once again the paper flew.

Coltrane waited for a few minutes once the song ended. He had planned to leave long before Cami did. If he had gotten up right then however, he would have taken a chunk out of the table.

Coltrane waited an additional few minutes then threw some bills on the table to cover his tab plus a tip. It was time for a cold shower.

"Julio, we didn't get it. The *chica* didn't answer the door. I think she's gone."

"What do you mean you think," Julio asked.

"Well, me and the guys went to get something to eat. We thought maybe she put the car in the garage."

"So you let her leave? How stupid could you be?"

"Look, me and the guys were hungry so we stopped by McDonald's."

"You aren't getting paid to stop by McDonald's. Keep an eye out and be ready to make a move when Peter comes back tomorrow."

"You sure he'll come back?"

"Positive," Julio replied chuckling. "Peter's a do-gooder. He'll come back. Trust me."

Chapter 29

Cami looked around her block before she got out of her car. The block was quiet with a few lamps on in a couple of houses. The night was cold and windy with snow flurries swirling down from the sky.

Cami spied Coltrane's lights on inside his house and remembered his insistence that she call. It was just after 1a.m., but he did tell her it didn't matter what time it was. And the fact of the matter was that she really did want to talk to him. Cami might have even missed him if she examined her feelings, but that would make her admit that she cared. She wasn't sure if she was ready to face that fact yet.

Hurrying through the snow, she bounded up the porch steps, checked her surroundings one last time, then unlocked the door. One could never be too careful living in a city like Detroit. Just last month Mrs. Monroe's daughter had gotten robbed at gunpoint coming home late one night two blocks from Cami's house. The crime filled city was going from bad to worse. And like Cami, people had gotten stuck in a rut and learned to accept the crime as everyday happenings. As long as the bad things happened to everyone else, it wasn't that bad. At least that's what people like to tell themselves. For Cami, it was difficult to leave what was familiar, and down right scary. Detroit was all she had ever known. But she wanted more. She deserved more, and so did Tisha.

Throwing the deadbolt, Cami hung her coat in the closet then sat on the edge of the couch and stared down at Tisha. Her baby was growing up so fast. Sometimes staring at Tisha was like staring in the mirror. She was an exact replica of Cami at age ten. Thank God she didn't look like Earl, Cami thought.

"Tisha, I'm home."

Tisha stretched sleepily throwing off the multicolored blanket. It landed atop an empty soda can, a bag of potato chips, a book Coltrane had given her on the subject of cats, and the kitten itself.

"Tisha, come on and go to bed."

Tisha cracked one eye open enough to realize her mother was actually home and she wasn't dreaming after all.

"Hi Mom. Man you stink," Tisha said and waved a hand in front of her nose.

"I know baby. I'm sorry. I didn't shower because you asked me to come home early."

"That's okay. I was really scared when that man came to the door. Mrs. Monroe said he had a package for you, but he wouldn't give it to her. He left a note. It's on the coffee table."

Cami eyed the slip of paper and wondered what the guy wanted, and more importantly who he was.

"I'll take care of it. Go on to bed now."

"Okay. Don't step on Boots Mom. He's on the floor. Love you."

"Goodnight baby. I love you too."

Cami picked up the slip of paper and read the short, but powerful note.

I have important information from Belinda.
Call A.S.A.P.
Peter Wallace
313 555-3596

Cami didn't recognize the name or the phone number scribbled at the bottom of the note. She wondered if Peter Wallace was somehow connected to Caroline. She also wondered if it was too late to call. Picking up the cordless and holding the weight of it in her hand, she decided to call first thing in the morning. Even though she badly wanted to know what the information was, she didn't think that Peter Wallace would appreciate a call at 1am.

Instead Cami punched in the seven digits that she had memorized earlier.

"Hey baby," Coltrane answered.

"You always answer your phone 'hey baby'?"

"Only if it's you. How was work?"

Cami wondered what to tell Coltrane. Eventually, if they kept seeing one another she'd have to tell him she was a dancer, but not now. How *was* work, she asked herself. She couldn't very well tell him she jacked off a bottle of Vodka into three men's mouths. That wouldn't make for good conversation. She opted for the subtle approach.

"Work was fine. I'm tired though."

"Want me to come tuck you in?"

Cami laughed. She actually laughed and it felt damn good.

"Yes and no," she answered.

"What does that mean," Coltrane asked chuckling.

"Yes, I'd like you to tuck me in, but no I'm not going to let you."

"I see. But that does me no good at all."

"Sorry. Besides I'm about to jump in the shower."

"That's right, leave me with images of you rubbing soap all over your naked body. Cami, I never thought you could be so cruel. See you in a few hours baby."

"You don't have to walk Tisha to school you know," she told him.

"Sure I do. I made a promise, and I never break my promises. My word is my bond Cami. You will realize that soon enough. Goodnight baby."

The line went dead and Cami was left wondering about Coltrane's cryptic statement. So much about him was puzzling, but he was sticking around. She was impressed by that. Very impressed.

Chapter 30

Cami eyed the neon green numbers on her alarm clock. She'd been awake for nearly thirty minutes, already having gotten Tisha up for school.

As soon as the green numbers changed to 7a.m., Cami picked up the phone on her bedside table. She'd waited long enough to call Peter Wallace, all night in fact. If she woke him up she'd just apologize. But anything pertaining to Belinda was very important.

Cami punched in the telephone numbers and waited for the phone to ring.

One ring.

Two.

Three.

After the fourth ring, Cami was about to hang up when she heard a deep male voice answer the phone.

"Wallace here," Peter answered fumbling with the headset of his cellular phone. He was immersed in traffic, trying to make his way to work just like every other Detroiter at 7a.m.

"Uh, yes, good morning. You left a note in my mailbox last night," Cami said a bit nervously. Anything regarding Belinda terrified her. The letter was enough to freak her out, not to mention murder. Then there was Caroline, and now more information. Things were definitely weird lately.

"Camilla," Peter asked expecting an older sounding person. The woman on the other end of the digital connection sounded all of about sixteen.

"Yes, this is she. What information do you have and how did you know Belinda," she asked cutting to the chase.

"She was my sister's best friend since high school. My sister asked me to deliver a package to you because she wanted to make sure you received it."

"Who's your sister and how do I know I can trust you?"

Peter didn't need this shit this early in the morning. He was overworked and underpaid. He was tired, he was cranky, and he was horny as hell. In light of his recent single status, he hadn't had any in two weeks, and it was grating on his nerves. To top it off he was trying to do a favor for his sister, and he could see that Camilla was going to be difficult.

"Look Camilla, I can't make you trust me. If it helps, I *am* a police officer. But what's important is finding out whether or not Belinda was murdered. Now according to my sister, the package I have may prove that."

Cami covered the mouthpiece with her hand and told Tisha to wait downstairs as she listened to Peter. When he mentioned the word 'murder' she took a quick indrawn breath. Cami was the only one that she knew of, besides Tony, who knew Belinda was murdered. Just the thought of someone else believing Belinda didn't die of a drug overdose gave her hope and strength to carry on her quest for the truth.

"Okay. Where can we meet?"

"I can bring it back by your place around 6 p.m. How's that? I know it's late, but I'm due in court today. I don't know how long I'll be."

Cami knew 6 p.m. would be cutting it close. She had to be at work by 7 p.m. But come hell or high water, she was going to get that package. She'd just have to be a few minutes late.

"That's fine. I'd appreciate it Peter. Thank you."

After hanging up with Peter, Cami went downstairs to find Coltrane sitting at her dining room table placing an Egg McMuffin in front of Tisha. He was wearing faded blue jeans with a dark green ribbed turtleneck, and he looked absolutely delicious. She could even smell the tantalizing scent of his cologne from across the room.

Never in Cami's life had she wanted something so badly. And she wasn't kidding herself any more. She wanted Coltrane. He was the only man that paid any attention to Tisha. Within the last several days, Coltrane and her daughter had become thick as thieves. It was wonderful to know that Tisha liked him. Besides, most men would have run in the opposite direction when they found out she had a kid. Coltrane not only knew Tisha existed, but he brought her gifts as well.

"Mom," Tisha called as she noticed Cami lurking quietly into the living room. "Coltrane brought us breakfast. He even got you one of those yogurt things you like. He said he didn't want you blaming him again for trying to make you fat. Pretty cool huh?"

"Very cool," Cami agreed.

Coltrane took in Cami's flannel night gown and thought he'd never seen anything as sexy. Of course he'd never thought of flannel as sexy but on Cami it looked good. The soft, warm fabric clung to her curves and outlined her breasts and butt. Even though Coltrane knew what her breasts looked like, just the outline of them underneath the material made his jeans feel as if they were cutting off his circulation.

"Morning, baby," Coltrane greeted intertwining his hand with hers.

In response, Cami leaned down and planted her lips on Coltrane's.

For her the kiss was like none she'd ever engaged in before. Ever. It was slow and deep and emotional. There was a wealth of meaning behind the kiss and it was the only way Cami was able to convey her feelings, her trust, and her desire. For Cami the kiss was like unlocking an old cellar door and clearing away the cobwebs to discover something wondrous inside.

"Dang Mom! Give the man some air so he can breathe," Tisha playfully scolded as she took a bite of the signature oval-shaped, potato hashbrowns.

The kiss ended all too soon as Tisha yanked them back to the present. But when Coltrane looked into Cami's eyes this time, he detected something new. He recognized it immediately as trust mixed with something else he couldn't describe. Something that he'd felt himself lately but couldn't put a name to it.

"All of that for a cup of yogurt? What'll I get if I feed you steak," Coltrane joked.

In answer to Coltrane's question, Cami dipped her white plastic spoon into the yogurt and granola mixture and pulled out a heaping spoonful. She swirled her tongue provocatively into the white mixture before putting the spoonful into her mouth. Darting her tongue out a couple of times, she licked the spoon clean, then repeated the process.

Coltrane's mouth went dry at the sight of Cami's tongue, and his loins ached painfully. The way her tongue darted out and licked all that white stuff evoked images that were better left unexplored.

"You want steak for dinner?"

Cami just laughed and went into the kitchen to make Tisha's lunch. Laughing was easier when she was with Coltrane. It felt damn good to laugh, especially since she'd probably be crying by night's end.

If she couldn't prove that Tony murdered Belinda she didn't know what she'd do. Murdering Tony was number one on the list, but she had Tisha to think about. Besides, murder was too easy for that bastard. Cami wanted him to sit in a tiny cell and rot to death. Slowly. Very slowly.

SALES RECEIPT

ATAPSCO BINGO
VENING SESSION   Mon Aug 8, 2005

Invoice : 1053115

Qty	Item	Price	Total	Pts
4	Pick 8	1.00	4.00	

PMT: CASH   TOTAL   4.00

PICK 8

1137635*	03	04	11	12	20	49	50	75
1137636*	02	04	06	08	10	11	22	23
1137637*	01	02	03	05	06	08	10	29
1137638*	19	27	29	36	38	53	56	62

STN : POS1   Mon Aug 8, 2005 9:05 pm
CLERK: PATAPSCO;

        THANK YOU - Please Come Again!

PLAY SHEET

PICK 8

03 04 11 12 20 49 50 75

02 04 06 08 10 11 22 23

01 02 03 05 06 08 10 29

19 27 29 36 38 53 56 62

Chapter **31**

Helen took the People Mover into Greektown after leaving her lawyer's office. Since she had taken the rest of the day off from the real estate office, and was already downtown, she figured she'd treat herself to lunch. Taking the train seemed to make the most sense. Besides, Helen had something to celebrate.

She had filed for a legal separation nearly an hour ago. Earl would be served with papers while he was at work because she had no idea where he was staying. As long as Earl didn't contest the upcoming divorce, she'd be a single woman within a year. Helen thought it ironic that a marriage that had lasted well over a decade could be dissolved in so little time. She hadn't even decided if she wanted the house or not. Her lawyer said they could sell it and split the money. However, she would love to keep the house because she wouldn't have a mortgage, but the house held so many memories that were good and bad. Helen thought that maybe a clean start was in order. She'd have enough money from the sale of the house coupled with alimony to move into another one.

Helen grasped the handrail tighter as the train slowed to a stop. It was extremely crowded because several people were going to lunch. Every seat was filled and there was very little standing room. Gratefully, she was getting off the train with the throng of people all headed for Greektown, as the waiters shouted 'OPA!'

191

while serving the traditional flaming cheese that put Greektown on the map.

As Helen entered *Niki's*, her favorite Greektown restaurant, the smell of searing lamb and feta cheese wafted past her nose. The delectable aroma made her stomach growl. The hostess led her through a maze of diners, waiters, tables, and booths to seat her at a table for two. Removing one of the place settings, the hostess told Helen that her waiter would be with her shortly.

Taking a look around the restaurant made her feel a bit lonely. Each table or booth had at least two people. But Helen reminded herself of the reason why she was alone. She'd rather be alone than be with Earl. He would never change and she'd known it for some time. He was always going to chase a skirt married or not. Helen didn't need that and she certainly wasn't going to put up with it. Without Earl, she would be able to respect herself. Without Earl, she would feel free to live, and she absolutely wanted to live.

After placing her order for a Greek salad, a Gyro, and of course the flaming cheese, Helen took the current novel she was reading entitled *Black Mother's Milk* out of her leather bag. Removing her bookmark, she picked up where she left off.

She barely thanked the waiter when he brought her salad and a glass of water. Helen was slightly annoyed when she felt a tap on her shoulder.

"Excuse me?"

She was at such a good part in the book that she hated to put it down. Helen looked up to find a handsome black man with skin the color of a toasted walnut standing before her, tall and muscular, who looked to be about forty years old slightly graying at the temples. His camel colored overcoat was unbuttoned and the lapels of a black, double-breasted expensive looking suit peeked through.

"May I help you," Helen asked placing the bookmark between the pages to hold her exact spot.

"I was wondering if you're enjoying the book," he asked gesturing toward it on the table.

"Oh," Helen exclaimed surprised. "Yes, I am. I've never read this author before, but so far he's really good. The main character is a real bitch, but she's honest and upfront about everything. I like that about her."

The man smiled and displayed a row of pearly white teeth. They looked natural, not like Earl's teeth that had been capped several years ago, when he'd said his smile wasn't perfect anymore.

"I could autograph it for you, if you'd like," the man said gesturing once again toward the book.

"Autograph it," Helen asked puzzled before realization dawned bright and clear. "*You're* Ashton Prichard?"

"Yes," Ashton answered still smiling. "Sometimes when I see people reading my book I can't help but to ask if they're enjoying it. It's a completely masochistic habit I have that my mother keeps telling me is impolite."

"I'd love your autograph. It would make my day. I'm Helen Turner by the way."

Ashton shook the proffered hand then reached into his inside coat pocket and produced a pen. He autographed the book then handed it back to Helen.

"I guess I'll let you get back to your lunch, and the book," Ashton said reluctantly.

"Actually, I'd love the company. That's if you don't have other engagements."

"No, I just got here. Thanks for the invitation," Ashton said and pulled out the chair opposite Helen. Calling the waiter over, Ashton received a place setting, silverware, and placed his lunch order.

"So, what's it like knowing your book is a bestseller," Helen asked over the hubbub of the busy restaurant. Raucous lunch crowds were shouting 'OPA!' every couple of minutes. It *was* a tradition after all.

"It's great actually. It's more than I had hoped for to tell the truth. Did it take you long to write it?"

"Actually, not long at all. The book kept my mind focused on something while I was going through a divorce," Ashton replied.

"So you're divorced," Helen mumbled more to herself than to Ashton. She even glanced at her leather bag remembering her copy of the legal separation papers she'd stuffed in there earlier.

"And you're married," Ashton observed indicating the thin solid gold band encircling Helen's left ring finger.

Helen followed Ashton's gaze to her ring finger. It was funny that something so tiny could mean so much. She remembered when Earl had slipped that wedding band on her finger, vowing to cherish her and honor her. What a joke ! Earl honored himself and cherished every other woman except her. Something that Helen had thought was so right had ended up horribly wrong.

"I'm not married," Helen replied twisting the gold band around her finger, an action she'd done for years. "I'm newly separated, and soon to be divorced. I just hadn't gotten around to taking the ring off yet."

"I remember those days," Ashton commiserated. "You end up spending a lot of time wondering what to do with the damn thing. Do you keep it? Do you throw it away?"

"And what did you do," Helen asked curiously as she took a bite of salad.

"My ring is in the Detroit Sewer System actually. I figured the marriage went to shit so why not the ring."

Despite the seriousness of the topic, Helen laughed. And before long Ashton joined in too. They talked well into the afternoon, amicable conversation flowing easily without any lulls. They spoke of likes and dislikes, dreams and goals. They even spoke about their failed marriages, the common thread being infertility.

Helen couldn't believe someone as virile and dashing as Ashton would have trouble making a baby. And to think that his wife left him over that was deplorable. Helen had always believed in adoption. Well, not always, but she had recently begun thinking about it. A man like Ashton seemed to be perfect husband material. Helen learned the hard way that that was most important.

After only baklava crumbs littered their plates and the last drops of coffee were sipped from their cups did they even think about saying good-bye. Even then it was Ashton's 4 p.m. meeting that made him cut the afternoon short. Well, not exactly short. They had talked for nearly three hours.

"Would you like to have dinner with me Friday night," Ashton asked before he departed. Hooking up with Helen couldn't have been a chance meeting. He wasn't ready to let her go so soon.

"I'd love to," Helen responded to the invitation. She hadn't been asked on a date, a *real* date, in years.

"Great. Why don't you call me and we'll firm up the plans."

Ashton handed Helen a business card with his home number written on the back, and wrote her number on another business card.

"Thanks for the terrific lunch Helen."

"Thank you for the autograph."

Ashton lifted Helen's hand to his mouth, kissed it, and then he was gone.

Not bad, Helen thought. Not bad at all.

Chapter 32

Cami waited anxiously as 6 p.m. had come and gone. It was already a quarter after six and Peter still hadn't shown up. She was definitely going to be late for work and Macky was going to be all over her ass. But anything about Belinda was more important than the club any day. She had to get the package from Peter or she'd spend another night tossing and turning and worrying about the damn thing. She'd slept less than 4 hours a night since Belinda's death and she just couldn't afford to lose any more.

"Mom, is that man coming back again tonight when you're gone," Tisha asked without breaking eye contact with the television screen.

"No, he was supposed to be here already," Cami replied.

"I don't think you should work tonight in case he comes back. Besides that, I got a bad feeling."

Cami stopped looking at her watch and out of the window long enough to sit next to Tisha on the couch. She draped an arm around her daughter's shoulders and pulled her close. Tucking a long strand of hair that escaped the single thick plait behind Tisha's ear, Cami placed a kiss near her daughter's temple.

"Tell me what's wrong," she asked Tisha. Her daughter was rarely worried when she left for work. The same daughter that told her she was old enough to put herself to bed at night and didn't need Mrs. Monroe to sit in the house.

"Can't Coltrane stay here 'til you get home from work," Tisha asked hopefully.

"I don't think so honey. You really like Coltrane don't you," Cami asked.

Tisha shrugged her shoulders, a gesture that was familiar to children of all ages. It was as if they were shrugging boulders, the rise and fall was so utterly exaggerated.

"Yeah, I do. It's better when he's around. You're better," Tisha admitted reluctantly. "Not that you were bad Mom, 'cause you weren't. It's just that you're...you're happier."

Cami didn't quite know how to respond to that one. What could she say? But she was spared from answering when the snow crunched loudly in her driveway. The distinct sound of a large truck engine hummed outside, then suddenly stopped.

"Go upstairs Tisha. I don't want Peter seeing you until I know I can trust him," Cami explained quickly.

"But he's a cop," Tisha complained.

"I know honey, but that doesn't mean we can trust him. Now go."

Cami waited for Tisha to run upstairs before she answered the door. She watched through the peephole as Peter's tall, lean form climbed from a blue Ford Explorer. She saw Peter glance around the neighborhood, spending a little extra time on Mrs. Monroe's house. He was probably remembering the double-barreled shotgun Mrs. Monroe had pointed at him, Cami thought. It was a miracle he hadn't asked to see a gun permit.

When the doorbell pealed Cami yelled, "Who is it?" through the thick steel door just to be on the safe side. Just because she knew Peter was coming didn't make the man on the other side of the door him.

"It's Peter Wallace, Ms. Abernathy," he replied blowing on his hands to keep them warm.

"Do you have identification," she asked before opening the door. She saw the large FedEx envelope, but she wanted more.

Peter reached into his pocket and produced his badge along with picture identification and held it up to the peephole for Cami. He didn't blame her for checking. If more people were as cautious before opening the door perhaps some home invasions wouldn't occur, along with the deaths that often accompanied them.

Once Cami was satisfied, she threw the deadbolt and unlocked the door.

"Hi Camilla, I'm Peter," he began by extending his hand. "Sorry I'm late, but I got caught up at work."

"That's okay. Please have a seat."

Cami motioned toward the couch and waited for Peter to sit first before perching on the edge of her seat. She watched Peter adjust his overcoat, which made the front flap of his suit jacket fall open to reveal the butt of a gun in a shoulder holster. Peter was very attractive, his roan skin reddened a bit from the frigid air. But he wasn't Cami's type. Or maybe she'd already found her type in the form of one Coltrane Kennedy.

"Thank you for coming by," she said to break the silence.

"Oh, of course," Peter replied off-handedly. He was a bit preoccupied. Camilla Abernathy wasn't what he had expected, at all. For one, he hadn't thought she'd be so damn beautiful. And for two, he didn't think *she would be so beautiful.* He expected a drug kingpin's niece to be flashy, with gaudy jewelry and sack chaser earrings, the ones that were thick gold hoops that were so heavy that they pulled on the woman's earlobe. Peter didn't expect the soft spoken, gorgeous woman beside him with the baby blue cable knit sweater and worn Levi's. Apparently, she hadn't been tainted by Anthony Jackson's crimes. She was, however, Belinda's blood and not Anthony's. Perhaps that made the difference.

"This belongs to you," Peter said relinquishing the package over to Cami. "I hope you can figure out what's in here and how it can help to put Anthony Jackson behind bars."

"I hope so too," Cami agreed accepting the package from Peter.

"If there *is* something in there and you need help with it, call me. I'll make sure it gets to the right people," Peter offered before standing and readjusting his coat.

"I appreciate it. I may take you up on that offer," Cami said earnestly. Peter Wallace looked trustworthy.

She walked him to the door and they exchanged farewells. Cami watched Peter pull out the driveway then called Tisha back downstairs. Unfortunately it was late and before going to work she wouldn't have time to open the package. She thought about calling in, but she needed the money. She had to get Tisha's college fund finished before spring. Cami had to work.

"Tisha, I have to leave honey."

"Aw Mom! Why can't you stay home? Just tonight?"

"I can't honey. If I don't work, we don't eat. You know that Tisha. Please don't make me feel guilty."

Tisha sighed heavily and plopped down on the couch. She grabbed the remote angrily and began flipping through the channels.

"I'm already late Tisha, I have to go."

"Bye."

"I love you Tisha."

When Cami didn't get a reply she slipped on her coat dejectedly and didn't bother zipping it. She tucked the package under her arm and grabbed her purse. Sometimes she just wanted to climb under the covers and not come out.

"I'll page you when I get to work honey."

Slinging the strap of her purse over her shoulder Cami left the house, locking the door behind her.

"Julio, it's me."

"So, what's the story?"

"You were right," the man said. "Detective Wallace did come back to deliver the package. The only problem is that the chica left with it right after he left."

Julio slammed his fist into the wall. The bitch was making his life difficult. Everybody was on his back and Tony was waiting to slit his throat. If Julio didn't get that package he was a dead man. Hell, his wife would probably be better off without him. She'd no doubt spend his life insurance money on her current boy toy. Julio wasn't going out like that. Especially not so his bitch of a wife could buy a small villa in Colombia.

"Fuck," Julio exclaimed frustrated. "Follow that puta and get the package the first chance you get."

"Already on it. We'll have it tonight. For sure."

"You'd better or we're all dead."

Coltrane watched out of the window as the blue Explorer pulled out of Cami's driveway. She'd told him earlier that a friend was delivering something that he'd thought would help her with the 'Belinda situation'. Coltrane knew she hadn't been telling him the whole story. He just wondered what the whole story was, and what was in the FedEx package. He'd bet his ass that whatever was in that package meant a lot to several different people, with Anthony Jackson, a.k.a. Snow King at the top of the list.

Coltrane didn't know who the guy was that left Cami's house, but he was sure of one thing- the guy was a cop. He looked like a cop, he walked like a cop, and he'd cased the neighborhood like a cop. Coltrane wondered if Cami knew exactly what she was getting herself into by opening so many cans of worms. She had to have no idea how many people were involved. But he didn't blame her for wanting to try to bring Belinda justice. They were, after all, like mother and daughter.

Coltrane pulled back the beige drapes at his front window to look down the block. The guys were still watching Cami's house. They were in a silver Honda Accord, a different vehicle than the one they were in the day before, but the same guys nonetheless. Coltrane wanted to know what the hell they were doing. Whatever it was, wasn't good. That was for certain.

Taking out his cell phone, he placed a call to Yuri.

"Hey it's me. They're still watching Cami's house and they're in a silver Accord today."

"The tag I ran yesterday belonged to a Maria Gonzalez, age fifty-seven of Dearborn," Yuri replied reading the information out of a pocket notebook.

"Well it doesn't look like Maria is in the car right now," Coltrane joked as he watched Cami get into her car and pull away. Then a few seconds later the silver Accord followed. "They're on the move Yuri. They're following Cami to work and she took the package with her. Make sure Sully's on it."

"He's already in route buddy," Yuri assured him. "Just relax. I know this whole assignment is screwy, but she'll be fine. Especially while she's at the club."

"I know, but I don't like it. I feel like they're coming back. Something's missing and we don't know what it is. Those guys seem to know more than we do, because they want that package and I don't think Cami knows what the hell that is. I think the guys are going to make a play for the house to see what they can find. Call me crazy, but that's my gut feeling. I almost forgot- have we found something on this Caroline woman?"

Coltrane ran a hand over his face and sat down on the couch. Who the hell was Caroline and what did she know about the Snow King?

"We'll find her Coltrane, whoever she is. Sit tight and we'll get back to you after we dig around a little more. I think I'll pay Maria Gonzalez a visit and find out who's been driving her car," Yuri told him.

"I can't lose her Yuri," Coltrane confessed to his long time friend.

"I know buddy. You won't."

Chapter 33

As soon as Cami walked through the doors of the club, the thick rancid smoke made her eyes water. The blaring music reverberated through her chest and the jeers of men with a finite amount of women assaulted her ears. It was another night at The Chocolate Factory.

"Cami you're late," Macky complained as he accosted her in the dressing room. "I got a club full of men with ten V.I.P.s and they're all asking for you. But my best girl isn't here. Just fucking great."

Cami ignored Macky as she stuffed her coat, purse, and the FedEx package into her locker. She didn't need him breathing down her throat. She had enough to worry about. And she sure as hell didn't care about the men at the club. Most of them were a bunch of sexually frustrated perverts who were borderline stalkers.

"Don't give me any shit Macky. I'm never late and you know it. You know what my life has been like lately, so cut me a break. Now I'll be out on stage when I'm ready."

Macky grumbled something under his breath as he checked the mirror to make sure his hat was still cocked to the side. He had to hunch his six foot frame down low because the mirrors above the vanity counter were low, but Macky never passed a mirror without looking in it. His bronze colored skin had always been flawless, and his beard was always perfectly manicured. The coarse hairs lay flat and were trimmed expertly.

Macky then adjusted the vest of his dark purple three piece pimped out suit. He thought he looked ghetto fabulous, but not even Prince himself would have touched that suit with a ten foot pole. It was all part of an image he'd created for the club.

Macky showcased the finest forms of chocolate the city had ever seen, and the club's patrons loved him for it. Macky played the role of 'pimp daddy' every night because it seemed to generate more business.

Cami was the only one who knew the absolute truth. Macky, a.k.a. Dr. Theodore (Theo) Mackenzie outside of The Chocolate Factory was nothing like the character he portrayed at the club. Theo Mackenzie was extremely Republican and had a medical degree in Obstetrics and Gynecology from none other than Yale University. She still didn't know why he had turned in his white lab coat and latex surgical gloves. Or why he'd begun looking at the vagina more in terms of gyration and less in terms of procreation.

Cami sped through the dressing room and changed into her costume, a little red cowgirl number with a fringed red leather jacket and a skirt to match, a red cowgirl hat, and thigh high spike-heeled patent leather boots.

The dressing room was full with girls doubled in front of the vanity mirror and sitting in every available seat. A few were on their way out to the stages, so Cami grabbed a seat quickly and paged Tisha.

I'm here honey
Ok
Still mad?
Yes
Sorry honey. U doing ok?

Ate pie from Monroe and chillin' with Boots and Miss Daisy

GTG honey. ILU

LU2

Cami knew Tisha must have been really angry if she was playing with Miss Daisy, a childhood doll. Tisha only played with Daisy when she was upset. She claimed the doll made her feel better, which was the case most times. Tisha had named every doll she'd ever gotten, but then again so did Cami. It was good to know that some things never changed, she thought as she went to tell Redd her music selection.

"We're still following her. She's a stripper and she's hot."

"I don't give a shit what she is, just get the motherfucking package," Julio yelled. He was in a piss poor mood and the bitch with the package wasn't making him feel any better.

"I told you we'd get it tonight and we will, so relax. The Snow King's not going to kill us, so stop thinking that. Tomorrow morning he'll be singing your praises and we'll have fat pockets."

"You'd better be right or I'll kill you myself."

After only a few short hours Cami was exhausted. It was because she didn't get much sleep the night before. Hell, she hadn't gotten much sleep since Belinda's death, and before that she had spent her nights worrying about her pregnancy. It had been a couple of shitty months and Cami wanted the nightmare to end.

As Cami danced on stage, the movements were automatic and rehearsed. Her mind was going a mile a minute though. She thought about Earl, and Coltrane, and Tisha. Mostly Tisha. Cami needed to find a way to talk to her daughter. They still hadn't truly discussed the fact that Earl was her father. That was probably the reason Tisha was still so angry. Hopefully, Miss Daisy would make her feel better though. Cami remembered how Belinda had given her a doll when she was just six years old. Cami's real mother was still alive then. Belinda had told Cami that the doll was for making her feel better. Cami had named the doll Caroline and passed it along to Tisha when she was born.

The memory was like being doused with a bucket of ice cold water. Cami was so jarred by it that she missed a dance step, but quickly covered it up. She made herself focus on the song and was grateful that it was near the end.

How could I have been so stupid!

Cami berated herself as money was stuffed into her G-string. *Caroline* was her doll. That's what Belinda meant in the letter. Something had to be inside of the doll, which was completely possible. Caroline was an old rag doll that had been stitched up numerous times over the years. And Caroline was in Tisha's bedroom, a part of the massive doll collection her daughter had.

When the song was over Cami hurried off stage and began to dress. It was only 11pm but she didn't care. She had to leave and get home immediately. She had to find the damn doll and see what Belinda had put inside of it. She also had to open the FedEx package. She was too close now to finding the proof she needed to wait a moment more.

As Cami pulled the cable knit blue sweater over her head, Macky came into the dressing room. He regarded her coolly as he took in her clothes, and her shoes.

"This a new act Cami," Macky asked sarcastically as he watched her pull her coat from the locker.

"I have to leave Macky. It's an emergency," Cami informed him quickly. Her tone of voice brooked no argument, but Macky delved into one anyway.

"What the hell Cami? You're late and now you want to leave early," he argued.

"Look Macky, I've never given you one problem in eight long years. Now, I *have* to leave. Please don't fight me on this. I know you're better than that get-up you're wearing. I know you're a nice man."

"Fine," Macky relented. "Just don't go around telling people that I'm nice. It'll ruin my image."

Macky brushed an imaginary piece of lint off of his purple sleeve and thought about all that Cami had been through. First the death of her aunt, and then the loss of her baby had really sent her for a loop.

"Sorry for giving you shit Cami," he whispered. "Take all the time you need."

"Thanks Macky. Gotta go."

Cami grabbed her purse and shoved the FedEx package under her arm for the second time that day. She enlisted Tiny, one of the bouncers at the club, to escort her to her car then thanked him with a kiss on the cheek. Tiny was nothing but a big, cuddly, brown teddy bear. He only acted like a gorilla for the club's benefit.

Cami sat in the Miata and let it warm up. Snow swirled down from the sky accumulating rapidly on the ground. The wind howled fiercely as it rent the night air. It almost looked like a scene out of a cheesy horror movie, she thought. Cami thought that the ironic scene would have been a movie director's dream: *Stripper leaves club on a cold wintry night to avenge aunt's death only to be mauled by the abominable snow creature.*

Cami laughed aloud. It was either laugh or cry. Whatever she was about to find could quite possibly kill her. Then she'd be as dead as the night and as cold as the fallen snow. And she knew this.

Coltrane cut the television on as he slipped out of his green turtleneck and threw it on the couch. The snowy white wifebeater T-shirt he wore underneath shone brightly in the darkened living room. The pristine sleeveless tee shirt allowed him to feel a little air on his mahogany skin. He thought about stripping down to his boxers but he wanted to wait until Cami got home before he got comfortable.

Coltrane had just checked out the window and saw that the silver Accord was back. He hated to see that car again, because that meant that his gut had been right. The guy definitely wanted to scope out the house. The shadowy figures were barely silhouetted against the moonlight, but it looked as if there were now four men.

For the umpteenth time Coltrane wondered who they were. He, Yuri, and Sully had no leads thus far. Yuri went to check out the one lead they had about the woman that owned the car in Dearborn. It was a dead end however, when Yuri found the woman strangled to death, and her body stuffed in a small coat closet.

As the opening bars of *The Tonight Show*'s music began, Coltrane went to use the bathroom. A couple more hours and Cami would be home.

Chapter 34

Cami was thankful to be home. Visibility was low because it was snowing so heavily. It had even picked up as she had turned into her driveway. These were the nights that she wished she had an automatic garage door opener, she thought as she cut the ignition.

It was only twenty minutes until midnight, which was relatively early by her standards. Cami saw the beckoning light that spilled from her living room. Tisha always left a light on for her, and on this cold snowy night she was very grateful.

Cami stuffed the package as best she could into her purse. It stuck out badly, but some protection from the snow was better than none. Then she remembered her gym bag on the floor of the passenger side. Cami decided at once to put both the package and her purse into the gym bag, which would eliminate the hassle of either getting wet. She looked down the block before she exited the Miata, but couldn't see much of anything. Only a fool would be outside in this weather, she uttered aloud as she opened the car door. Besides, she didn't even think a criminal would bother coming out in the thick snow. It was a proven fact that crime always went down in Detroit in the winter time.

The snow crunched underneath her shoes, the sound echoing around the dark street. The night was completely silent except for the constant howl of the wind and the moaning wail of dense, blowing snow flakes as its companion. Most people had a lamp post in their front yard, but even that soft illumination seemed invisible.

Cami held the banister tightly as she carefully made her way up the porch steps. She slipped once on the layer of ice underneath the snow, but righted herself immediately. The last thing she needed right now was to bust her ass in the middle of the night. Grasping the front door key between her thumb and forefinger, she unlocked the first lock then switched keys to unlock the deadbolt. She could hear Jay Leno's opening monologue on the television which meant that Tisha had tried to wait up and was asleep on the couch.

Cami lent her weight to the door, huddling against the snow and the arctic blast. But as the front door opened she heard an unfamiliar sound. She heard what she thought were muted footsteps, but they came from all different directions. That didn't make sense, but in the back of her mind she knew something was wrong. Someone was on her porch and maybe behind her. Someone was somewhere and she couldn't see a goddamn thing.

Everything began happening in slow motion. Seconds stretched slowly into molasses coated minutes, and then time began to stand utterly still. All of her senses sharpened and the blood keenly roared through her ears. Her heart hammered in her chest and she fought to remember to breathe. Someone was on her and she didn't know who the hell it was.

Shadowy figures appeared out of thin air looming over her like monsters in a nightmare. Three, no four pair of eyes stared accusingly at her through holes cut into black skull caps. She turned quickly, willing herself to twist the door knob and get inside of the house. When her hand connected with the brass knob she heard a slicing motion behind her then immediately felt pain between her shoulder blades. The padded down-filled winter coat she wore didn't shield her from feeling the full impact of what she intuitively knew was the butt of a gun.

Cami fell to her knees heavily, freezing snow, ice and rock salt biting into her knee caps. Her gym bag, which was looped across her body, slammed into her hip making her two combination locks gouge her thigh.

"Give us the fucking package or you die!"

The man behind her shouted the order right before the butt of the gun slammed into her shoulder blades again. The force of the blow caused her right hand to twist involuntarily, the same hand that was on the doorknob.

The front door burst open with a thud, jarring Tisha awake from a sound sleep. She rubbed her eyes and realized that she was on the couch and was momentarily elated that her mother had come home early.

Then Tisha sat up and saw what was happening.

Cami lay sprawled half in the door and half out on the porch. She was being kicked everywhere by men wearing all black with big steel-toed boots. It had to be a nightmare.

"Mom!" Tisha screamed as Cami came to her knees.

Hearing Tisha's frightened scream snapped Cami out of whatever feeble paralyzed state she was in. She didn't care whether it was the need for self preservation or a mother's protective instinct, but the bastards were *not* hurting her baby.

Cami didn't grow up in Detroit her entire life and not learn anything. She'd seen the talk shows demonstrating self-defense tactics for women and she knew in her heart that she could not let them get her daughter.

"Tisha run!" Cami screamed at her daughter.

"Mom!"

"Run dammit! Run!"

Tisha scrambled off the couch and ran through the kitchen to the side door.

"Get the girl," the man behind her yelled to one of the other men beside her.

"No!" Cami screamed.

Cami felt around on the ground frantically for her keys and mercifully found them. Grasping a key between her thumb and forefinger she plunged it forcefully into the man's thigh as he started to run after Tisha.

"You bitch!" the man yelled grabbing desperately at the keys stuck in his thigh.

"Get the fucking kid," the man with the gun yelled to the third man.

Cami kicked out quickly and the heel of her shoe landed in the gunman's groin. He yelped out in pain, but the kick didn't deter him. This time the butt of the gun hit her squarely on the left side of her head. A wave of dizziness engulfed her, but she vowed not to pass out. She had to get Tisha before the other guy did.

The man with the key stuck in his thigh recovered enough to rip it out and that only pissed him off further. He lifted her off the ground by the front of her coat.

"Where is the fucking package bitch," he spat in her face.

"I don't know what you're talking about," she cried, desperately trying to wrench free of his hold. She didn't know how long it would take before they left her alone. But she had a feeling the man with the gun would kill her.

"Where's the package you got this evening," the gunman asked then hit her again.

She barely held onto consciousness, but she was coherent enough to see a flash of white other than snow out of the corner of her eye. It almost looked like a man jumping over her porch railing. It almost looked like Coltrane.

It was a moment before Cami realized that it was Coltrane and he actually was on her porch and he held a gun pointed directly at the gunman.

"Drop the fucking gun," Coltrane ordered. The deadly tone of his voice brooked no argument.

A silent standoff ensued for a few heart stopping moments, which felt like hours. Then the man with the key in his thigh dropped Cami and lunged himself at Coltrane grabbing for the gun. The fourth man had been stock still for the entire struggle until now. He too joined in the battle to overtake Coltrane and the gun.

Cami immediately tried to get to her knees but the gunman knocked her backward and placed a booted foot against her chest. Her breasts were crushed under his foot and she could barely breathe. She gasped for breath twice, but was unsuccessful at sucking air into her lungs.

The gunman pointed the gun at her head and said, "You have until the count of three to hand over that package or you and the kid are dead!"

"One..."

"Two..."

"Three!"

A single gun shot tore through the air.

Chapter 35

Coltrane shoved upward with the heel of his left hand into one guy's nose, shattering bone and rupturing membranes instantly. The man lay writhing and screaming on the ground. Coltrane only needed one alive to question later. Three would have to die. He wasn't going to let them walk away from hurting Cami and Tisha. *That* was unacceptable.

Coltrane's full attention turned toward Cami. He'd heard the threat and knew the bastard was going to shoot her. Placing his current adversary into a sleeper hold, Coltrane wrapped his left arm around the man's neck and squeezed. The man tried to claw at Coltrane's forearm for release, but Coltrane was immovable.

When Coltrane heard numbers being counted and saw the silver gleam of a .38 pointed at Cami's head, he raised his own .9 mm and fired. The man's body slumped over and landed on top of Cami.

When Cami heard the single gunshot she screamed, then screamed again. She thought for sure she was dead, but then the man fell on top of her and his gun dropped onto the snow covered front porch.

Once she realized she really was alive, all thoughts turned to Tisha. Her daughter was out there somewhere, and the son-of-a-bitch was chasing her. Cami wasn't even sure if Tisha had made it out of the house. All Cami knew was that she had to find her daughter.

"Get him off of me," she cried finding it damn near impossible to lift the huge man off of her. As she pushed against his body a warm sticky substance oozed through her fingers. She realized it was blood, *his* blood and it seeped into her coat mingling with her own. The thick crimson liquid threatened to penetrate her coat and reach her skin.

"Get him off!" she cried again hysterically, only to find her burden suddenly lifted.

Coltrane physically lifted her from the ground as if she weighed no more than a child. Her legs felt wobbly and her knees hurt like hell, but she quickly regained her footing. The only thing that mattered was finding Tisha.

"Tisha!" Cami shouted and her voice echoed throughout the snowy night. "Tisha!" she screamed again, only to be stopped short by an imperceptible shake from Coltrane.

"Cami, I'll find her. Now be quiet so I can listen," Coltrane instructed.

Cami quieted abruptly, but didn't hear a damn thing besides the blowing wind. In her mind Coltrane was making them waste precious seconds. Her baby was out there somewhere.

Coltrane cocked his head to the side and heard the sounds he knew were racing footsteps behind the houses. Granted they were distant, but there nonetheless.

He took out his cell phone and hit the send button. The line was answered immediately on the first ring. Coltrane spoke rapid Russian then shoved the phone back in his pocket. The exchange probably took ten seconds at best.

"I'll find her," Coltrane repeated just before he hopped off the porch and catapulted himself smoothly over the low fence and into Cami's backyard.

Cami didn't wait around twiddling her thumbs. She was hot on Coltrane's heels and pissed because the fence slowed her down. She didn't vault over it as easily as he did, but nevertheless, she was close behind. Tisha was *her* daughter and Cami would die trying to save her.

Coltrane followed the footprints in the snow until he saw Tisha running for her life in a pair of bright yellow pajamas. Those pajamas were like a beacon in the night and Coltrane thanked his lucky stars he found her so easily. The bastard dressed in black however was quickly catching up to her.

Coltrane picked up his speed and raised his gun. He saw his mark, aimed, and fired.

"No!" Cami screamed. "Tisha! Where are you?"

Cami pumped her legs even harder finding it difficult to run through the deep snow.

Please God don't let my baby die.

Cami kept running and drew up short when she came across one of her attackers, writhing in a pool of his own blood and grabbing at his lower leg. She'd seen Coltrane bending down after the gunshot, but she assumed he was bending over Tisha. That wasn't the case at all. That meant that her daughter was still alive.

Please God let her be all right.

"Tisha!" Coltrane called as he saw the yellow pajamas fall into the snow. "It's okay honey, come back."

"Tisha where are you," Cami yelled out as well, closing in on Coltrane's running form. The man didn't falter a bit. He said that he'd find Tisha and he did, she realized when she saw bright yellow pajamas appear through the blowing snow.

Tisha got to her knees and turned around. She heard first Coltrane's voice then her mother's and she didn't see the scary man that was chasing her.

"Coltrane, I'm here," Tisha called out, and when she got to her feet Coltrane was there in front of her. She'd never been so happy to see him.

Coltrane lifted Tisha into his arms and hugged her. She seemed to be all right, and for that he was thankful.

Coltrane carried her back in his arms until Cami nearly collided with him. She yanked her baby away from him and cradled Tisha's head in her hands.

"My God, Tisha are you okay? Are you hurt baby? Answer me!"

"I'm okay Mom, I'm okay. What's happening? What's going on? Mom, you're bleeding."

"We have to keep moving. Let's get to the house," Coltrane told them and ushered their bodies forward until they were nearly running.

Coltrane wanted to get them back to the safety of the house and out of the cold. He also had a few questions for the bastard still squirming on the ground trying like hell to slither away with a blown out knee. His left leg dragged behind him, and it was clear that he'd never walk normally again.

Coltrane pushed Cami and Tisha behind him then drew his gun. He pointed it squarely at the man's head then began his interrogation.

"Who sent you," Coltrane asked and flipped the safety on his weapon to the off position.

The man started sputtering in rapid Spanish, pleading for his life.

"Who do you work for," Coltrane pressed and placed his gun on the center of the man's forehead. Spanish words flew out of the man's mouth and Coltrane caught every last one of them.

"You bastard," Coltrane spat after cajoling the entire story from the man. He wanted to see the man's brains splattered in the dark alley. He needed to do something to make the blood boiling in his veins settle down and return to normal.

"He's not worth it Coltrane," Yuri called out to his friend.

Cami pushed Tisha behind her and would have had her body melded with her daughter's if she could have. She didn't know who the white man was that appeared suddenly in the alley, but apparently Coltrane did.

"Take them back to the house Coltrane. Ms. Abernathy looks as if she's going into shock and Tisha's freezing. Her feet are going to be frostbitten soon."

The concern in Yuri's voice for Cami and Tisha snapped Coltrane out of his crazed state. The most important thing was that they were alright.

Coltrane lifted Tisha into his arms and shifted her to his back. She wrapped her legs around his waist and her arms looped around his neck. She held on tightly as Coltrane looped an arm around Cami's shoulders to get her moving.

"Let's keep this quiet Yuri and get it cleaned up fast," Coltrane told his friend and co-worker.

"Way ahead of you. Sully's at the house and an ambulance is on its way."

Coltrane turned and pulled Cami along in his wake keeping up a break neck pace. She was panting heavily once they reached her fenced backyard. Coltrane lifted Cami over the low fence then vaulted over easily even with Tisha on his back. He moved like a well oiled machine.

Once they reached the house Cami saw another white man hoisting two men into a white van that was parked in her driveway. She assumed it was two of her attackers because her porch was empty, except for the gunman that Coltrane shot.

"Close your eyes Tisha," Coltrane instructed as he stepped over the body and into the warmth of the house.

Cami's body felt like jelly once the heat hit her. All she wanted to do was sit down for a minute and gather her bearings.

Coltrane took charge inside the house and Cami let him. She was still trying to collect her thoughts as he set her gym bag on the floor, then stripped her out of her blood soaked coat and stained sweater. She sat down on the couch as Coltrane wrapped the Afghan around her upper body clad in only a black lace bra.

Next Coltrane worked on Tisha by taking off her rubber soled bunny slippers that were soaked from the snow, and began chafing her feet with his hands. Her toes were nearly blue, but after a few short minutes they were turning pink again as the blood began to circulate.

"Who the fuck are you," Cami asked calmly. Her voice was so flat that it scared him. She was definitely going into shock.

"I'm DEA," Coltrane replied just as calmly.

"*What?*"

"I work for the Drug Enforcement Administration in the Washington, D.C. field division Cami. We'd been investigating Anthony Jackson for three years when one Monday morning last month Belinda came into our office and said that she could get us the evidence we needed to put Anthony behind bars for life. But when we came to Detroit with the operation in place, Belinda was dead."

"So you *used* me," Cami stated, her temper escalating quickly. "I let you into my home and you *used* me! This was all a job to you."

"That's *not* true," he denied forcefully. "I was in that house next door because Belinda refused to help us unless you and Tisha had protection. She said that you would never agree to police protection or being tailed. She personally asked if I would be the one to watch out for you. Belinda didn't want Anthony to hurt you."

Cami heard everything that Coltrane said but it didn't make it any easier to digest. She sat ramrod straight holding on to Tisha for dear life. Her entire body was wracked with severe tremors. And she felt betrayed.

"Everything's a lie! Your parents don't even live in Bloomfield do they? And what was the cat for? Trying to butter me up maybe?"

Tears leaked from Cami's eyes and she couldn't control them. She felt a string of emotions swirling inside of her. Fear, anger, and hope all combined to form a powerful maelstrom that nearly made her faint dead away.

"Goddamn it Cami, everything is not a lie! I didn't tell you who I was because Belinda asked me not to. I didn't mean to fall in love with you either, but the shit happened anyway."

"Bullshit," Cami yelled.

"Prove it," Coltrane yelled right back.

Tisha had been silent the entire time and plastered against her mother during the shouting match. But she couldn't take it anymore. She loved both her mother and Coltrane and didn't want to hear them hurting each other by saying mean things.

"Stop yelling at each other," Tisha screamed at them. "You're acting like kids. If Coltrane didn't love us Mom, he wouldn't have saved us. You're being unreasonable 'cause you're scared. Well I'm scared too, but Coltrane's the one with the gun. We need him," Tisha proclaimed with maturity well beyond her years.

Tisha sat back down and snuggled back against her mother. Her teeth were only chattering a little now from being out in the cold, but her foot was hurting from stepping on something in the alley. They were also beginning to tingle badly the more they warmed up.

"The man in the alley said that he worked for Julio, and Julio worked for the Snow King. So that means that Tony wants that package and he's willing to kill me for it."

Cami made the statement as if she were talking about the weather. The fact that her uncle was trying to kill her didn't put her into a fit of hysterics. It was almost as if she'd expected Tony was the culprit. It made her mad as hell, and the anger worked miracles at reducing the fear.

"You speak Spanish," Coltrane asked surprised.

Cami quickly nodded her head.

"Mom speaks a lot of languages," Tisha informed Coltrane proudly. "She's got a high I.Q. She's almost a genius," Tisha boasted and smiled at the look on Coltrane's face.

"What do you speak," he asked curiously.

Cami shrugged her shoulders and replied, "Spanish, French, Italian, Korean, and a little Chinese."

"Why the hell do you speak Korean?"

"Because I wanted to know what they were saying while I got my nails done," she shot back.

"If you're so smart, why the hell do you work at the club?"

"Don't judge me," Cami yelled, but cut off anything else she was about to say when Tisha jumped up prepared to chastise them again.

Before Coltrane could say anything else, Yuri knocked once on the door then let himself into the house. The atmosphere was highly charged, but Yuri was used to all kinds of situations, especially in their line of work.

"Cami, Tisha, this is my friend and co-worker Yuri Petrivkov," Coltrane introduced.

"Nice to meet you," Yuri replied with a heavily Russian accented voice.

"I'll be right back," Coltrane said and started for the door.

"Where are you going?"

"No, don't go!"

The question from Cami and the exclamation from Tisha made Coltrane turn back around. He hated to hear such fear in their voices, but knew soon they'd be alright. After their ordeal tonight, it was expected that they'd be frightened.

"I'm coming right back. I need to run next door for a few things, but it will only take five minutes. I promise.

"In the meantime, Yuri will stay with you until I come back. You can trust him Cami."

Cami nodded her head jerkily and pulled the blanket around her shoulders even more. She was chilled to the bone and not from the cold.

Yuri and Coltrane spoke quietly by the door in Russian and Cami was pissed for not knowing the language. She did hear Mrs. Monroe's name and gathered that the woman was outside or something. Cami wasn't prepared to see anyone at the moment. She had too much on her mind.

"Mrs. Monroe wanted to see you, but Coltrane is taking care of it," Yuri explained after Coltrane left.

Cami got her first good look at Coltrane's Russian friend. He was tall and lean with a jagged scar on his right cheek. Coal black hair curled about his face with a wavy lock that fell just over his brow. He was handsome in a mysteriously rugged way.

"Mom, you're bleeding," Tisha said and pointed to Cami's forehead.

Yuri produced a handkerchief from his back pocket and gave it to Cami.

"Things will seem better in the morning," Yuri told her.

"Do you really believe that," Cami asked cynically.

"No, but it sure sounded good when my mother used to say it to me when I was a kid."

Yuri smirked a bit and it reached his silver gray eyes.

"You're going to be okay Ms. Abernathy. I'm certain of it."

Chapter **36**

Coltrane came back into the house after having spoken with Sully and the paramedics. He was pissed about the fact that the man he shot was actually still alive. He kept his mind focused on Cami and Tisha though. That helped a lot, but his blood now felt like a slow burn. He knew he was a federal agent, but Coltrane was a man first. Any man would feel as he did if something bad happened to their loved ones. It was only natural.

Coltrane set down his coat and a duffel bag on the couch, then placed Patch, his kitten, on the floor next to Boots. It was a miracle Boots hadn't run out of the house while the door was wide open. Tisha would have been heartbroken had that happened.

Thank God for small favors.

Yuri gave Coltrane a once over, taking in the duffel bag and the cat. His friend definitely had it bad. If only Yuri could have been on time for Natasha as Coltrane was for Cami. Perhaps then she would have been alive for him to love. Perhaps then he would not feel like emptying the clip from his .9mm into his skull every night. Yuri envied his friend's punctuality.

In his native Russian language, Yuri told Coltrane his thoughts about the situation. Whatever statements needed to be made could wait until morning. Cami was useless to them while she was in a state of borderline shock anyway.

"It was nice to have met you Ms. Abernathy and Miss Tisha," Yuri said then patted Coltrane on the shoulder and left.

"Coltrane are you staying over," Tisha asked while pulling her piece of the blanket tighter around her arms.

"Yes," he replied bluntly.

"Is your gun loaded," she asked seriously right after Coltrane's reply.

"Yes," he answered again.

"Good," Tisha sighed. "I'll sleep better knowing that you're in the house with a loaded gun."

Coltrane shook his head to hide his smile. If he ever had a daughter, he wanted her to be just like Tisha. She wasn't afraid to speak her mind. And her candor was so refreshing.

"How are you feeling Tisha? Do you think you'll be able to sleep once you're cleaned up?"

Tisha shrugged her shoulders and looked down at her feet. Even though they were a lot warmer, her right foot still felt bad. It almost felt like something was stuck in her foot.

"My right foot still hurts, but I think I'll sleep okay. I'm more worried about my mom. She's bleeding if you haven't noticed," Tisha replied in that grown-up way of hers.

Coltrane immediately turned toward Cami. He'd been so distracted with trying to kill those bastards that he hadn't truly taken in Cami's dishevelment. He thought the blood on her coat and sweater was from the man he shot, but now upon closer inspection he saw the small gash on the left side of her head just below her hair line. He also noticed the tremors that seemed to permeate her body.

Coltrane turned on his heel and went into the kitchen and when he noticed the open side door, he closed and locked it. Opening every cabinet in sight, he found first a glass then the bottle of brandy, which was the main target of his search. Splashing a little into the glass, he carried it into the living room and placed it into Cami's shaking hands.

"Drink it baby," Coltrane instructed. "It will help."

Cami lifted the glass to her mouth, holding it precariously in her trembling hands. She managed to gulp down the amber liquid then set the glass on the coffee table.

"Now, let's take a look at your foot Tisha," Coltrane said as he knelt down on the floor. Lifting Tisha's right foot and tilting it toward the lamp, he found the reason for her pain. A tiny sliver of green colored glass was stuck in her foot. It jutted out just enough for Coltrane to get a grip on it and pull it out.

"Ouch!" Tisha cried out at the twinge of pain, but then it was over and her foot felt a lot better.

"What was it," Tisha asked when she heard Coltrane lifting the lid on the garbage can in the kitchen.

"A piece of glass," he replied. "All right, everybody upstairs. Tisha, you clean up first then get in the bed. Your mother and I will clean up after we get you tucked in."

As Coltrane helped Cami up from the couch he noticed that her nerves had calmed down. Her shaking had lessened and her breathing had returned to normal. Some of the color had even returned to her face. For a while, he thought for sure that she would faint. But Coltrane was wrong. Cami was very tough, and she'd proved it by not giving up the package that was probably in her gym bag. They would have a talk about that once Tisha was all squared away.

Cami opened the door to her bedroom and waved Coltrane inside after leaving Tisha in the bathroom to wash up and change her pajamas. She sank down onto the edge of her queen sized bed adorned with a vertically striped denim blue and canary yellow comforter. The walls were also vertically striped, alternating the blue and yellow except for the wall behind the headboard. It was a solid blue. Canary yellow curtains hung at the window and were accented with a blue denim swag. A vertical striped blue and yellow lamp completed the décor.

Coltrane thought the room was decorated nicely. He would have been surprised if her room was shabby, when the rest of the house was so cozy and comfortable.

She still clutched the blanket around her shoulders, but abandoned it with a sigh. Clad in only her black lacy bra and jeans, she turned curious eyes on Coltrane. She had so many questions, but didn't know where to start. She also knew the feeling was mutual.

Cami watched as Coltrane deposited both his duffel bag and her gym bag on the floor next to her computer desk. The gym bag that contained the infamous package that almost got her and Tisha killed.

She moved from the bed and bent to unzip the bag. She had to know what was inside that package. She'd put it off enough already. She also had to get Caroline out of Tisha's room. The doll and the package had to be the key to convicting Tony.

"Why don't we wait until Tisha's in bed and we're cleaned up," Coltrane advised. "I have a feeling it's going to be a long night."

"Okay," Cami agreed huskily. Her voice sounded scratchy from screaming. She could use a hot cup of tea after she got out of the shower. By then her hands should have stopped shaking completely. Or enough so that she could at least drink the tea and not burn herself.

"Mind if I take a quick shower while you get Tisha in bed?"

"Not at all," she replied as Tisha walked into her room washed and changed. "Towels are in the linen closet."

Coltrane knelt down and kissed Tisha on her forehead.

"Are you sure you're okay Tisha," he asked again to make certain nothing had changed.

"Yes, I'm fine. I told you as long as you got a gun, I'm not scared. Mom's the one who'll have trouble sleeping."

"Don't worry, I'll make sure she gets some sleep," he told Tisha then grabbed a pair of gray jogging pants out of his bag and headed for the shower.

"Love you Coltrane," Tisha called after him and got the same reply.

Cami tucked her daughter in bed only after each assured the other that they were going to be fine. Cami couldn't help staring at her miniature clone and realizing that she came very close to never seeing Tisha ever again. The prospect of that happening brought a fresh sheen of tears to Cami's eyes. She had to stay alive for Tisha, because there was no one else to take care of her. Earl sure as hell wasn't going to turn into 'Father of the Year' overnight. It was her responsibility to stay alive and Coltrane would help her with that. He'd already proved that he was worth his salt. Without him tonight, Cami knew she would have been dead.

"Sorry I was so mad at you today Mom. I never meant to hurt your feelings, and I just know I did. I saw it on your face when you left for work.

"I thought those men were going to kill you and I-"

Cami stopped her daughter from talking when she saw Tisha's eyes fill up with tears.

"I love you Tisha and nothing, I mean nothing, in this world could ever change that. Now try and get some sleep."

Cami kissed Tisha's cheek and pulled the covers up to her neck. Her daughter was nearly already asleep.

Cami plucked Caroline from the doll collection and quietly left the room.

Placing the doll next to her pillow, Cami undressed and slipped on her red terry robe and belted it at the waist. Then she did something so completely out of character that she would have laughed had it been another day.

Cami joined Coltrane in the shower.

Coltrane felt the cool air on his body when the bathroom door opened and closed. There was no need to reach for his gun, which rested on the ledge of the tub. He knew it was Cami. He'd smelled traces of her perfume and he knew the sound of her walk. He was a little surprised that she'd come into the bathroom. He was even more surprised when she stepped into the shower with him.

Cami sidled up next to Coltrane's sinewy muscled body to share the spray of water from the showerhead. Neither spoke, but as they silently communicated each began to soap the other passing the slippery white bar between them.

After Coltrane had rinsed Cami's hair of shampoo and conditioner, she broke the silence.

"So what took you so long to save me Mr. D.E.A.?"

Coltrane looked slightly embarrassed, but answered the question honestly anyway.

"I was in the bathroom," he replied guiltily.

"You were in the *bathroom*," she repeated with a look of chagrin.

"Yes, the bathroom."

Cami burst into hysterical laughter that quickly turned into gut wrenching sobs. She'd had to be so strong for so long, and she was so very tired. Hot water streamed down her face and mingled with her tears. Coltrane held her tightly against his chest until her tears were spent.

Cami didn't know how long they'd stayed in the shower, but she felt so much better when Coltrane shut off water that had grown tepid. He toweled them both dry then helped her into her terry robe.

Coltrane slipped on his jogging pants then made Cami sit on the toilet seat. He wanted to treat all of her cuts and bruises with the first aid supplies he'd found in the medicine cabinet before his shower.

Cami winced several times when he began to apply the antiseptic, but Coltrane kept a steady hand and did as best he could. Even blowing on the cuts to minimize the sting didn't seem to help. Through it all as usual, Cami was a real trooper.

Coltrane led Cami back to the bedroom after she blow dried her hair and pulled a tee-shirt over his head while she traded in her robe for her flannel nightgown. It was finally time to get down to the business at hand.

The package.

Cami got the package out of the gym bag and set it on the bed next to the doll. Grabbing a pair of scissors from atop her desk, she took them back to the bed and sat down next to Coltrane.

Taking Caroline in her hands, she sat and stared at the doll. It had been her childhood friend and confidant, and now whatever was inside the doll would quite possibly get her killed.

"You okay Cami," Coltrane asked.

"Coltrane, I'd like you to meet Caroline."

"*That's* Caroline," he asked incredulously. He, Yuri, and Sully had been searching for Caroline for three days. Never would they have imagined that they were looking for a doll. Caroline was a simple chocolate colored rag doll with hair made of black yarn, and she wore a pink dress.

"Have you known about the doll the entire time," he asked curiously. Coltrane would feel better if Cami hadn't connected the 'Caroline' in Belinda's letter with 'Caroline' the doll until recently.

"I should have, but I only figured it out tonight at work," she replied. "Well, let's see what's inside the doll shall we?"

"By all means."

Cami released the Velcro closure on the back of the doll's pink dress and took it off. Using the scissors, she started at the doll's neck and carefully cut downward, taking great pains not to disturb the contents beneath the stuffing.

Wrapped in a wad of white cotton stuffing, was a small rubber-banded stack of folded documents. Cami flipped through each one marveling at the fact that she knew nothing about the information and Belinda hadn't told her about it.

There was a fifty thousand dollar life insurance policy with Cami listed as the primary beneficiary and Tisha the secondary, in the event of Cami's death. There was also a deed to a house in Washington, D.C. with Cami listed as the owner, as well as a bank statement with Tisha listed as the account holder of thirteen thousand dollars. And last but not least there was a plain white sheet of paper with a man's name, and an account number. The last document was by far the most puzzling.

"Do you recognize that name," Coltrane asked.

"No, but it sounds familiar."

"Yeah, it does. Everything else is pretty clear though. The address on that deed belongs to a brownstone in Georgetown. I'm pretty sure Belinda left you a very nice townhouse in D.C. worth a lot of money, at least half a million."

"Are you serious," Cami asked looking at the deed again.

"Very. Now open the envelope and find out what's there. We'll figure out who Johnathan Cumberland is later."

Cami ripped open the Fed-Ex envelope and pulled out a manilla file folder. Riffling through quickly, she found a list of about thirty or forty names, more account numbers, and what looked to be computer passwords. There were bank statements from offshore accounts and another plain sheet of paper with 'JC Development Company' and an account number written on it.

"Do you think that Johnathan Cumberland owns JC Development Company," Cami asked. The whole thing was an enigma, but it was worth enough to Tony to have her killed.

"It's a good guess, but I wonder about the people on that list. Who are they and why would Tony kill me over them?"

"Well, let's see if we can find out a little about them," Coltrane replied.

Cami booted up her laptop and sat down in the small black office chair. She was immediately connected to the internet as her fingers flew over the keyboard.

Changing places with Coltrane, Cami watched as he first logged onto the D.E.A. website, and then entered his password for what appeared to be a special database of drug trafficking suspects. Coltrane entered the first name on the list in the search function and they both waited anxiously.

Five matches with the name 'Cleophas Matthews' appeared on the screen with five pictures, all of whom were black men living in Detroit.

"Oh my God! I know Cleophas number two," Cami said and pointed to the second picture on the computer screen. "Everybody calls him Nymph. He's Tony's right hand man. He usually runs the car wash when Tony's not there, as well as anything else Tony tells him to do."

"If that's the case, then everybody on this list works for Tony. The suspects in this database have never been linked to Tony because he's very good at covering his tracks. This is huge," Coltrane mumbled. The D.E.A. had been waiting for a break like this for years.

"Let's try another name," Cami said and Coltrane's hands flew over the keyboard yet again.

Julio Rodriguez's picture appeared on the screen and identified him as a homicide detective for the Detroit Police Department. They read the short bio that told of Julio's Colombia origin, and from the way it looked, Homicide was a new department for him.

"He's a crooked cop from one of the largest drug trafficking countries in the world," Cami muttered.

"Don't sound so surprised baby. The only way Tony could sustain an operation like this is to have cops in his back pocket. Unfortunately, it happens more than it should.

"All these people on this list have to be on Tony's payroll. I'll bet I can link these accounts to not only the car wash, but dummy companies that Tony uses to launder money. J.C. Development is probably one of them."

"Hell, Al Capone was caught for tax evasion. As long as Tony goes to jail I don't care what the charges are. Do you think this is enough evidence," Cami asked hopefully.

"I think so baby. I need to call my boss and update him, but I think this is the break we've been waiting for," Coltrane told her confidently. He'd never expected Belinda to have gathered such major evidence alone. Things never worked that way. But, as he was coming to realize, anything was possible.

"You know this means Tony will come after you and Tisha again. Are you sure you can see this through?"

"I'll do it Coltrane," Cami said with determination. "I want Tony to rot in a square box for the rest of his life. He murdered Belinda and he tried to have me killed tonight. If you don't get him first, he'll sure as hell get me."

"I won't let that happen."

Coltrane looked up from the laptop and into Cami's eyes and nodded. She saw his conviction, his determination. She also saw his love, and surprisingly enough, that didn't scare her. She'd never been loved by a man before, so she really didn't know how to react to it. But being with Coltrane felt natural and right. If anything, that was a good sign.

"Well, I guess we know why Johnathan Cumberland's name sounded vaguely familiar."

Cami looked at the screen and inhaled sharply. She'd been so busy thinking about Tony in jail, that she forgot Coltrane had typed in another name – the only name that had appeared twice, in the doll and inside the package.

"Oh Jesus," she groaned.

"That's right. It looks like *the* Johnathan Cumberland, our current Drug Czar. He advises the President on our national drug control strategy. This just keeps getting better," Coltrane said.

"And he's from Detroit. That's why the name's familiar. He's damn near a local hero around here for all his philanthropy and community involvement. I remember now, he was always getting interviewed on Channel 7, promising to get drugs off the city streets and protect our children," Cami stated in disbelief.

"And he's connected to Tony," Coltrane chimed in.

"Ain't that a bitch."

Chapter 37

Tisha crept down the hall to her mother's room. She was so glad that it was daylight. When she thought about the scary things that had happened last night, it was easier coping with them with the sun shining. Tisha wasn't scared when she went to bed however, because she knew Coltrane was in the house. He'd shoot anyone who tried to hurt them, just like he shot the man chasing her last night. They were safe with Coltrane.

Tisha knocked twice on her mother's door and waited. She wasn't stupid. She knew what grown-ups did in bed together. Of course her mother had never had a man sleep over before, but Tisha knew what other grown-ups that loved each other did in bed. And her mother and Coltrane loved each other so there was no reason why they wouldn't be doing sex. Maybe once they did sex, Coltrane would officially become her father. That would be crazy cool.

Tisha heard Coltrane's whispered 'come in' and twisted the doorknob. Coltrane sat in bed with a blue tee-shirt and jogging pants on, but her mother was sound asleep.

"Morning honey. Aren't you tired," he asked as Tisha sat beside him on the bed.

"Not really 'cause I have to go to school."

Cami began to stir at the sound of her daughter's voice. Her eyes felt gummy from lack of sleep and her body ached everywhere. She didn't even remember getting in bed. The last thing she remembered was watching Coltrane type in account numbers to offshore locations such as the Grand Cayman Islands. That was at nearly 4 a.m. She must have fallen asleep somehow. Coltrane must have put her in bed.

"Why are you up so early Tisha," Cami croaked from bed.

"It's 7 a.m. Mom. If we don't hurry I'll be late for school."

"Oh honey, you can stay home from school today. I know you're tired."

"I know Mom, but I have a math test today and I studied really hard for it," Tisha explained positioning herself between her mother and Coltrane. "I am a little tired, but I'll take a nap when I get home. Or I'll page you and you can pick me up after the test."

Cami gingerly pushed herself erect. Her head was sore and the spot between her shoulder blades where she'd been hit with the butt of the gun was tender and probably bruised. The bandages on her knees were slightly askew from having rubbed against the bed sheets. But the most important thing was that she was alive. Everything else would heal in time, no matter how badly she ached at the moment.

"Are you sure Tisha?"

"I'm sure Mom. I'll page you at lunch and let you know how I feel."

Cami threw the covers from her body and placed her feet on the floor.

"Give me a few minutes Tisha to get dressed."

"Actually," Coltrane began breaking his silence, "I'll take Tisha to school. You're in no condition right now to brave the cold."

"That's okay, I can take her," Cami stated half-heartedly. She had a huge problem with relinquishing control.

"Camilla, I'm taking Tisha to school and you're staying home."

Cami gracefully relented and pulled on her terry robe. She left Coltrane in the bedroom to dress as she shuffled downstairs to make her daughter's breakfast and plait her hair for school. Not having to deal with the cold and snow was a welcome reprieve, especially considering how she felt.

Cami cracked two eggs into a small stainless steel bowl and beat them with a fork mixing in salt and pepper gradually. Just as she put the skillet on the stove Coltrane came into the kitchen.

"I'm sorry baby, but you're going to have to ride along with us. Yuri and Sully can't make it over here in time, and you're not staying in this house alone."

"Okay, I'll only be a minute. Let me scramble these eggs for Tisha first and make some toast."

Coltrane thought for sure that he was going to have a fight on his hands, but he was obviously mistaken. He wondered how she'd react however when he tells her they're going to have to leave the house once Tisha gets home from school. So much had happened last night that he didn't think Cami could have dealt with that cold reality at 4 a.m.

Today was a new day however, and all bets were off. Tony had to know by now that the bastards didn't get the package. If he didn't know, he'd know soon, and Coltrane wasn't going to sit around and wait for Tony to retaliate. He, Cami, and Tisha would be gone by nightfall.

Tisha came bustling into the kitchen with her backpack slung over one shoulder and carrying a vanity case filled with tons of hair accessories.

"You didn't have to cook Mom. I could have eaten a bowl of cereal."

"I know honey, but this will jump start all those math problems in your brain."

Cami carried Tisha's plate to the dining room table and started on her daughter's two French braids as Tisha ate her breakfast.

When Cami left to change clothes, Coltrane took the opportunity to tell Tisha about having to leave the house. He'd come to realize what a good ally she was if he could win her over. Besides that, he only wanted to have to deal with Cami. One female arguing with him was better than two.

Coltrane knew for a fact that Tisha wasn't the type of kid that you needed to beat around the mulberry bush with. He plunged head first into the topic of discussion.

"Tisha, after we pick you up from school today, whatever time that may be, we're going to come here and pack because it's not safe to stay in the house another night."

"You think those men will come back again," she asked around a mouthful of eggs.

"Even the ones you shot?"

Coltrane laughed. Children were always so literal.

"No, not them, but different ones. That's why we'll have to leave."

"Why do we have to leave?"

The question came from Cami as she stood in the archway between the dining and living rooms. She was back sooner than Coltrane had imagined. She'd apparently pulled on a Wayne State University jogging suit and carried a pair of snow boots in her hand.

"When Tisha gets home from school we're going to a new location," Coltrane informed her. "It's not safe to stay here. I allowed it last night, but not tonight. We'll have time to pack some clothes later this morning."

Cami took in all that Coltrane said slowly. She hated to leave her house. That seemed like such a sign of defeat. Where were she and Tisha going to live? And for how long? She supposed just until Tony was arrested. Then maybe her life would return to normal. Whatever *normal* was. Then maybe she would finally get the hell out of Detroit. Maybe she and Tisha would move to Washington, D.C. and live in the expensive townhouse that Belinda left her. It would be a new start, and a welcome one.

For that reason among many, she didn't give Coltrane any problems.

"If you think we should leave, then we'll leave," Cami agreed. "I want Tisha to be safe."

"I want you safe too Mom."

"I know sweetheart," Cami replied. Tisha had been her life for ten years, and Tony was *not* going to take that away from her.

Julio pulled into Tony's car wash at 8 a.m. and cut the engine. He hadn't heard from his boys at all. He'd gone to each of their houses and blew up their pagers and cell phones. They hadn't answered and were nowhere to be found.

Knowing in his gut that something went drastically wrong, Julio had driven by Cami's house and what he'd seen nearly made him shit his pants. Although the scene had apparently been cleaned up, there were still traces of bloody red snow on the porch and on the ground. Lights were on inside the house, so Julio had to assume that the blood belonged to his guys. Especially since he couldn't reach all four of them.

So now he took a deep breath and gathered his balls to go and talk to Tony. He figured if he confronted Tony about the fuck up, then Tony might give him a chance to correct the situation and get the package himself. J.C. was breathing down his neck, asking if he'd gotten the package yet. If Tony ever found out that Julio had been going behind his back and dealing directly with J.C., Julio would be a dead man.

He definitely didn't plan on dying anytime soon. He planned on quitting the police department and moving back to Colombia. He'd start his own drug cartel and rake in the Benjamins. He and J.C. had a few plans and if things worked out they'd both be filthy rich – not that J.C. wasn't rich already. Tony had seen to that.

Nymph watched Julio from just inside the entrance to the car wash as he listened to his ear bud. Tony was downstairs in his office hammering away at a new philly they'd recruited named Pauline. She was a junior at an East Side high school and so far she'd managed to bring in two grand a week like clockwork from her school buddies. Tony had to reward her for her efforts of course, and he never turned off his ear piece just because he was boning some ho. Tony liked to know what was going on at all times. That's why Nymph informed him that Julio was on his way inside.

"T-Money, that punk bitch Julio's on his way to the door."

"Bring him down," Tony huffed then groaned loudly as he came.

Nymph didn't give Julio a chance to say anything. He immediately escorted him down to Tony's office. The new girl, Pauline, was zipping up her jeans when Nymph and Julio walked into the office.

"I tell all my girls to leave the panties at home when they come to see me. It saves time. Remember that," Tony told Pauline as he buttoned his shirt."

"Sure thing Tony. See ya."

Pauline pranced out of Tony's office like the young philly she was, her hips swaying seductively. She looked like a sex kitten that had lapped up a bowl of cream – Tony's cream to be exact.

"Ah hell Tony! She's just a kid," Julio protested and was met with raucous laughter.

"He must not know our philosophy when it comes to women T-Money. Go 'head and educate him," Nymph said still laughing at Julio. The motherfucker had the nerve to be *outraged* and he was a crooked drug dealing cop.

"There are three things a man should always remember when it comes to women. Am I right Nymph?"

"Most definitely T-Money."

"First thing you need to know Julio is that I don't love hoes, hoes love me. Secondly, you can't love 'em and stay above 'em."

Tony turned toward Nymph and smirked.

"And as far as fucking the girl," Tony began lacing his fingers together behind his head, "if there's grass on the playing field, it's time to play ball."

Julio tried to conceal his contempt for his so-called boss. Drugs were one thing, but he drew the line when it came to screwing young girls. But what did he care? He was only in Tony's office to ask for a second chance. Julio swore to himself that he was going to get the goddamn package then split. Once his plan was in place, Julio knew his pockets would be fat.

"So Julio, let's cut to the chase. Your arms look mighty empty, which leads me to believe that you don't have my package."

Julio began to fidget with his hands, then stuffed them in his pockets. His eyes cast downward as he answered Tony.

"I don't Tony, but I stopped by to tell you that I'm on my way to get it for you."

Nymph looked skeptical and gave Tony a negative shake of his head. One thing he knew to be true: Julio was a pathological liar.

"So you're standing there telling me that your guy has it in his possession right now and all you have to do is pick it up?"

"Well, not exactly," Julio mumbled.

"T-Money I told you his bitch ass wasn't going to deliver. Let me cut him while I got the chance," Nymph interjected.

"Where exactly is the package Julio," Tony asked as he pulled open a drawer in his desk filled with silver, prehistoric looking medical instruments.

Julio began to sweat profusely. His tie felt as if it were choking him, and he couldn't breathe any air into his lungs. All he could think about was Tony or Nymph using those tools on him. He was a fool to think that Tony would give him another chance.

"I imagine Camilla still has it," Julio answered. "But I'm going over there now and I promise you that I'll get the package this time."

Before Tony could say anything his telephone rang. It was his personal line in his office, and at present only one man had the phone number.

"Yes," Tony answered on the second ring.

"Did you get the package," the caller asked in a low raspy voice.

"No, but I'm sure you already know that. I mean considering how you and Julio have become best friends."

"I don't have time to play games," the caller warned. "One word from me and your entire operation will crumble."

"I told you about threatening me Cumberland," Tony hissed into the phone.

"I told you never to use my fucking name," Cumberland spat. "If that package gets into the wrong hands I'm through. And if I go down you're going down, *Anthony.*"

"I suggest you order a casket for your wife. She'll be dead by morning."

Tony hung up the phone after his parting retort. J.C. was apparently starting to get nervous. And a nervous man made mistakes.

"Nymph do you think we should give Julio another chance," Tony asked rifling through the metal tools.

"Hell no!"

"My thoughts exactly. Apparently in order to get things done the right way, I need to do it myself."

"Fuck you Tony," Julio yelled and turned to leave. He wasn't going to volunteer himself to get cut up by Tony and Nymph. He never should have come into the car wash. He never should have gotten mixed up with Tony in the first place.

Nymph stopped Julio from leaving and muscled him into the chair in front of Tony's desk. A nasty gleam sparkled in his eyes because he was about to have some fun. Nymph loved to have fun.

"Here," Tony said and handed Nymph the scalpel he'd been searching for. "Be creative, but don't fuck up my office. The maid just cleaned yesterday."

Nymph accepted the scalpel with a smile. Forcing Julio's right hand palm down on top of Tony's desk, Nymph sliced off Julio's middle finger. The scalpel made short work of the finger, cutting it easily and cleanly through flesh and bone. Laughing, Nymph threw the finger into Julio's lap.

Julio doubled over in pain. He unknotted his tie and slid it from around his neck so he could tie up his hand to keep from bleeding to death.

"What the fuck did you do that for," Julio croaked using all his energy frantically trying to staunch the flow of blood.

"Because I wanted to give you the finger," Nymph replied and burst into laughter with Tony joining in. The two men laughed so hard tears of mirth shone in their eyes.

"You wanted to give him the finger," Tony repeated. "That's why you my MoFo Nymph. Now take this bitch out the back door then get K-Dog and Queenie. We need to pay my niece a visit."

Chapter 38

Coltrane led Cami upstairs after having had a minimal breakfast of toast and coffee. He needed to call his F.B.I. contact, and then he needed to report in to his boss. With all the information on Tony and his crew, as well as the Drug Czar, he expected to have an arrest warrant by nightfall. They had proof of Tony's operation, end of story. Coltrane didn't want to hear any bullshit excuses that were usually the norm. He wanted Tony's ass in jail by midnight. Until that happened, Cami and Tisha were far from safe.

Cami went to her closet and pulled out a small black pilot suitcase and opened it on the floor. She gathered some clothes with Coltrane's help and gingerly knelt down on her scraped knees to arrange them in the suitcase. When she was satisfied that there were enough clothes to last several days, she went into the bathroom and gathered toiletries for herself and Tisha. When that was done, she took a green pilot suitcase out of Tisha's closet and repeated the process. Now all they had to do was wait for Tisha to get out of school and then leave.

"You have everything you need for a couple of days," Coltrane asked as he zipped Tisha's suitcase and set it in the hallway next to Cami's.

"I forgot Tisha's Gameboy and the Harry Potter book she's reading. Other than that, I think that's it."

Cami retrieved the book and the portable video game out of Tisha's room and gave them to Coltrane to put into her suitcase.

"Come on Cami, you're exhausted. There's time enough for you to take a nap."

Cami stood in the hallway with a dazed expression. She was still so numb. Her mind was still having trouble wrapping itself around the whole situation. Did she really almost die last night? Was Tony going to keep trying until she *was* dead? Coltrane was right, she was exhausted.

"I am tired," she replied. "But I'm too keyed up to sleep."

"Well at least rest."

Coltrane grasped Cami's shoulders from behind and walked her into her bedroom. Once there he spun her around so that the backs of her knees touched the edge of the mattress. Pushing gently, Coltrane held Cami's shoulders firmly as he lowered her to the bed.

"How's your head," he asked lifting her chin and surveying his handiwork. The small gash on the left side of her head had long since stopped bleeding. A tiny amount of dried blood had seeped through the white gauze bandage. Coltrane made a mental note to change the bandage later and clean the wound.

Cami shrugged her shoulders and said, "It's okay I guess. There's a dull ache that won't go away. I took some ibuprofen a little while ago. I'm hoping it helps."

"What about the rest of you?"

"Are you kidding? I feel like I've been hit by a mack truck."

Cami turned her lips into Coltrane's right palm and planted a kiss. His other hand cradled her cheek and its warmth felt so good on her face.

"When you said what you said last night, did you mean it?"

Coltrane didn't try to pretend he didn't know what Cami was talking about. They were both way past that point. And there was no turning back.

"Yes I meant it Cami. I do love you."

Cami searched Coltrane's eyes and hoped like hell he was lying because she was so afraid of the truth. His sexy brown eyes were so intense that they bore a hole straight into her soul.

On this morning filled with the aftermath of revelations both shocking and bittersweet, Coltrane became her rock and her strength. He was a beacon of light guiding her through a dark tunnel.

Coltrane was her salvation.

"I've never said this before to anyone," Cami began hesitantly, "but I need you Coltrane."

Coltrane felt the enormity of that statement way down deep in his chest and for a moment his lungs threatened to seize up.

Still cradling Cami's cheek, he bent his head and kissed her deeply. Coltrane's tongue delved artfully into her mouth while his hands slid down to her sweatshirt. Lifting it up and over her head, he took his time drinking in the sight of her breasts, something he couldn't do in the shower the night before.

Before long they both lay naked in bed with Coltrane raining skillfully placed kisses all over her body. There wasn't much he'd left unexplored she thought, until he parted her thighs and began kissing his way up to her very core.

"What are you doing," she panted unable to deny the pleasure that coursed through her body. No man had ever kissed her there, not even Earl. She'd always pleasured him orally, but he'd never bothered to return the favor. She'd never known what she was missing until now.

"Let me taste you," Coltrane breathed from between her legs, fanning the thin strip of hair that adorned her womanhood. Everything was waxed and smooth and it turned him on.

Cami grasped Coltrane's mahogany shoulders as he worked his magic between her thighs. Each thrust of his tongue threatened to send her over the brink. She had never known such raw ecstasy.

Guttural moans filled the bedroom when at last she erupted and dissolved into a quivering heap, her inner muscles still clenching Coltrane's tongue for fear that the sensations would end.

With one hand Coltrane ripped open the foil packet with his teeth, his other hand preoccupied with fondling, touching, teasing. He sheathed himself with the condom then positioned his lower body between her legs. Moving slowly, Coltrane drove deeply, filling her to the hilt.

Cami's indrawn breathed forced her muscles to tighten about him. Her body stretched to accommodate him as he filled her completely. Coltrane moved rhythmically, caressing her inside and out, leaving his imprint and erasing all past memories of anyone except him ever touching her.

He made her feel such joy. So much so that it pushed past the numbness and the loneliness that had manifested itself inside of her for so long.

Coltrane made her feel whole again as they crested that wave together, molding their bodies so that where one ended the other began. She glided her hands up the flat sinewy plane of his back and felt the light sheen of perspiration as he kissed her passionately. She tasted her essence as their lips locked and their tongues intertwined.

Coltrane brushed a lock of hair away from Cami's jaw and kissed her on the cheek. He'd never in his life told a woman, other than his mother, that he loved her. But it felt right with Cami. Lord knew *she* felt right. And he adored Tisha. Given the chance, Coltrane knew he could make life better for them. All they had to do was stay safe until Tony was in custody.

"You are so beautiful," he told Cami and kissed her gently on the lips.

"You too. Well, you're handsome that is," she replied with a smile.

Coltrane's lighthearted expression turned serious and businesslike when his cell phone rang. He muttered an expletive as he rolled to his side breaking their connection.

"Kennedy," he barked while sitting up in one smooth motion. The sheet slid from his body as he planted his feet on the carpeted floor.

"Wagner is here in Detroit," Yuri spoke quickly, "and he's on his way to the house. Sully and I are to meet him there."

"Wagner's *here*? But I just briefed him last night about the information. He's supposed to get a warrant together so we can go after Tony and Cumberland."

Coltrane's puzzled expression made Cami uneasy. Something wasn't right and she wasn't sure she wanted to hear about it.

She picked up her jogging suit and ran to take a quick shower and get dressed. If she had to hear bad news about Tony then she wanted to hear it without being naked.

"We all know that, but that didn't stop Wagner from hopping on a flight did it? Something stinks Coltrane and I don't like it."

Coltrane couldn't figure out why his boss would be in Detroit. Yuri was right about something being up.

"How much time do I have," Coltrane asked.

"Ten, maybe fifteen minutes. He's exiting the freeway now."

"Shit! All right I'll see you then."

"If I were you old friend, I'd make sure my feelings weren't on my shirt sleeve when Wagner shows up."

Yuri ended the call and Coltrane threw his cellular into his duffel bag. It's a cut and dried case Tony and Cumberland are guilty, end of story. Once they had a warrant they could arrest Tony and take down the car wash. Tony's whole drug empire would crumble, but they needed one goddamn slip of paper first. It was all such bullshit.

"What is it," Cami asked standing at the foot of the bed fully dressed.

"My boss is on his way over along with Sully and Yuri. He wants to meet with us. I'm hoping he's delivering the warrant personally."

Cami turned toward the dresser and picked up her hair brush. Using the mirror, she gingerly pulled the brush through her hair and then pinned it up with a hair clip in back.

"I'm really sorry about this baby. I wish the circumstances were better, but they aren't."

Cami shrugged her shoulders. "None of this is your fault."

"I know, but I still feel like shit right now. I will make this up to you. I promise."

Cami ran her fingers through the springy coarse hair on Coltrane's chest then rested her head there.

"It's okay," she reaffirmed. "And I'll be looking forward to the makeup. Especially if it's as good as it was this morning. Now get cleaned up before your boss catches you naked and hard."

Helen answered ringing phone lines and greeted clients at the small real estate company where she worked as a receptionist. The morning was hectic, but she didn't mind. It made the time go by faster, which was a plus. The sooner Helen made it through Thursday she'd be one more hour closer to Friday and her date with Ashton. She couldn't wait.

Ashton had already called her last night to tell her to sleep well. Then he woke her up this morning to inquire about how she slept. Helen had never felt so giddy in all her life. She felt sixteen all over again, wondering if the boy she liked, liked her too. It was crazy and fun at the same time. Helen hadn't had fun in such a long time, and it felt really good.

The door chime dinged as Helen looked up from her computer. The beaming smile on her face faded as Earl walked in carrying a large white envelope. Helen knew he carried his copy of the separation papers. He must have received them first thing this morning while he was at work.

"I guess you know what these are," Earl stated holding up the white envelope.

"I have a pretty good idea," she replied, her expression impassive. She couldn't tell if Earl was happy about the separation or upset.

"Are you sure you want to go through with this," Earl asked.

"Positive."

Earl shrugged his shoulders and slid the papers out of the envelope. Taking a pen from Helen's desk, he signed on the dotted line agreeing to dissolve their marriage.

"It's your loss," he quipped and threw the pen back on the desk.

"Actually, it's my gain Earl. Thank you."

"You'll never make it without me you know."

retorted immediately placing a call on hold. It was rude, but the sooner she was done with Earl the better.

"No other man will want you. You're only half a woman. You can't even carry a baby. But that's okay because I already have a kid. I've never needed you for anything."

Helen didn't even flinch. She steeled herself against the hurtful words that had caused her lungs to constrict. Earl had a baby already. Some woman had already given him what she could not. She concentrated on breathing normally so Earl wouldn't know how his painful statement had cut her to the quick.

Helen's mind immediately went to Tisha, Cami's daughter. It all made perfect sense. Tisha was the spitting image of her mother, which was a good thing. Helen wondered if Tisha even knew. She couldn't help but to feel sorry for the girl. No child deserved to be in the middle of a love triangle, if that's what it even was. It was more like the middle of the Bermuda Triangle.

"I'm sorry that you're Tisha's father. She deserves a better man for a dad. I hope Cami finds her one real soon."

The mention of Tisha and Cami turned Earl's fair-skinned face a dark crimson.

"Bye Earl. I have work to do. You can make arrangements with my lawyer to pick up the rest of your things."

Earl turned on his heels and stormed out of the real estate office.

"Scumbag bastard," an elderly client with salt and pepper hair yelled from her chair in the waiting area. "Those sons of bitches ain't shit honey. You did the right thing and don't ever think different. I took my second husband to the cleaners for cheatin' on me back in '67. Made him pay child support for the baby I was carryin' too. That kid took every dime he had. And you know the best part?"

"What's that," Helen asked admiring the seventy-something woman's spunk.

"The kid wasn't even his. She was my third husband's baby, but no one needed to know that 'til she turned eighteen."

The old woman burst into laughter. Her boisterous cackles filled the small office and Helen couldn't help joining her.

Chapter 39

Christopher Wagner was a balding fifty year old man that resembled Al Bundy. Cami kept expecting him to stuff his hands down his pants at any moment. The effect was ruined however when he opened his mouth. The deep southern accent oozed politeness and hospitality. His tall lean form was agile and graceful, and when he smiled his face changed completely. He actually was quite attractive when he smiled.

"Thank you," Wagner said as he accepted the cup of coffee Cami handed him.

"Sir, what's this all about," Coltrane asked, his face a mask of professionalism.

Wagner sipped his coffee and took his sweet southern time about answering the question. He eyeballed everyone over the rim of his cup and began to talk only after he was ready to talk.

"This is going to piss y'all off," Wagner began, "but we're off the case. The Feds got wind of it and want it turned over to them."

"You can't be serious," Sully spat. He ran a hand through his curly blonde hair that was already out of control.

"It gets better," Wagner commented before continuing. "I'm here in person to collect any information you have on Johnathan Cumberland. We can't touch him. He and the President were roommates at Yale and studied law together at Princeton. They're best friends. He'll of course deny any affiliation with the Snow King and the President will make sure everyone believes it."

"So he's going to get off free and clear because of political bullshit," Coltrane burst out.

"There is good news though. I have the warrant for Anthony Jackson's arrest. The Feds as well as the Detroit Police Department should be in position as we speak to take down the car wash."

"We do all the hard work and the Feds always get the credit," Yuri complained. "Never fails."

"As long as Tony goes to jail, I could care less about Johnathan Cumberland. I just want him to pay for his crimes, because Belinda should not have died!"

Cami stood abruptly and went into the kitchen to refill her coffee cup. As she got the cream out of the refrigerator her eyes caught Tisha's school calendar. Apparently Tisha was scheduled for a half-day. They'd both forgotten with the recent events.

Today was the half day.

Cami's eyes flew to the clock in the kitchen. Tisha should have gotten out of school exactly thirteen minutes ago. Cami had never been a superstitious person, but that number thirteen left a lump in her throat. She checked for her pager on her hip, but she'd forgotten it on her nightstand.

Through the dining room window Cami saw school kids on their way home. The kids were few and far between because most parents usually let them stay home on half days, but they were there nonetheless.

Cami looked down the street toward the school, but she didn't see Tisha. Hopefully her daughter was waiting inside the school. But when Cami looked again she saw Tisha's multi-colored knit hat bobbing up and down as she hurried down the sidewalk alone. Cami also saw Earl's Cadillac pulling up alongside the curb in front of Mrs. Monroe's house. That didn't bother her nearly as much as Tisha walking home alone did. She'd deal with Earl later.

But when Cami turned to glance down the opposite end of her street, the lump in her throat grew, nearly choking her to death.

The license plate that read 'SNWKING' was getting closer to her house. Tony's Benz cruised down her street as if it traveled the block everyday. When the car began to slow near her house, Cami's heart pounded as she raced into the living room.

Wagner was on her front porch telling Yuri he had to grab something from his car as she sprinted through the front door. Then everything happened so fast it was a blur.

Shots rang out from different directions shattering the windows in Cami's living room. Shards of glass littered the carpet and furniture and stuck to their hair and clothing.

"Get down!"

Coltrane and Sully yelled at her simultaneously as they both produced weapons out of thin air.

Wagner spun suddenly and was thrown into Cami, knocking them both backwards into the foyer.

"Wagner's hit! Cover me," Yuri shouted over the deafening sounds of gunfire.

"Who the fuck is shooting," Sully asked positioning himself beside the broken windows to try to get a better view of their attackers.

Coltrane laid down cover fire from the front door and pushed Cami behind him just as a bullet grazed his right shoulder. Yuri ducked inside and bodily dragged a bleeding Wagner into the house and behind the sectional.

"It's Tony," Cami screamed as Coltrane and Yuri checked to see how badly Wagner was hit.

Finding a shoulder wound, Coltrane rolled Wagner onto his side while Yuri checked for an exit hole.

"Got it," Yuri called out. "Went straight through."

"Tisha's out there," Cami announced hysterically. "Tony will kill her. I have to get her before he does!"

Cami jumped up and headed for the side door but Coltrane pulled her down hard.

"What the hell are you talking about?"

"Tisha had a half day and she's walking home! She's out there!"

Cami took off just as another round of gunfire shattered the dining room windows. Coltrane grabbed her around the waist and dove to the floor just as hot metal seared the flesh of his left shoulder. He grunted as he landed on top of Cami, his shoulder already seeping blood where the bullet grazed him.

"Somebody get me up and to the window," Wagner croaked. "I'm hit but I'm not dead. I'll help with cover fire while you go for the girl."

Yuri hefted Wagner up and to the broken dining room window and placed a gun in his hand.

"Lean on this chair if you get dizzy," Yuri told him placing a dining room chair within reach. "There are four or five guys that got out of the car, so make every shot count."

"I've been firing a gun since before you were born Yuri. I aim to kill. Now get the girl."

"Let me go," Cami screamed. She clawed at Coltrane's hands unsuccessfully. He had her lower body so tightly that it was nearly impossible for her to move.

"Goddamn it Cami! Listen to me," Coltrane hissed in her ear. "I'll get Tisha, but you have to stay the fuck down. I don't need to worry about you too right now."

"Okay, but hurry. He'll kill her. I know he will."

"What do you see Sully," Coltrane hollered into the living room.

"There are four. I recognize Tony and the one they call Nymph. There's a tall wiry one ducking for cover on the east side of the house. And there's the biggest, blackest, motherfucker I ever saw guarding Tony behind the Benz. He's hit in the chest and the leg, but he didn't go down. If he's high it might take twenty bullets before we lay him down. I also got a civilian man cowering behind a Cadillac next door.

Coltrane checked his ammunition. He was half empty and his extra clips were in his duffel bag, which was upstairs. How did everything get so fucked up so fast? Tony was supposed to be at his car wash getting arrested, not shooting up Cami's house.

Shit!

"Sully, cover Coltrane. He's going after Tisha. I'll keep pumping bullets into the big motherfucker until he falls. Yuri, go out the back door and sneak up on those sons-a-bitches from behind."

"My thoughts exactly boss," Yuri called out running toward the back of the house.

"Gentlemen, I want these sons-a-bitches in body bags by lunchtime. I'm shot, I'm hungry, and I'm pissed. Get to work," Wagner ordered leaning against the dining room chair.

"Stay here Cami," Coltrane instructed then headed toward the back of the house with Yuri.

They each made sure the back of the house was clear before going out the side door, Yuri to the right to sneak up from behind and Coltrane to the left toward Tisha. Coltrane wouldn't make the same mistake as the night before and leave the bastards alive. As Wagner put it, they were going to be in body bags by lunch.

K-Dog had disappeared behind the house somewhere and only came out to fire his gun occasionally. Nymph ducked out from behind the bumper to return fire, and he was clearly pissed.

Why in the hell were men firing back at them? Cami was supposed to be home alone. Tony had planned to spray the house with bullets in hopes of killing her, then get the package in question. What the fuck was going on?

"What should we do boss," Queenie asked as he watched his own blood drip onto his brand new Timberlands.

After a few seconds Queenie repeated the question.

"Just shut the fuck up and let me think," Tony yelled. He'd never in his life been up against the wall, until now. He'd dealt with Colombian drug lords without a scratch. He had cops in his back pocket and at his beck and call. He'd even gotten himself political connections. But never in a million years would he have though he'd be in this predicament. He was caught in a shoot out with Belinda's niece. How ironic. The bitch probably planned it from the grave. What other reason was there?

"I think we should get the fuck out of here Boss," Queenie said wiping his palms alternately on his jeans, his gun still pointed at the house.

There was no way in hell he was going to run home with his tail tucked between his legs like some punk ass bitch. He was nobody's bitch that was for damn sure.

They had to shoot their way out. There was no other choice since two of his tires were blown out.

At least that's what Tony thought until he saw Earl cowering in his Cadillac.

What the fuck is he doing here?

And as luck would have it, Tony saw Tisha rooted to the sidewalk not far away. She was his ticket out of here. Cami might want him dead but she'd never shoot her own kid.

"Nymph, get the girl," Tony ordered, "then get that Cadillac over there. That's our way out."

"Won't be but a minute T-Money."

As Earl hunkered down on the floor of his car he heard the distinct sound of Tony's voice. He'd recognize that voice anywhere. Which meant that Tony was shooting at his niece. And now he wanted a girl, which upon glancing through the passenger side window, was Tisha.

His daughter.

Earl's chest constricted at the thought of Tony shooting Tisha. The little girl that looked so much like his beautiful Camilla. Earl couldn't let that happen. Wouldn't let that happen.

Nymph came out blasting. He took a hit in the arm and felt the bullet ripping through the meaty flesh of his bicep. Nymph steadied himself and returned fire as best he could. At least he wasn't shot up like Queenie, who'd taken at least seven hits and was still going strong. Nymph hadn't planned on dying any time soon. He still had hundreds, maybe even thousands of girls left to fuck.

No, today wasn't a good day to die.

Nymph saw Tisha's feet glued to the cement. Her eyes were as big as saucers and a backpack lay at her feet. Tears were sliding down her cheeks and snot dripped from her nose because of the cold. She looked absolutely terrified. That made it even more convenient for Nymph to snatch her up. If he knew T-Money, the girl would serve well as a human shield. It was a good ass idea. Then they'd all pile into the Cadillac and get the fuck out of Dodge.

girl would serve well as a human shield. It was a good ass idea. Then they'd all pile into the Cadillac and get the fuck out of Dodge.

Nymph pointed his gun at Tisha and said, "Come over here right now."

Tisha was paralyzed and scared. She didn't know what to do. She didn't even know if Coltrane and her mother were okay. She tried to move her feet but they felt so heavy. And she was afraid of getting shot if she went any closer to the house.

"If you don't bring your ass over here right now, I'm going to shoot you."

Tisha felt a sensation of warmth and then wetness spreading between her legs and trickling down her thighs as her bladder let go.

Nymph didn't feel like taking another bullet, but the kid was the only way they'd make it out alive. People were still laying down heavy fire from the house and getting the kid meant putting himself out in the open.

"Get the fucking kid," Tony yelled nearly kissing the dirt on the ground. Queenie was taking hits and he was starting to falter, leaving Tony unprotected. He needed Tisha and he needed a goddamn car. Two of the Benz's tires were blown out and it was full of bullet holes. Tony only had one option, and that was making it out alive.

"Get over here kid or I swear I'll shoot you," Nymph tried again ducking his head as a bullet pierced the back panel of the Benz.

"No you won't," Earl stated calmly as he stepped in front of Tisha. He spoke as if Nymph held nothing more than a water pistol.

Shit! Nymph didn't need this shit right now. He took a deep breath, jumped from behind the Benz and fired.

Earl looked down at his chest in amazement. Crimson blood bloomed across his shirt, quickly soaking the fabric. He was shot. He couldn't believe it. He never thought he'd go out like this, but if he was going to die at least he'd die knowing that he saved Camilla's daughter.

His daughter.

Earl sank to his knees and then fell forward, the pain too great. That left Tisha unprotected, but hopefully she'd be safe. She had to be for Camilla's sake.

As Nymph bent to grab Tisha his body jerked two, three, four times. He was hit everywhere. His body bled from his upper torso and the grip he had on his gun lessened instantly. When Nymph looked at his hand, he saw a hole the size of a quarter in his palm.

They shot the fucking gun out of his hand. This was not a good day, and he was going to die.

When Tony saw Nymph go down, then Queenie, he knew it was up to him to make it out alone. K-Dog's punk ass was still hiding behind the house somewhere. If K-Dog made it out alive Tony was going to personally kill him for being so weak. He didn't pay his crew to run away with their tails tucked between their legs.

Tony kicked Nymph out of the way, his dead body still bleeding profusely. Still firing with his right hand, Tony reached out his left arm and grabbed Tisha by the front of her coat and lifted her thin body up in front of him. Let Cami figure out how to protect her daughter *now*.

Chapter 40

Cami hovered beside Wagner at the dining room window. From there she had a better vantage point than anywhere else in the house. She saw Tisha frozen amid the gunfire, and there wasn't a damn thing Cami could do about it. This was the second time that she was entrusting Coltrane with Tisha's life. He hadn't let her down before, but Cami was still scared as hell.

She peered through the bottom of the bay window in enough time to see Nymph pointing the gun at Tisha, and lost it. He was about to shoot her baby and she didn't see Coltrane or Yuri anywhere in sight.

As Cami jumped up from the window to run outside, a strong hand tightened about her wrist halting her flight. She looked up into Wagner's eyes and saw his plea. She was surprised by the strength in his arm considering he'd been shot. But he was a fool if he thought she was going to let her baby die before her eyes.

"Let my men handle it," Wagner firmly instructed. "He'll be dead in a few more seconds."

Cami checked the window again and saw Earl hauling ass out of his Cadillac. He'd pushed Tisha behind his back and the next thing she knew blood was spreading rapidly across Earl's chest.

Everything started happening so fast that Wagner let go of her wrist to fire his gun. That's when she made a fast break for the side door. Tisha was not going to die. A parent was not supposed to bury a child, and Cami didn't plan on doing any such thing.

Cami got outside just in time to see Nymph pumped with bullets, but it wasn't enough. Tony had snatched Tisha from the sidewalk and was using her for a shield.

"Oh God! Oh God! Oh God!"

"Tisha," Cami screamed. "Tony no!"

"Tell them to stop shooting Cami or Tisha is dead," Tony yelled still holding Tisha in front of his upper body.

"Stop shooting," Cami screamed and pleaded.

She only got a couple of feet into the driveway before Coltrane grabbed her arm and shoved her behind him. She hadn't even seen him until he grabbed her. His gun was aimed directly at Tony *and* Tisha.

"Please help her Coltrane," Cami begged.

"Baby, I love you but you need to be quiet."

Coltrane made the statement as he slowly pressed forward down the driveway. He was focused on every move Tony made. He just needed Tisha to move half an inch so he could plant a bullet in the middle of Tony's head. Tisha had to move or Tony would try his best to take off with her, all the while using her as a shield.

"Tony please let her go," Cami yelled totally disregarding Coltrane's order to be quiet.

"Mom!" Tisha called out frantically amid all the chaos. She heard her mother's voice but she couldn't see her.

"I'm right here honey. You're going to be okay. I promise Tisha."

"Coltrane," Tisha called out, her voice a bit calmer now that she wasn't alone. "Can you please hurry 'cause I'm really scared."

"I will baby. Just stay very still."

"I will."

"Shut the fuck up! Everybody shut up!" Tony yelled becoming more and more agitated. There was a man on the porch aiming a gun at him as well as the prick in the driveway with Cami. There were too many angles left uncovered. These guys had to be Feds, and that meant they were bound to be trigger happy even if he did have the girl. He had to get into that Cadillac.

"Whoever the fuck you punk bitches are, at least you lasted longer than the sorry motherfuckers that showed up at my office this morning. They came to The Sanctuary to find God, and found Death instead!"

"Take the goddamn shot," Yuri yelled in Russian from across the street.

"I need another inch," Coltrane replied in Russian as well. "It's too close."

"I've seen you do this before. Now take the goddamn shot and keep your heart out of it!"

Coltrane realized Yuri was right. He was so worried about Cami and Tisha that it was clouding his judgment. Tony was only about thirty feet away, which wasn't far at all. Coltrane could take the shot, and he was going to take the shot. Tony was a dead man.

"Stay back or I'll kill her," Tony shouted trying to work his way over to Earl's Cadillac.

"Tisha, how about taking a trip to Disneyworld with me and your mom after Christmas," Coltrane asked raising his voice above Tony's and advancing down the driveway ever so slightly. "Would you like that baby?"

"Yes," Tisha mumbled preparing herself for something to happen. She wasn't stupid. She saw the murderous look on Coltrane's face. Tony was in big trouble.

"Good. I'll buy the plane tickets then."

Coltrane fired his .9mm and struck Tony square in the forehead. Tony's arms went slack and Tisha fell to the ground as Tony fell backward into the street.

Yuri ran back across the street to check on Wagner and Sully dragged a handcuffed K-Dog out into the open.

"Tisha!"

"Mom!"

Tisha ran into Cami's open arms and hugged her tightly around the neck. She promised herself that she would always help with the dishes whenever her mother asked, because she very easily could have died today. She wasn't ready to see her Aunt Belinda yet. Thanks to Earl and Coltrane she wouldn't have to for a very long time she hoped.

"Mom, what about Earl? Is he okay?"

Cami turned her attention to Earl who lay on the ground near the front bumper of his Cadillac. Coltrane rolled him over to check his pulse and to see how badly he was wounded. When Coltrane laid two fingers against his neck, Earl's eyes fluttered open and he tried to speak.

"Tisha okay?"

"She's fine Earl, thank you."

Cami held Earl's cold hand in both of hers. Even through all that had happened over the years, Earl was still her first love and she did love him in the beginning. Earl was the first man that had ever paid any attention to her, but instead of becoming a father figure, he had become her lover. And without Earl she never would have had Tisha. For that reason alone she was grateful to him.

"Sorry I haven't been a father," Earl rasped. "But I was there when it counted right?"

"That's right."

"Maybe...won't go to hell after all."

Earl tried to laugh but choked on his own blood.

"Take care of them," Earl told Coltrane right before the blackness claimed him.

"I will," Coltrane reassured him too late.

Cami hung her head with sadness. So many had died. Her street looked utterly devastated. Blood was everywhere and the street and sidewalk were littered with bodies. It looked like a scene out of the Godfather movies. This was not her life. She wanted no parts of death and destruction, but it apparently wanted her.

"Come on Cami."

Coltrane went to lift Cami from the ground but she shook off his hand.

"We can't just leave him here," she said referring to Earl.

"We won't baby. The ambulance is on its way."

She allowed Coltrane to help her up after she extracted another promise that an ambulance was on its way. By the time she reached her side door, true to his word, an ambulance pulled up in front of her house.

"Why don't you get them out of here," Yuri told Coltrane. "We'll take care of everything including boarding up the windows. Tisha doesn't need to see all of this. It's not good for her."

"Good idea. You know how to reach me," Coltrane told Yuri and clapped him on the back.

Coltrane wasted no time at all. He loaded Cami's and Tisha's bags into the trunk of his car along with a few extra things Cami threw into another duffel bag. He threw his own bag and computer into the backseat beside Tisha. Once everybody was buckled up, Coltrane took off. Cami never looked back, not even once.

Chapter 41

Coltrane pulled into the driveway of his parents' Bloomfield Hills home. His father opened the front door before Coltrane had even cut the ignition. He had apparently been waiting for their arrival.

Stan Kennedy's lean six foot frame loomed in the doorway. His birth certificate said that he was sixty-two, but he didn't look a day over fifty. Stan thought that hard work and clean living kept a man young.

His hands were stuffed in his front jeans pocket, a habit he'd gotten into since losing his two fingers at the plant. The sight of his mangled hand didn't bother many people, but it still bothered him. Closely cropped thick gray hair shone in the sunlight and sort of matched the gray pullover sweater he was wearing.

Coltrane had called before leaving Cami's house and gave his mother an abbreviated version of what had taken place. His parents were both obviously worried after hearing about a gun fight. They were also quite curious about the first woman Coltrane had ever admitted to loving.

"Is this your parents' home," Cami asked. She'd been silent the entire drive. She just kept seeing Tony holding her daughter in front of his body and Earl's dead body bleeding on the sidewalk. But if it weren't for Earl's sacrifice, Nymph might have shot Tisha.

"Yes. I thought you and Tisha would be more comfortable here than in a hotel."

"So the first time I meet your family is taking place after a shooting spree? And you walk through the front door shot in the arm because of me? Are you crazy?"

"I'm not shot Cami. The bullet grazed my shoulder. There's a difference. And no, I'm not crazy. My parents will understand so stop worrying."

Cami covered her face with her hands. She was a mess emotionally and physically. First impressions were everything. She knew that from personal experience. Her clothes were soggy and covered with mud where she knelt in the snow.

Cami's hair wasn't curled or even brushed properly. She knew she looked like something the cat had dragged in. Then again, no self respecting animal would have anything to do with her right now.

"Come on baby. Trust me," Coltrane told her.

He removed her hands from her face and wiped at a smudge of dirt on her cheek. He saw the deep purple spots beneath her eyes, a sure sign of lack of sleep. Cami even looked exhausted. He was going to make sure that she went straight to bed.

"Please go inside Mom. I'm getting cold out here and I have to use the bathroom," Tisha begged from the back seat.

Cami shook her head and wiped the excess tears from beneath her eyes. She smoothed her hair the best she could and gathered her composure. There was nothing she could do about the situation anyway. It was what it was. The only thing she could do was make the best of it.

"Okay, let's go," Cami stated bravely, even though she was afraid of what Coltrane's parents would think of her.

Coltrane's father, Stan, met them at the trunk of the car to help with the bags. Coltrane looked exactly like his father. Cami could almost imagine Coltrane in his sixties, still macho and strong like Stan.

They saved the introductions until they reached the house. The main objective was getting out of the cold.

"Your mother's going to have a fit when she sees that arm," Stan said glancing at the blood running down Coltrane's arm soaking his sweater.

Cami stopped in her tracks. She didn't need a screaming mother to deal with on top of everything else.

"Maybe Tisha and I should go to a hotel after all."

"Nonsense," Stan blurted. Diana will have a bigger fit if you leave this house."

Stan ushered everyone into the house ahead of him. Before taking even three steps, they immediately ran into Diana. She summed up the situation in one glance and started issuing orders as if she hadn't retired from nursing five years ago.

"Leave those bags right there for now Stan. You fetch my medical bag and I'll put on the tea kettle."

Diana took in Coltrane's arm, Cami's sunken eyes, and Tisha's relief. There was no mistaking the two for anything but mother and daughter. They looked just alike. They also looked tired and hungry, and maybe just a wee bit curious.

"All right, everyone in the kitchen. I'll get you patched up, then we'll fix some lunch."

Tisha had never seen a house so large before, other than on television. It was like walking through one of her doll houses, but only real life. And Coltrane's mother seemed really nice. Tisha was glad about that because her mother looked ready to bolt at any moment.

Personally Tisha wanted to stay with the Kennedys. She liked Coltrane which meant that she would probably like his parents. That wasn't always the case with everyone, but so far Coltrane's parents seemed cool.

"Excuse me Mrs. Kennedy, may I use your bathroom please," Tisha asked.

"Of course you can. There's one through the kitchen next to the family room. And call me Granny D. All the neighborhood kids do."

"Cool! I've never had a grandmother before."

"Leave your coat here and I'll hang it up in the back closet for you."

Tisha did as she was told then ran off to the bathroom with a clean pair of underwear and pants folded beneath her arm.

Diana didn't waste any time issuing more orders. With raising four children she was used to running a tight ship. She had to or otherwise her boys would have driven her insane. Nothing had changed over the years either. Her boys still got into the most trouble, the kind of trouble that required stitches because of a gunshot wound.

"Let me have your coat Cami. I'll put it with Tisha's. And you can call me Diana."

Cami automatically did as she was told for fear that Diana would take off her belt and spank her. Now she knew where Coltrane picked up his talent for issuing orders.

Diana Kennedy was a tall, beautiful, willowy woman. Her copper colored skin was smooth except for a few thin lines at the corners of her eyes. Most people called them wrinkles or crow's feet, but Diana thought they gave a person character. She'd also heard them referred to as laugh lines. That name was at least a little better, because having a few lines at the corners of the eyes meant happiness. She'd be wary of anyone over fifty that didn't have them.

Diana's salt and pepper hair was twisted into a bun at the nape of her neck. She wore a pair of black jeans and a black tee-shirt with an open multi-colored flannel shirt. She looked stylish, and comfortable, and motherly.

Cami had never personally experienced being mothered. Her own mother spent more time with a bottle of Vodka than she did with Cami. And Belinda just wasn't the mothering type. Belinda loved her like a mother, but it wasn't in Belinda's nature to handle children. Cami would never take Tisha to a strip club on her eighteenth birthday for a job, even if she'd had a baby. They would just have to find another way to support the baby other than welfare. And Cami sure as hell wouldn't marry a drug dealer. But Belinda did love her and that was all that mattered.

Stan and Tisha entered the kitchen together. Stan carried Diana's medical bag and Tisha carried extra bandages and a bottle of antiseptic. They set the supplies on the kitchen table for Diana.

"You okay Cami," Coltrane asked. He lifted his ruined sweater over his head then sat down at the kitchen table. "You look as if you're going to faint."

"Mom you do look a little weird," Tisha observed.

Diana cupped Cami's elbow and lead her to a chair opposite Coltrane.

"I'm really messy Diana. I'd rather stand."

Cami made a valiant effort to stand her ground, but her body ached and she was so incredibly tired. The chair did look comfortable with plush seat cushions.

"Don't be silly sweetheart. Go ahead and sit down."

Once Diana got Cami situated in a chair she turned her attention to her son. Glancing at his left shoulder, it looked as if he would need eight or nine stitches. Thank God the bullet only grazed him.

Diana searched through her medical bag and gathered everything she needed. Placing a make-shift suture kit on her kitchen table, she went to work cleaning the wound and preparing it for stitches.

"I don't have a local to inject around the wound Coltrane. You're going to feel every stitch and you need about nine."

"Go ahead Mom. I can take it. I'm trained to block out pain remember? That's what being a S.E.A.L. is all about," he half joked.

"Just because you block it out doesn't mean it hurts any less," Cami chimed in testily. She was tired of all the macho man bullshit. Coltrane could have been killed, and it would have been her fault.

Stan gazed at his wife as he carved sandwich meat from a leftover roasted chicken for lunch. She was busy treating their son, but he saw the grin that flittered across her mouth upon hearing Cami's comment.

When Diana started the stitches Cami looked away and stared at the butter yellow kitchen walls and the ivy border. But Tisha on the other hand stood right by Coltrane's side and held his hand for support. She visibly flinched and sucked in her breath at each pass of the suturing needle.

"It's almost over Coltrane," Tisha promised and patted his hand. "I'm proud of how brave you are. I know if I had to get stitches I'd cry. I cry when I have to get a shot at the doctor's office."

"Thank you Tisha. I wouldn't be able to sit here if it weren't for you. Yep, you helped a lot."

Diana finished after only eight stitches. She surveyed her handiwork then bandaged Coltrane's left shoulder and bicep.

After placing everything back in her bag, Diana shook out a painkiller from a prescription bottle.

"Take this and don't do anything that will rip my stitches," Diana sternly told her son.

"Thanks Mom."

"Now you," Diana said and turned toward Cami. "Let's bandage your head and clean the wound."

"Oh I'm fine," Cami lied.

"Like hell you are. You're about to fall out of that chair from sheer exhaustion and you walk like your entire body aches.

"I'm going to help you whether you like it or not. You're as stubborn as the rest of my kids."

Diana's harshness was downplayed by the soft motherly smile on her mouth and her gentle touch. She even smelled like a mother if that made sense. Some flowery fragrance wafted past Cami's nose as Diana bent over the gash on her head. She smelled like lilacs or maybe magnolias.

"Cami's been complaining that her head hurts and her body is sore."

Coltrane sounded all of five years old running home so he could tattle first. The smug expression on his face told her that he was enjoying himself too.

"I took some ibuprofen this morning," Cami admitted reluctantly.

"Did it help," Diana asked. She placed a strip of tape over the small square bandage she'd replaced.

"No."

"Hmm," was all Diana said before giving Cami a painkiller too. "It will probably make you sleepy, but you need the rest anyway.

Stan set a platter of roasted chicken sandwiches on the table, along with a pitcher of fresh squeezed lemonade. He lowered his tall form gracefully into a chair while Coltrane placed ice filled glasses on each placemat.

"Roasted chicken with mayo and lettuce," Stan announced while Coltrane filled the glasses. After the glasses were filled, everyone held hands as Stan blessed the food and thanked God for keeping everyone safe.

"Everybody dig in."

Tisha was the first to put a diagonal half of sandwich onto her plate. She was so hungry that she felt like she hadn't eaten in days. And when Coltrane found a bag of her favorite potato chips in the cabinet, Tisha got her grub on.

"You should eat something Cami," Coltrane told her when he noticed that she hadn't touched her sandwich. She'd at least taken the painkiller without a fight.

"I'm not that hungry."

Cami rubbed her eyes with her thumb and index finger trying to keep the tears at bay. She felt so weepy all of a sudden. The anger and fear had passed, but she still had flashbacks of what had happened and it constantly made her want to cry. And Earl was dead. That was the biggest shock of all. She'd never meant for him to get hurt. And she never should have let Tisha go to school. It was all her fault.

"Don't you dare sit there and take the blame for any of this Cami. I can see it all over your face," Coltrane admonished. He wasn't about to let her sit and mope for the rest of the day.

"The most important thing is that we're all alive. There's no need to feel guilty that Earl is dead either. I'm glad he risked his life to save Tisha. If she were my daughter I would have done the same thing. It was a noble way to die."

"Ease up son," Diana pleaded. Cami seemed to be at her limit already.

Cami pushed away from the table and stood abruptly. The movement nearly upset her plate. It wobbled precariously on the edge before righting itself.

"Don't you think I know that Coltrane? I'm glad Earl did what he did, but it doesn't make it any easier to swallow. Helen is still left without a husband because of me."

"No, not because of you. It's because of Tony."

Coltrane stood and pulled Cami into his arms.

"You'll be okay Mom," Tisha commented and hugged both her mother and Coltrane together. "In Mary J. Blige's words, 'I don't want no more drama'. Can everybody handle that?"

Tisha put her hands on her hips and waited for an answer.

"Yes, we can handle that," Cami replied with the beginnings of a smile.

"Mary J. Blige? Who's that?"

"Granny D, she is only *the* Queen of R&B Soul, and she is fabulous. Mary J. tells it like it is. She's my favorite."

"You two get some rest. Tisha and I are going to have a music lesson while you're sleeping. I'm going to introduce her to my good friend Ella Fitzgerald."

"Ella who?"

Diana sighed and made a few tsking noises with her teeth.

"Ah, today's youth. Gotta love'em."

Chapter 42

Coltrane had declared over dinner that night that Friday was going to be 'family fun day'. They were not to think about anything bad or he was going to personally think of a fitting punishment for all transgressions.

So, bright and early Friday morning they all went out to breakfast at a favorite local restaurant, his parents included. Over grits, eggs, toast, coffee, and orange juice, Cami got to know Coltrane's parents a little better. And his parents got to know Cami better too. They had a million questions, but were holding off for a better time to ask them. They didn't want to scare away the only woman that had captured their son's heart.

Cami had spent most of Thursday sleeping and trying to purge herself of the images that constantly bombarded her mind. By dinner she had relaxed a little, and by morning she'd almost felt normal – almost, but not quite.

"So, was Coltrane a good kid?"

Stan laughed at Cami's question and swatted his hand on his knee.

"Yeah Coltrane was good. Good at being bad," Stan said in between laughs.

"Dad, I wasn't that bad. I remember Miles being a lot worse. He's the one that jumped off the garage not me."

"That's because you pushed him," Diana spoke up. "That's why God made angels Cami. They protect fools and little children."

Coltrane thwarted his father's protests and threw some bills on the table to cover the cost of the meal. When Cami also tried to pull money out he took the twenty dollar bill and gave it to Tisha.

"What's this for," she asked excitedly.

"For popcorn and candy at the movies later."

"Cool! Thanks Coltrane."

"That was really rotten," Cami whispered in his ear.

Coltrane's reply was a quick kiss on the lips.

"Mom, Granny D and Grandpa Stan taught me how to scat yesterday. It's so much fun."

"Tisha has such a wonderful voice. I was very impressed," Diana said. "I've never heard a ten year old sing the way she does."

"Thank you. Tisha has always loved to sing even when she was a baby."

Coltrane checked his watch then finished his orange juice. He promised Cami that he'd take her by Helen's house. She was hell bent on seeing Earl's wife before they went anywhere. He had to damn near beg Cami to eat breakfast first. She'd said something during the night about needing to clear her conscience.

"We need to go baby if we want to make the 11a.m. Disney movie," Coltrane warned.

"Well, I hope you have fun. Stan and I will be waiting for you Tisha. We have lots of fun things planned for this evening."

"That's right I almost forgot. Mom and Coltrane are going on a real date tonight."

"That's right kiddo, but first we're spending the whole day together, so let's get going."

Coltrane ushered Tisha and Cami through the restaurant and out the door, waving goodbye to his parents through the glass window.

Helen stared out her kitchen window as she rinsed vegetables in the sink. So much had happened in the past twenty-four hours. Her life had been completely changed forever and turned upside down.

Helen found herself trying desperately to wrap her mind around the latest events. She had filed for a legal separation, met a wonderful new man, found out that her husband already had the child that she could never give him, and received a call that he had been shot to death.

Ironically, Ashton sat at Helen's dining room table making calls about the funeral arrangements for Earl. When she'd called him from work yesterday to tell him that Earl had been shot to death, Ashton had immediately shut down his computer and picked her up. He had been a godsend. Helen probably wouldn't have been able to handle everything if it hadn't been for Ashton. Even though they'd just met, he'd been such an outstanding friend.

Now while she fixed them an early lunch, Ashton made appointments with the funeral home and the cemetery. Both of them had been awake since the crack of dawn. Helen had welcomed his help because she didn't know what to do first. Besides that, she'd been too shocked to even think clearly.

Helen set two bowls of broccoli cheese soup on the table and then carried in two plates filled with mixed greens and all the usual salad trimmings.

"How are you holding up," he asked and began to eat.

Helen shrugged her shoulders. She didn't quite know how to answer the question. She was doing okay, but she felt so guilty for some of the thoughts that had entered her mind.

"I'm alright," she mumbled around a forkful of salad.

"But?"

Helen threw her fork down and twisted the big bangle bracelets she always wore on her wrists. She wore them everyday specifically to hide her scars – scars that could never be removed. Scars she acquired while she was married to Earl, the man who probably never even truly loved her. Helen had been a mere convenience, someone to cook, clean, and do laundry.

"Ashton, to tell you the truth I don't know how I feel. I'm sorry that he's dead. No one deserves to die so violently. But part of me remembers how badly he treated me then I don't feel bad at all. And then the big kicker is that I don't have to go through the divorce, and I feel *relieved* about that. Isn't that awful? So now instead of alimony, I'm getting a hefty life insurance settlement."

Ashton covered her hand with his own. Helen wiped daintily at the corners of her eyes and then returned her napkin to the table.

"You have permission to feel any way you want and not to feel guilty about it."

"I'm glad you're here Ashton. There's no way I could have handled all of this alone."

"I'm glad I could help."

Before Helen could take another bite of salad the doorbell rang. Dread immediately filled her chest. What if Reverend Whitaker had already spread the word around the church about Earl's death. Helen wasn't prepared to play the grieving widow yet. She needed time. She'd hoped to get through the weekend unscathed. She'd made the arrangements for Tuesday, not quite a week, but before Thanksgiving that Thursday.

"Do you want me to answer it?"

"No, thank you. I'll get it."

Helen scooted her chair back from the table and went to the front door. She was surprised by what she saw, although on some level she had expected it. Cami stood on her doorstep alone. Curious, Helen immediately opened the door.

"Camilla? What are you doing here?"

"May I come in?"

"Of course."

Helen held the door wide and let the younger woman enter into the house. For years Helen had tried to figure out what was so wrong with her and so right with Cami. But it wasn't about right or wrong, it was always about Earl. Helen understood that now.

Cami took a quick glance around. She'd always wondered what Earl's house looked like inside as a teenager. That was way back when, when her head was filled with fanciful thoughts about Earl divorcing Helen and marrying her. What a fool she'd been.

"I'm sorry for dropping by unannounced, but I didn't think you'd agree to see me if I had called."

Helen honestly didn't know what to say. For years she'd replayed scenarios in her mind about a confrontation with Cami. But now that Earl was dead, it didn't seem worth it. It didn't really matter anymore.

"I'm not angry with you Cami. If anything I admire you for making the choice to have your daughter. Not many teenagers would have taken that road."

"For me there was never a choice to make," Cami replied shrugging her shoulders. "How long have you known?"

Helen smiled slightly remembering Earl stopping by her job just the day before. He'd tried his best to hurt her by saying such nasty things, but for the first time it hadn't mattered to her what he'd said. Now he was dead.

"That Tisha was Earl's daughter?"

Cami nodded her head yes.

"I just found out yesterday. Right after Earl signed our separation papers. For the life of me though I can't figure out why you didn't sue Earl for child support? Or even make it known that he was Tisha's father?"

Those were questions Cami couldn't even answer for herself. She should have gotten child support, but that would have meant everyone finding out about their relationship, including Belinda. Cami hadn't been ready to handle all of that at sixteen with a newborn baby.

"As stupid as it sounds, I didn't want to hurt you, let alone my Aunt Belinda. I've seen you at church on Sundays for years. I couldn't bring myself to do it. And I had Earl telling me constantly that no one could know. Maybe he was the driving force behind the ultimate decision. I don't know."

Cami fidgeted with the buttons on her coat. She'd wasted enough time already. She'd come to Helen to say one thing and it was high time that she quit stalling. Besides, Coltrane and Tisha were waiting for her in the car and Tisha had begged her not to make them late for the movie.

"Helen what I really came to do was apologize. For what it's worth I'm sorry that I had an affair with Earl years ago. And I'm sorry he died. But I'm not sorry that he protected Tisha. My daughter would have died if he hadn't taken that bullet. Tisha's my life and I'm so grateful that he saved her."

To Helen's utter surprise Cami reached out and hugged her quickly. Helen's scenarios over the years had never ended with a hug, a cat fight maybe, but never a hug.

"There's nothing we can do about the past Camilla, but we can move forward. And there's nothing to apologize for. If I had known about Tisha sooner I would have made Earl do the right thing. Even if I had to write the check myself every month."

This time it was Helen who hugged Cami and wrapped her in a big embrace. All the pieces of the puzzle were complete for both women. They could both move on with their lives now and neither would feel guilty about it. When Helen thought about Cami in the future, she'd remember this specific moment and nothing more.

"Let me know if I can do anything to help with the funeral arrangements," Cami mumbled as Helen let her go. "I've taken up enough of your time, so I'll get out of your hair now."

Cami made her way to the front door and down the porch steps, but turned around when Helen called her name.

"Do you think Tisha would sing at the funeral? She has such a beautiful voice and it's quite fitting, don't you think? No one has to know anything about anything."

"Sure, Helen, I'll ask her. I'm sure she'd be glad to sing," Cami replied and then stepped into the idling car.

Cami threw up her hand as the car drove away. She finally had closure and it felt so good. She could finally move on with her life with a clean conscience. Cami regretted not doing it sooner. Maybe then Earl wouldn't have died. But, Tisha was alive she reminded herself. That was all that mattered.

Chapter **43**

Cami and Coltrane sat engrossed in conversation in the parking lot of Café Noir, a Detroit hot spot. Neither had stopped talking since kissing Tisha goodbye and leaving his parents' house. They talked over dinner in Greektown and as they strolled back to the parking garage after dessert. Now that the stress had passed, they were free to have fun and take a little time to learn more about each another.

"Where are we," Cami asked when she noticed they had stopped driving and were parked.

"Café Noir," Coltrane replied. "I heard about it on WJLB while you were talking to Helen. Tisha thought I should bring you here because they showcase local talent and they're having a poetry reading tonight along with a local jazz band I think. Tisha said you really love poetry, so here we are."

Cami was going to get her daughter good when she got back to the house. Tisha would tell all her mother's secrets if given the chance. And Coltrane obviously gave Tisha the chance quite a bit.

"I'll bet they make a mean cappuccino. Tisha said you like those too."

"What else did Tisha tell you?"

"I'll never tell. Let's go in before it gets any more crowded."

A mellow vibe floated around the café as patrons listened to the jazz band. The lights were low creating a warm, seductive glow. Heads bobbed and feet tapped the floor as the saxophone player launched into a soulful wail. So far they both liked what they heard.

Coltrane spotted the last available table up near the stage and grabbed it before the crowd grew. Placing their coats on an empty chair, they sat down and were soon approached by a waitress.

"So tell me about D.C.," Cami asked as they waited for two cups of cappuccino.

"Washington, D.C. is great. There's a lot to see and do. There's the Smithsonian, The White House, small bistros in Georgetown...you name it and D.C.'s got it."

Coltrane surveyed the tables around them. There were people of all ages, from the young to the old. Conservatives and liberals mixed to form a very engaging crowd. Conversations buzzed all around them including a raunchy group of woman beside them. They were discussing each other's current sexual conquests.

"What about the schools? Are they good?"

"Well I don't know the stats, but I have friends with kids who attend public schools in D.C. As far as I know they seem to be doing okay."

"Hmm," was Cami's only reply before the waitress set two cups of cappuccino in front of her and Coltrane.

Cami blew on the foam before taking a small sip. She hadn't had a cappuccino this good in a long time. It reminded her that she needed to get out more. Now that things were settling down, she promised herself that she would get out more. She'd take Tisha to some of the places she'd been hedging on for years. Places like Disneyworld, which Coltrane had already promised, and Virginia Beach so Tisha could dip her toes in the

Atlantic, and to New York City to see *The Lion King* on Broadway. It was way past time to start living life.

"Penny for them," Coltrane told her.

"Do you think Tisha and I would be happy in D.C.?"

"Absolutely. And besides, I'll be there every step of the way."

"You're sure about that?"

"Very sure."

Coltrane lifted Cami's hand to his lips. Neither had brought up the future before tonight, but he was very happy with her decision. It would have been a pain to move back to Michigan. But Coltrane would have done it for Cami. He would have been crazy to do it, but he would have been happy.

The host announced the start of 'Open Mic Night' and so began the local talent and then the not so talented. Some of the regulars were really good, but then there were those that were way out in left field. But all together it was a lot of fun.

One of the women at the table beside them got up at the urging of her friends amid giggles and outright laughter. She took the mic from the host then smoothed down her form fitting black skirt.

"My name is Theresa and I'm going to title this poem *'That Man'*."

Theresa pointed her finger at Coltrane as she titled the poem. People looked around at him and Cami with curiosity. Coltrane shrugged his shoulders not knowing what to do or say.

"I have no idea what this is about," he told Cami when she gave him 'the eye'. "Honest, I don't," he added.

Theresa launched into her poem keeping her eyes centered on Coltrane the majority of the time, except when there was a direct attack on Cami:

"I wish I had a man like that right there.
Tall, dark, and handsome with perfectly cut hair.
His eyes caught mine, but only for a minute.
Hell, I'm not even sure if his girl even seen it.
She looks pretty cute, I'll hand her that.
But the question I have: Is he happy with that cat?
Does she rub you, kiss you, and hug you like I could?
Does she even know what to do with your morning wood?
Does she give you the love that I could dish out?
Does she know tricks to please you with her mouth?
I want a man like the one at that table.
I want him to know that I'm very capable.
I can cook for him, clean, and even pay the rent.
Just so long as in the bedroom he can make me limp.
Now I mean no disrespect to my beautiful black sista.
I just want to know about her mista.
Is he happy where he's at?
'Cause I need a man like that."

When Theresa stepped off the stage shouts and oohs and ahhs followed her. All eyes were now on Cami.

"Baby, I only glanced at her for a second, but it wasn't like *that*," Coltrane assured her.

"Does the sista have a reply," the host asked as he dangled the microphone in front of him.

"This is so juvenile. Baby, you don't have to stoop to her level," Coltrane said as he gave Theresa a dirty look.

"Did you see that movie *8 Mile* with Eminem," Cami asked as she calmly took a sip of her drink and then stood.

"Eminem? Cami, what does he have to do with this?"

"Coltrane, there's no way I'm going to let *her* punk me out. If she wants to battle, I'm up for it," Cami said decisively as she walked to the stage.

Cami had danced naked every night for eight years, but standing on stage now made her nervous, which made no sense. Perhaps actually having to think on the spot and talk about Coltrane made her nervous. It meant having to reveal things that she hadn't wanted to say just yet.

Grasping the mic as the audience egged her on, Cami looked at Coltrane and said, "This is called 'My Man'."

"I love the way my man appreciates me exclusively

I love the way my man worships me totally

In his arms I bask in a warmth so deep and intense

A desire so strong it doesn't make a bit of sense

His hands caress me tenderly, definitely, independently

A gentle tugging and kneading

A sigh escapes my throat, nearly pleading

I love the way my man calls me his queen

I love the way my man examines my body as if it's a sight

he's never seen

Admiring every dimple and curve

With a concentration that rattles my every nerve

My man gazes into my eyes while his hands slowly stroke

my thighs

Eyes are windows to the soul

And staring into my man's eyes makes me lose control

My man creates a magic that swirls around my being

Our culmination produces the blinding light I'm seeing

Each thrust of his body into mine

Sends a fire so hot up and down my spine

I love the way my man searches for a nectar so sweet

A bubbling cauldron at the core of me is what he seeks

The inferno rages
My love is contagious
Accepting the seed my man has planted
Accepting the mantra he continually chanted
I love you, I love you is what I so longed to hear
I love you, I love you is what my man chanted in my ear
I love the way my man appreciates me exclusively
My man is mine
Unequivocally
Undeniably
He belongs to me."

When Cami walked off the stage Coltrane pulled her into his arms, dipped her, and then kissed her in front of everyone. Cheers erupted and laughter surrounded them. Even Theresa clapped and waved a white paper napkin admitting her surrender.

When they took their seats again the jazz band resumed playing and attention was turned back to the stage taking the focus off them.

"Thanks for defending my honor," Coltrane joked.

"Anything for the man I love," she replied more serious than joking.

"We're going to have a good life together Cami. I promise."

"Yeah, I know."

Epilogue

Cami stood at the graveside service wearing her heavy wool overcoat for the second time in as many weeks. Earl's cherry wood casket was lowered into the six foot hole as Reverend Whitaker said a prayer.

Coltrane stood behind her and Tisha and lent his warmth as well as his support. Helen stood beside them holding Cami's hand, her wide brimmed black veiled hat shielding her face. Ashton was there too in the crowd, lending his support from an appropriate distance. No one had to know about the separation.

It was miraculous really that the two women were side by side holding hands. If Earl were alive to see the sight, it would have surely killed him. He'd always tried so hard to keep both of his lives separate.

Snow flurries swirled around the sky on this Tuesday before Thanksgiving. Cami had so much to be thankful for. Her daughter was alive, Tony was dead and she was leaving Detroit for a better life. Instead of giving lip service to her dreams, Cami was going to make them happen. She'd found several jobs online that she was qualified for and all of them had 401(k) plans. She and Tisha would be just fine.

After the prayer was over, Reverend Whitaker stepped aside for Tisha to take her place at the head of the casket. After a nod from her mother, Tisha threw the yellow rose she held into the grave. She stepped back, closed her eyes, took a deep breath and sang the opening notes of '*Amazing Grace*'. The voice of an angel carried on the wind as she said goodbye to her father.

Good evening and welcome to WXYZ Channel 7 Action news. It looks as if the snow has fallen today. Not outside, but inside a Detroit crematorium. Anthony Jackson, also known as the infamous Snow King, was cremated today ending his reign as Detroit's most notorious drug lord. Jackson owned AJ's Car Wash on 7 Mile, which is now closed following a massive explosion that killed several members of a joint task force that was attempting to apprehend him. Sources state that the car wash was the base of operations for Jackson's drug empire.

In other news tonight, Drug Czar Jonathan Cumberland, a local hero, has resigned his post amid a rash of allegations that he was somehow linked to Jackson. Cumberland stated he simply wants to spend more time with his children and with his pregnant wife who is due on Christmas Day.

The President released a statement supporting Cumberland's decision and thanking him for his 3 years of service.

The White House has not announced an immediate successor to Cumberland's position....

Distributed By:
Afrikan World Books
2217 Pennsylvania Ave
Baltimore, MD 21217

Quick Order Form

Email Orders: orders@hope-harbor.com

Postal Orders: Hope Harbor Publishing
ATTN: Order Processing
P.O. Box 4942
Annapolis, MD 21403-4942

Name _____

Address _____

City/State _____ Zip _____

Phone _____ Email _____

Ship to (if different from above):

Name _____

Address _____

City/State _____ Zip _____

Phone _____ Email _____

Please send the following copies of *Fallen Snow*:

_____ copies X $14.95 each = $_____

MD res. add 5% sales tax   _____

U.S. shipping via Priority mail:
    $4.00 first book, then $2.00 each additional   _____
International shipping:
    $9.00 first book, then $5.00 each additional   _____

Total Due   _____

Payment: ___Check ___Visa ___MasterCard

Card number _____

Name on card _____ Exp date _____

Thank You For Your Order!